Previous Praise for *No One to Trust*

"Being the first novel in a brand-new series, all that can be said for this author is that she certainly started out with a 'bang'! For any reader looking for 'edge-of-your-seat' thrills, this series is the perfect gift."

—Suspense Magazine

"The author doesn't let up until the end, making *No One to Trust* extremely difficult to set down. I enjoyed her Deadly Reunion series, but this book surpasses those by far, and I hope this is only a glimpse of what we can expect from the Hidden Identity series. Fans of Eason's and readers of Christian suspense will definitely want to check out this new series. I, for one, cannot wait to get my hands on the next installment."

—Fiction Addict

"Eason begins an exciting new series with action and thrilling chase scenes. . . . The conclusion is excellent, and mystery lovers will enjoy this suspenseful novel."

—RT Book Reviews

"With betrayals and bodies piling up and more than their own lives at stake, Summer and David will have to rely on their faith, their wits, and maybe even each other if they're going to survive. They may have *No One to Trust*, but their author proves she can be trusted to add another solid story to her already impressive resume."

—Crosswalk.com

NOWHERE
TO TURN

Books by Lynette Eason

WOMEN OF JUSTICE

Too Close to Home

Don't Look Back

A Killer Among Us

Gone in a Flash (ebook short)

DEADLY REUNIONS

When the Smoke Clears

When a Heart Stops

When a Secret Kills

HIDDEN IDENTITY

No One to Trust

Nowhere to Turn

NOWHERE TO TURN

A NOVEL

LYNETTE EASON

Revell

a division of Baker Publishing Group
Grand Rapids, Michigan

Published by Revell
a division of Baker Publishing Group
P.O. Box 6287, Grand Rapids, MI 49516-6287
www.revellbooks.com

Printed in the United States of America

Library of Congress Cataloging-in-Publication Data
Eason, Lynette.
    Nowhere to turn : a novel / Lynette Eason.
        pages cm. — (Hidden identity ; book 2)
    ISBN 978-0-8007-2209-8 (pbk.)
    1. Abused wives—Fiction. 2. Single mothers—Fiction. I. Title.
PS3605.A79N69 2014
813'.6—dc23   2014016608

Published in association with Tamela Hancock Murray, The Steve Laube Agency, 5025 N. Central Ave., #635, Phoenix, AZ 85012.

14   15   16   17   18   19   20   7   6   5   4   3   2   1

Dedicated to my Lord and Savior,
Jesus Christ.
I love you.

But the Lord is faithful,
and he will strengthen you
and protect you from the evil one.

—2 Thessalonians 3:3

1

Danielle Harding pressed the ice pack to her bruised cheek and watched her husband back out of the driveway. He was gone, headed to a two-day conference downtown, and she was ready. No time for tears or for the hatred she felt for the man.

Instead, she turned from the window and rushed up the stairs to the master bedroom. From the closet, she pulled her midsize suitcase and tossed it onto the king-size bed. She bolted into the large walk-in closet and grabbed the clothes she'd already planned to take. Next, the toiletries.

At the slam of the door she froze. Terror thrummed through her veins.

"Dani?"

He'd come back. No, no, no. Lightheaded with the rush of terror, Dani grabbed the suitcase and shut it, zipped it.

Heard his footsteps on the stairs.

"Dani!"

A cold sweat broke out all over her body. She pulled the suitcase into the closet and shoved it toward the back.

Breathless, she called, "I'm up here, Kurt." What was he doing back? He'd already come home for an early lunch and to grab a few more things, including the box of toy snakes he'd had her buy that morning.

She should have waited.

Icy fear slugged her in the gut. She backed out of the closet and pulled the door shut. She made a beeline for the bathroom and grabbed the brush from the sink seconds before he stepped into the room.

"What are you doing?"

"Brushing my hair. It needed it." She dragged the bristles through the tangles he'd left when he'd grabbed her by the back of the head. Her hand trembled. She set the brush on the counter and turned to face him, hoping no emotions showed. "What are you doing back? Did you forget something?"

"Yeah. My wallet. Have you seen it?"

"You put it in your coat pocket."

"You sure?"

"I'm sure."

He stared at her. Before she could stop herself, she raised a hand to cover the forming bruise beneath her right eye. "I'm sorry," he said, his dark eyes reflecting a remorse she'd seen too many times in their twelve years of marriage. A remorse that would vanish as soon as he perceived she'd done something "wrong" again.

"It's okay," she soothed. "You didn't mean it. It was my fault anyway. I shouldn't have pushed the issue."

She'd wanted to have a birthday party for Simon, their son. Kurt had said no. She'd begged him to reconsider and he'd punched her in the face.

He reached toward her and she couldn't help the small flinch. His jaw tightened and his eyes narrowed.

Quickly, she stepped forward and placed a kiss on his lips. "I'll see you when you get back."

His features softened and he nodded. He glanced at the clock. "I gotta get out of here. You're sure it's in my coat pocket?"

"Positive."

"Right. Bye."

"Bye," she whispered.

He loped back down the stairs. She watched him from the balcony overlooking the foyer. He turned back and she caught her breath.

"I'll be home day after tomorrow."

"I know. Be safe." She tried not to choke on the words.

He gave her a two-fingered salute and slipped out the door. Dani sank to the floor, her legs no longer able to support her. "Oh Lord, I don't think I can do this."

Jenny Cartee had assured her she could. Jenny. Dear, sweet Jenny, who'd recognized an abused wife and confronted her about it. Jenny, who'd showed Dani that she had worth, didn't deserve to be a punching bag, and helped her find the courage to leave before her husband killed her. Or Simon.

Just thinking her son's name gave her the strength to rise to her feet.

Eleven-year-old Simon. If she couldn't do this for herself, she had to do it for her son. Simon deserved to grow up without the constant fear and pain he lived with on a daily basis.

Dani waited fifteen minutes to make sure Kurt was really gone this time. Then she moved fast. She dragged the suitcase from the closet and finished packing it with her things, added Simon's, and then carried the luggage down the stairs and into the garage.

The black SUV sat in the far spot, just waiting. Any other day, she wouldn't have dared drive the car. Kurt kept a log of the mileage, when she drove, how far she drove, and demanded a list of each person she talked to. Today was different. Today she didn't care. Today she and Simon would finally be free. Simon rode to and from school with a friend and he was due home soon. As soon as he walked in the door, they'd leave. Because Kurt would call Mitchell's mother to make sure she'd delivered him. All under the guise of being a loving father, of course.

Dani went back into the house and up the stairs to the guest bedroom. She moved the nightstand and pulled up the swatch of carpet covering the small hole she'd cut into the plywood. The small box beckoned to her from its resting place on the two-by-four. She grabbed it, covered the hole with the carpet, and moved the nightstand back into place. She had managed to gather a few hundred dollars and stash the money along with some other items in the little box. But she needed more.

Back in the master bedroom she set the box on the bed, then looked at the picture on the wall. Before she had a chance to talk herself out of it, she removed the picture and looked at the dial on the safe. She'd played with the combination a few times before when the thought of leaving had consumed her. Always before she had come up empty. If this time was the same, she'd just have to take what she had and go.

Again, she tried birthdays, anniversaries, the time Simon was born. Kurt's brother's birthday, his mother's. Nothing. Frustration clawed at her.

Then it hit her. Kurt was a narcissist. It wouldn't be about his family. It would be about him. His pride. What did he cherish the most?

His job. His status. She tried his birthday, his graduation day from the academy. Her fingers stilled.

His badge number.

4892.

But she only needed three numbers for the combination.

She shot a glance at the clock. Time ticked away. Maybe she should just give up.

But not yet.

Something pushed her to get into the safe. She spun the dial. 4-8-9.

Nothing.

She ran her sweaty palms down her jean-clad thighs. Heart pounding faster than usual, she went back to the combination. 8-9-2.

Nothing.

48-9-2. She pulled the handle.

Click.

The door opened with a quiet whoosh.

A thrill shot through her. She'd done it. The door to the safe stood open. She wasted a precious ten seconds just staring at the piles of cash in front of her. Then raced to grab a bag from her closet. Almost weeping with gratitude, she swept the money into the bag, and after only a moment's hesitation, emptied the entire safe.

Which included a Glock 17 and other items she didn't have time to identify.

Her blood hummed as she saw the stacks of twenty-dollar bills. Elation flowed. She would be able to take care of Simon without worrying about money until she found a job. A new name, a new place, a new life. The thought nearly made her giddy.

She shut the safe and replaced the picture.

And the clock continued to tick away its minutes. Minutes to freedom. Her heart beat hard and she heard herself panting.

Taking a moment to compose herself, she breathed in through her nose and out through her mouth. "You're almost there, Dani. You're almost there."

She raced back down the stairs and out into the garage once

more. She hid the bag with the money under the backseat. She returned to the house to fix a cooler of food when the phone rang. She jumped. Froze.

Then glanced at the caller ID. Kurt. Her hand hovered over the handset. What would he do if she ignored it?

Turn around and come back.

She snatched it up. "Hello?"

"Stuart's coming by in about five minutes," Kurt said by way of greeting.

"What? Why?" Her stomach cramped. That would ruin everything.

"He's coming to get something I left in the safe. He should almost be there."

The safe? Really? Today? Stuart came by occasionally to get something from the safe, but today? Fear screamed through her. She spun to look at the clock. "Couldn't he get it tomorrow?"

"Why? You got plans?" The low threat in his voice warned her not to push him. Not when she was this close.

Dani swallowed hard. "Of course not. Tell him that's fine, I'll be here."

"That's what I thought you meant." He hung up.

She ran to the window and glanced out toward the driveway. No sign of Stuart. Did she have time to get the bag out of the car and put the contents back in the safe?

Movement at the end of the street caught her eye.

Stuart.

No time.

Her mind spun and the only plan she could come up with was to play it cool. But what could she say when he saw the empty safe?

Just thinking about being alone in the house with him made her shudder. Three years Kurt's senior, the man made her skin crawl in spite of the fact that he'd always treated her with nothing but respect. Blessed with outrageous good looks, he had the personality of a viper. And the reflexes. Striking when one least expected it. Silent and sneaky with cold eyes she couldn't read and avoided looking at.

Her fingers shook, her blood raced. *Oh dear Lord, what do I do?*

Tears surfaced. How had she ever thought she could get away with this?

Stuart pulled into the drive.

Anxiety made her nauseous. She ducked away from the window as Stuart got out of his car.

"You can do this. Don't stop to think, just do it."

She hurried toward the stairs and grabbed the handrail to steady herself.

The doorbell rang.

2

Six months was long enough to recover from a gunshot wound and the betrayal of his uncle. At least that's what he told himself. Adam Buchanan leaned back in his chair and stared out the window. A former US Marshal, he now worked for Operation Refuge, an organization founded by David and Summer Hackett. Adam liked his new job. He enjoyed protecting those who couldn't protect themselves—and bringing down those who thought they were above the law.

Like his uncle. The man had been in the pocket of Alessandro Raimondi, the head of an organized crime family. Raimondi was now dead, as was Parker Holland, Adam's uncle—thanks to Adam. Adam's mother's way of communicating was to shoot him wounded looks. His father had fallen into a depression.

"How you doing?"

Adam spun to face the door. Summer stood there, concern etched on her pretty face. Her right hand rested on the bulge that announced an impending birth.

"Hanging in there." Adam gave a slight smile. "How are you?"

Summer grimaced, but her physical discomfort couldn't hide her joy. "Ready to pop, I think."

"How much longer?"

"Four weeks."

"You going to make it?"

Summer laughed. "Guess we'll see."

Adam felt loneliness pierce him. All he'd ever wanted was a career as a marshal and a family of his own. He sighed. At thirty-three, the family part could still happen. He ignored the shaft of grief when he thought about his career. He stood. "I need a case."

"You just finished one. Don't you want to take a couple of days to regroup? Take care of any personal things?"

"No." That was the last thing he wanted. When he was working, he didn't dwell on his family situation. He could totally focus on his job and leave his personal troubles behind.

Summer frowned at him as though trying to read his thoughts. "All right. I'll see what we have."

They always had something. Adam relaxed a fraction, knowing he would soon be back in the swing of it. No more thinking about what he wanted and didn't have. He'd found that helping others took his mind off the fact that he couldn't seem to help his own family. Helping others was his therapy, the balm to his wounded soul. David and Summer's faith had sparked Adam's and he'd finally stopped blaming God for his parents' decisions. They were both grown-ups and could make up their own minds. He wasn't accountable for their choices, only for his own. If they chose to continue to blame him for his uncle's death there was nothing Adam could do about it except pray. Which he found himself doing a lot. It helped some, but he couldn't deny he really wanted a reconciliation with them. Maybe one day.

Simon Harding stared out the window, then glanced at the clock. School was almost over. Most days he wished he could just stay there. He hated going home. The only good thing about home was his mother. And his video games. One more day of school and summer vacation would start. A ball formed in his gut at the thought. He hated the long breaks from school. He shifted and his hearing aid whistled. Simon pressed the mold more firmly into his ear and grimaced. He needed new molds, but his dad hadn't said his mother could take him to get them yet.

But his dad would, because if he didn't, people would talk. And if his dad thought someone would say something negative, he'd do anything to make sure that didn't happen.

The teacher stomped on the wooden floor and the vibration jerked Simon back to the present. Mrs. Brown fit her name. Brown hair, brown eyes, brown personality. She signed, "Simon, are you with us today?"

A flippant answer came to mind, but he resisted. Getting in trouble wouldn't be a good thing. He signed back, "Yes, ma'am."

Her brown eyes softened at the respect. "Good, I'm glad to hear it. Would you please come work the math problem?"

Simon looked at the board for the first time since he'd walked into the classroom. And smiled. He rose from his desk and easily solved the algebra problem, explaining each step as he went. When finished, he dropped the dry erase marker in the tray and looked at Mrs. Brown. Once again, he'd managed to surprise her.

She'd given him the hardest problem and he'd done it almost without thinking about it. He knew what a lot of people thought, including teachers. Deaf kids weren't supposed to be able to grasp some of the abstract concepts he'd mastered. Especially eleven-year-old deaf kids.

He glanced at the sea of faces before him. Confusion on a few. Resentment on others because he'd shown them up. Sheer boredom on most because the subject was above their heads. Only Mitchell Lee looked interested. And impressed. But Mitchell was like Simon. He didn't fit the mold hearing people had made for the deaf.

Simon took his seat and looked at the clock again. 2:45. As the minute hand ticked closer and closer to 3:15, his heart beat with the dread of going home.

Dani stepped back to let her brother-in-law in. He loomed over her, his big frame dwarfing the area. Stuart had always been nothing but kind to her. Gentle, sweet. But definitely creepy. She could just never get comfortable in his presence no matter how kind he acted. It was his eyes. They never matched his outward behavior. She said, "You know where the safe is." Go, go. She shot a glance toward the door. Just a few feet away, freedom waited.

"I do."

As soon as Stuart went for the safe—which he'd find empty— she'd have to grab the keys and race to the school to get Simon. A kink in her original plans to be sure, but she could do it. If he'd just go upstairs.

When he simply stared at her, she kept her face expressionless. *Play the game, Dani. Do it!* On shaky legs, she moved toward the kitchen when all she wanted to do was race for the door. Stuart followed her and she ground her molars, grasping to control her runaway pulse and stuttering nerves. The seconds ticked away. And every second counted.

"Can I get you something to drink?" she asked because she knew he expected it. She always offered food and drink when he came over. The steadiness of her voice shocked her.

"No, thanks." Stuart settled himself at one of the kitchen chairs, and while she wouldn't have thought it possible, Dani felt her tension escalate. Her head beat with the stress of trying to figure out how to get rid of him without making him suspicious.

The clock crept toward 2:55. The school was ten minutes away. When Stuart found the safe empty, she couldn't be here. Which meant she needed to leave now to get Simon before the dismissal bell. Otherwise her escape plan would be nothing but an epic fail. And it might even cost her and Simon their lives. "Can I get you anything?"

"No thanks, Dani, I'm fine. What time does Simon get home?"

"Around 3:30. Why?"

"Just thinking." He paused. "You could have done better, Dani."

His out-of-the-blue statement spoken ever so softly made her stare. "Done better?"

"I know Kurt doesn't treat you right." He stood and stepped toward her.

Dani took a step back as her pulse ratcheted up several notches. If this continued she would self-combust.

She forced a laugh. It came out more like a nervous titter. "What? I don't know what you mean."

Stuart's jaw tightened then he gave a short laugh. "Sure you do, but—Forget I said anything." He walked toward the steps. "I'll just get what I came for and be on my way."

A little breath of relief puffed between her lips. "Okay, you do that."

Dani waited, listening. As soon as he disappeared around the corner, she raced through the laundry room and into the garage.

She climbed into the Navigator and reached for the keys she'd swiped from the hook just inside the back door that led to the garage.

But wait. She froze. Stuart's car. He'd know exactly where she would go from here. He knew she'd never leave Simon. And he would follow. She went out the door that led to the driveway and hurried over to Stuart's vehicle, opened the driver's door, and popped the hood. Seconds continued to pass at a disturbingly rapid rate. Did he have the safe open yet? Had he discovered her theft?

Almost sobbing with her desperation, she reached under the hood and yanked whatever wires she could get her hands on. One of them came loose. She hoped it was enough to stall him. She raced back into the garage and stopped just before she got into the Navigator. Her purse! She'd left it on the counter. She ran back into the house.

"Dani?" She froze as his voice filtered downstairs from her master bedroom. "Hey! Where's the stuff from the safe? Is this one of Kurt's stupid practical jokes?"

She snatched her purse from the counter and bolted back to the garage, closing the door behind her as quietly as she could. She climbed into the Navigator, and reached to start the car.

"The key! Where's the key?" she whispered, panting, blood humming, nerves so tight she thought she might throw up. She looked down at the cupholder and nearly sobbed with relief as she pulled the key out, jammed it into the ignition, and started the car.

The dash clock said 3:02. Stuart would be looking for her any second. She pressed the button to open the garage door and put the car in reverse. "Please . . . please . . ."

The garage door opened behind her as did the door leading from the house. Stuart's face appeared and he lunged for the car door. Heart pounding, tears threatening, Dani slapped the lock button and pressed the gas pedal.

"Dani! Stop! What are you doing? Where's the stuff in the safe? Dani! Kurt's going to kill you!"

She ignored him, desperation fueling her. Dani backed out of the garage, tires squealing as she pressed the brake and threw it into drive. Within seconds, she arrived at the exit to the subdivision. In the rearview mirror she could see Stuart in the street, watching her. She knew he would head straight to the school once he got his car started. And she knew he would be on the phone to Kurt as soon as he could punch in the numbers.

Dani pulled out of the subdivision and into the median, wait-ing impatiently to merge with the traffic. Finally an opening. She shot into the opening and drove fast, weaving in and out of the traffic, but not so fast she'd get a ticket. As desperate as she was to get to the school, she simply couldn't afford to get stopped. She'd gotten her driver's license renewed online on a trip to the library two months ago. Kurt had been out of town for something and she'd accepted Jenny's offer to take them on the little outing.

Dear, sweet Jenny. But even Jenny didn't know everything. Dani finally turned into the school parking lot. Cars already waited in line. She bypassed them straight to an empty spot near the office. Simon was deaf, but he was mainstreamed into the regular edu-cation classroom. He had an interpreter that followed him from class to class. And two of his teachers signed. He liked school, but Dani knew he was bored with it.

She parked and raced into the building. At the office, she waited impatiently while the secretary helped a man in front of her. The bell would ring in three minutes. She waited, praying she'd pulled enough wires to stall Stuart long enough for her to get away. She wondered if he'd called Kurt. Her stomach cramped.

Two minutes. Dani stepped up. "I'm so sorry to interrupt, but we have a family emergency. Could you please buzz Simon's teacher and have him come to the office?"

"We don't allow early dismissals after 2:00, Mrs. Harding."

The lady looked like she wished she could help. Dani jumped on that. "Please! I've got to get him now! It's an emergency. A family crisis and I need to go. I have to catch him before he rides home with his friend." She knew she was begging, but Dani would have gotten on her knees if she thought it would help get her son. Because she sure wasn't leaving without him. *Please, God!*

"Come on, it's an emergency." The deep voice of the man she'd interrupted. Dani shot him a grateful look.

Again with the hesitation that had Dani ready to climb out of her skin. Then a faint nod. "Let me see if I can catch him."

Only a partial relief filled her. She hoped Simon would tell Mitchell he wasn't riding home, but frankly she didn't care, she just wanted to leave. Now.

The bell rang as the woman picked up the phone and Dani sucked in a deep breath. The secretary spoke, but the blood whooshing through her veins kept her from hearing what she said. *Please, God, oh please . . .*

As though in slow motion, the phone clicked back on the cradle. Dani looked at her as the woman smiled. "He's on his way to the office."

Now her knees felt weak. Wanted to buckle beneath her. Somehow she stayed on her feet and managed a nod. "Thank you," she whispered.

"I hope everything will be all right."

"I do too." Grim, she stared at the door her son would enter, willing him to hurry.

Simon raced down the hall, his backpack slapping against his hips as he weaved in and out of the students scrambling to go home. He'd read Mrs. Brown's lips when she spoke into the phone. She'd looked straight at him and frowned. "Family emergency? I'll send him right down." Simon had gathered his things and was out the door before she hung up.

Worry gnawed at him. Family emergency? Had his dad finally hurt his mother bad enough to send her to the hospital or had he even kil—

No. Tears clogged his throat. He burst into the front office and felt the air leave his lungs.

His mother stood there. Whole. Healthy. Alive. His eyes caught hers. She must have seen something in his expression because she reached for him and gave him a brief hug before turning to say something to the secretary. Simon didn't bother trying to understand her, he just let the relief flow through him.

Within seconds, she ushered him from the building. He could feel the tension vibrating through her body. His relief at finding her physically intact fled and the fear returned. What was wrong? When they stopped at the Navigator, she motioned for him to get in. He turned and stared at her. Signed, "You drove?"

"Yes," she signed back. "Get in and hurry."

"What's wrong?"

"In," she signed. "Please."

Her tight, drawn features drove his fear and confusion to new heights. Without another question, he climbed in and slammed the door while she did the same. Movement in the side mirror caught his attention.

"Why is Uncle Stuart here too?" he asked her, using his voice. He didn't like speaking in front of the other kids or adults, but with his mother he didn't care.

She jerked and slapped the locks, jammed the keys into the ignition and cranked the vehicle. Simon checked the mirror again and saw his uncle running toward them. But the car pulled from the curb and his mother drove with careful deliberation until they were free of the school zone.

She tapped his arm and signed, "Watch for him. Tell me when you don't see him anymore."

Realization dawned on Simon.

They were running.

Running for their lives.

3

"Birthday parties are a bore," Special Agent Joseph Duncan said as he slipped up beside Kurt.

"I agree." Kurt took a sip of Coke and watched the proceedings with interest. Kurt hated conferences and thought they were a waste of his time when he should be working a case, eagerly pursuing the next notch on his belt.

However, this conference wasn't as distasteful as others. At least here, he was going to have a little fun and do a little business on the side that would rake in a nice chunk of cash.

They were off duty as of thirty minutes ago and were at the bar. "Whose idea was this anyway?"

"Jack Fletcher's." Joe leaned against the wall and checked his phone. "You get Faraday a present?"

"Yeah. I did." Something in his tone must have caught Joe's attention.

His fellow agent eyed him warily. "What'd you do?"

Kurt lifted a brow—all innocence and light. "What do you mean?"

Joe snorted. "You know what I mean. You've got one of your famous practical jokes up your sleeve, don't you?"

"Why, Joseph, I have no idea what you're talking about."

25

Joe laughed. "Don't even try for the innocent look, you don't have one."

Kurt simply smiled. He loved practical jokes. The kind that people tried to laugh off, but underneath were seething because he'd "gotten" them. Practical jokes were even good for payback.

Gordon Faraday, the fifty-six-year-old birthday boy who was one year shy of retirement, grinned as he opened the packages and cards. Kurt couldn't stand the man. He was such a suck-up even when the situation didn't call for it. Kurt only sucked up when it benefited him.

Word had filtered down that Gordon had gone to the SAC about him to say he didn't feel like Kurt should have gotten his latest promotion. Kurt hadn't told Dani that they would be moving to Houston, Texas, that he was getting ready to be promoted to a squad supervisor. They would move in one month when the current one retired. Gordon's meeting with the SAC had been two months ago and Kurt had been waiting for a time to initiate some payback.

"What are we waiting on?" Joe glanced at his watch. "We've got stuff to discuss."

"Patience, my friend. Just a little bit longer."

Finally, Gordon reached for the blue-and-white-striped box that measured about two feet by three. He ripped the paper off.

Kurt tensed in anticipation.

The box opened, triggering the spring that released three hundred rubber snakes in all shapes and sizes. Time slowed for Kurt. He savored each second as the snakes flew in the air and then fell one by one to land on the now screaming Special Agent.

The man screamed again and ripped at them, flung them from his shoulders, his neck, his face. He danced to the side and screamed when he stepped on them. And then he froze for a brief second.

His eyes went wide and he grabbed his left arm.

His eyes fluttered closed and he slumped to the floor.

Kurt smiled. "Gotcha," he whispered.

Chaos ensued. Kurt listened to the voices. "Call 911!"

"Gordy! Hang in there, buddy, help's on the way!"

"Who did that? Who would do such a thing?"

Joe stared, then turned to look at Kurt, disbelief stamped on his square-faced features. "That was pretty intense. You know Gordon's deathly afraid of snakes."

"Yeah. Getting bit by one will do that to a person. His reaction was priceless, wasn't it?"

Joe blew out a slow breath and looked back to where Gordon lay.

Kurt nudged him. "Come on, I told you what he did. You know he deserved it."

Joe chuckled, but Kurt thought it sounded forced. "What if he dies?"

Kurt snorted. "Then he dies."

Wimp.

Joe watched the chaos, a slight frown on his features. Kurt followed his gaze and saw Ralph Thorn doing CPR. The next time Ralph lifted his head, his gaze locked on Kurt's, then his eyes slid to Joe. Then he bent back over his friend and continued to try to save the man's life.

Joe's phone rang. No one else noticed it in the chaos. Joe grabbed it and listened.

Kurt watched the color drain from Joe's face. When the man did an about-face and stomped from the room, Kurt followed. By the time they stepped into the hall, Joe had hung up.

"What is it?"

"We lost the guns."

Kurt stilled, sure he'd heard wrong. "What?"

"You heard me."

Kurt held in his rage with a rarely exhibited control. "What do you mean you lost them?"

"They had people waiting for us. We had to get out or be caught. I thought they were going to be able to get them back, but that was Liam. They didn't get them."

"Do you know how much those weapons are worth?"

"Yes, I know," Joe snapped back. He paced forward four steps, then back three. "We can get them back."

"How?"

"I have a contact. I'll get in the evidence room and get them."

Kurt scoffed. "You could probably find a way to remove money, drugs, whatever, from the room, but that many guns? No way."

"Then we'll just have to get more from somewhere else."

"I've already paid the supplier. I'm out fifteen grand, you moron!" He curled his fingers into a fist. "No, I'm out thirty grand because I was going to double my money. Then I need to pay for—" He broke off and lowered his voice. "I can't afford that kind of loss." He sighed. "Well, at least tell me you got rid of the witness."

"Yeah. She's taken care of."

"Then Kabakov will be sending payment for that."

Joe swore. "And I need it too."

A slight noise to the left had Kurt swiveling and dropping his voice, looking at the door. "You hear that?"

"Yeah."

Kurt gestured for Joe to follow him. He moved toward the door and, in one smooth move, swung it open. Alan James leaned against the wall, checking his phone. He looked up with narrowed eyes. "What's up?"

Kurt reached out, grabbed the man by the collar, and yanked him into the room. Surprise was on Kurt's side for a split second before Alan could try to bluff his way out of this one.

Kurt slammed him up against the wall. "Like to eavesdrop, do you?"

"Like to pull pranks that kill people, do you?" Alan snarled. He brought his foot up and rammed it into Kurt's knee.

Kurt screamed and dropped back. Alan lunged at a recovering Kurt and his punch caught him on the jaw. Kurt rocked back and lost his grip. He snagged his gun from his holster and spun to see Alan pull his weapon in response. Joe came from the left and tackled Alan to the floor. Alan rolled and a shot sounded. Joe cried out, grabbing his left ear. Kurt stood and swayed.

Alan bolted to his feet and Kurt went after him. He jammed a fist in the man's gut. Air whooshed from his lungs, but Alan still held tight to his gun.

Kurt swung his weapon up and aimed it at Alan. "You should have minded your own business."

Alan raised his weapon and fired. Kurt jerked. He pulled the trigger and saw the bullet hit Alan between the eyes. Kurt's vision blurred and he blinked. His blood pumped and he felt a sticky wetness under his shirt. The warm wetness moved down, soaking the waistband of his pants. He wondered why he noticed that. Yells reached his ears. Voices coming closer. They'd heard the shots.

Darkness pressed into him. He resisted. He felt his phone vibrating. Couldn't lift his arm to get it. Joe kept yelling at him, but Kurt couldn't process the words.

The door burst in as Kurt lost his balance and dropped over on his side. Darkness beckoned him.

It occurred to him that Dani would be glad to hear of his death. She would finally be free of him. The thought made him vaguely sad. He wanted to see her beauty just one more time.

Then he couldn't seem to think as heavy hands pressed on the wound in his chest.

Hot, so hot. Suffocating. Terror sliced through him at the smell of . . . sulfur? *No! I don't want to die! I'm not ready! God—*

Breathing became a memory and the world faded to black.

4

Stuart growled his frustration and watched the Navigator disappear, merged with the flow of the school traffic. He raced back to his white Lexus and gunned the motor. He'd finally checked under the hood and found the loose wires, which caused him to lose precious minutes as he reconnected them. He couldn't believe Dani had done this. For what? All he wanted to do was protect her from Kurt, because as soon as Kurt found the empty safe and his family gone, he'd kill them.

And Stuart couldn't let that happen.

Dani was running from Kurt and he had to stop her.

He'd figured she would go after Simon, he'd just been about two minutes too late. All eyes in the carpool line were on him now, including the school resource officer. He flashed his badge at the man, who nodded, but gestured for him to keep it slow in the school zone. Stuart gritted his teeth and nodded back.

He kept his speed right at the maximum allowed, gripping the wheel and steering into the traffic. He went as fast as he dared, having no desire to be pulled over and waste precious time showing his ID. However, he was determined not to lose her. It was time they had a serious conversation about her and Kurt.

His phone rang. "Hello?"

"Stuart? It's Peter Hastings."

"Yeah?" He knew he sounded distracted. He was. But he had to fight to keep Dani in his sights. His gut said she was running from Kurt. From him. "What is it? I'm busy."

"Kurt's dead."

Stuart slammed on the brakes and pulled into the nearest parking lot. He let Dani go. She wouldn't get far and he could always find her later. And she would have no reason to run once she learned Kurt was dead. She'd be back. "What happened?"

"He was shot at the hotel where the conference is. He died at the scene." Peter blew out a breath. "Man, I'm sorry."

Surprisingly, Stuart felt a huge hole in the vicinity of his chest. Then the feeling fled. He still had one more thing to accomplish.

He still had to make Dani his.

Completely and in every way. If he didn't, then Kurt would win. "I've got to go."

"You going to be all right?"

"Yes. Thanks for letting me know." A deep sigh overtook him. "I guess I'll need to let my parents know. Or has someone already called them?"

"I think the ASAC called them."

Patrick Kline, the Assistant Special Agent in Charge. "Good. Good. I'll, uh, head over there."

"Let me know if I can do anything."

"Yeah." He hung up, his mind still on Dani.

One thing bothered him. She'd cleaned out the safe. Why? What was in the box Kurt had sent him over there to get?

Stuart punched through the red light, a small smile curling his lips. Now he really needed to find Dani.

To tell her Kurt was dead and that she belonged to him now. That he was ready to step in and take care of her from now on.

The thought made him smile. "I won, Kurt. I beat you. She's mine." Now he just had to find her and tell her.

Dani had checked and rechecked her rearview mirror all the way to the hotel. At the library, where she'd spent as much time as possible when Kurt was gone and Simon was at school, she'd googled and mapped and planned her route. They'd made it to the first stop.

Inside the hotel room, Simon questioned her nonstop, his hands flying at warp speed. "Where are we going?"

"A long way from here."

"Across country?"

"Yes."

"To see your mother?"

A pang hit her. "No, that's the first place your father will look."

His shoulders drooped. "I want to meet my grandmother."

"I know, hon. And maybe one day that'll be possible. I know she'd like to meet you too." Dani kept her contact with her mother to a minimum. She was too afraid of what Kurt would do if he found out she was in touch with the woman.

Simon flipped on the television and picked up the remote. "I hope they have closed captions here."

"I'm sure they do." She didn't offer to see if she could get them working. Simon knew better than she did how to do that.

The room was nice. Nothing fancy, but it wasn't a dump either. The money from the safe would carry them for a while as long as she wasn't extravagant. But she refused to stay in a dangerous area. She'd had enough of danger for the past twelve years. It was time to find out what it felt like to feel safe again.

"Mom?"

She turned to find Simon's gaze fixed on the television screen.

And she saw why.

"Two FBI agents have been declared dead at the scene of the Crown Vista hotel. We don't have any more details at the moment . . ."

"That's where Dad is, isn't it?"

"Yes." She sank onto the bed beside him.

Simon looked at her. "You think it could be him?"

Dani signed that she didn't know. "Let's watch."

As time passed, she and Simon stayed glued to the screen, pausing only to order supper. Finally, a reporter came on the screen. "Alan James has been identified as one of the dead agents. The other agent's name has not been released yet because his family hasn't been notified. We'll be back with more news after this break."

Simon signed. "We need to find out."

Dani nodded. "Yes, you're right."

"Who can you call?"

"Your dad's boss."

5

Special Agent Joseph Duncan stepped through the doors and made his way to the small square room he called an office.

"Yo, Duncan, welcome back. Nice job on that last assignment. Took you long enough, though."

Joe turned and waved at Ralph Thorn, who nursed a cup of coffee on his way to his own desk. "Thanks, man."

"Six months is a long time."

"Too long, but not as long as I thought it would be." He tried to force a smile, but was sure it came out more in the form of a grimace than anything else.

"You been home yet?"

"Nope. Had to stop by here and get caught up a little. Then I plan to go home and sleep for about a week." Home. He should call it his hovel. Bitterness nearly engulfed him. Two years ago his father had died and left everything to Joe's older brother. The shining star. The Wall Street executive. The one who already had more money than he knew what to do with.

34

And Joe? He inherited a trailer park where no one paid the rent unless you hounded them or threatened eviction. Like he had time for that. It was one reason he liked the long undercover assignments. Actually six months wasn't all that long. He'd been hoping for a year or longer. Maybe next time.

"Sounds good. Let's get together for lunch when you surface."

"Right."

Thorn took a gulp of his brew and disappeared into his office across from Joe's cubicle.

Joseph Duncan. He shook his head. The name sounded weird. He'd used so many names over the past six months he wasn't sure who he was anymore.

His phone rang and he sighed. Word traveled fast. "Duncan."

"You're back." Peter Hastings's low voice rumbled in his ear.

"I am."

"Are we on for tonight?"

He frowned. "Tonight?"

"We've got a shipment coming in. And we have a buyer for the plates. So bring them."

Joe sighed and rubbed his eyes. "Tonight. I can't tonight."

"We need you there, Joe."

"I promised my sister I'd help her with something." He'd told Cheryl he'd bring her some cash. Her bum of a husband had left her with three small kids, and she was struggling just to put food on the table and hold down a part-time job that paid squat. Of course their older brother didn't care about that. He had only disdain for his two siblings who hadn't had what it took to make the big bucks. And their father?

No sense in going there, Duncan. "Never mind, I'll be there." Joe rubbed his gritty eyes. "I need the money." His sister needed the money. "Wait a minute. What plates?"

"The plates that Kurt hid and only you know where they are?

35

We've been waiting for you to come out from under so we could get them, but it's been a long, hard wait."

"Dude, I don't have the plates. Kurt had 'em, but he didn't give them to me."

Silence. "What?"

"He didn't give them to me." Joe repeated himself, enunciating each word as though talking to someone who didn't understand English.

"Joe—"

"You going to make me say it again?"

"Don't mess with us, Joe. You know what happened to Trennen." Raw anger filtered through the line.

Joe shook his head in disbelief as his adrenaline gave a sudden rush. He sat up, the weariness of the last six months falling from his shoulders. "You threatening me?"

"Should I?"

Joe felt his blood hum and the anger start to boil in his belly. "You don't want to go there. I said I don't have the plates and I don't."

A long stretch of silence. Joe waited him out. "Right. Of course. Sorry."

"Yeah." Another stretch of silence. "Why would you think I had the plates? Kurt had them last time I heard."

"Kurt talked about giving them to you for safekeeping."

"What? Why?"

"I don't know, man, I'm just telling you what he said."

"Right. Well, he didn't give them to me."

"So you said."

"Maybe he was planning on it and got killed before he could do it."

"Maybe."

Weariness pressed in on him. "Tonight. I'll be there. We'll talk more about this when I see you. You'll have to tell the buyer that the plates are unavailable and we'll contact him when we have them ready."

"Right. Like that's going to go over well."

"Look, just tell him there was a glitch in one of them, something that needs to be tweaked. He doesn't want faulty plates, does he?"

"I'll tell him."

Joe hung up and sat back, his mind spinning.

He reached for the stack of mail as he thought. Anything business related would have been opened by his designee. Anything personal would have been left alone. Also by his request. When he went undercover, he cut off all ties with any personal life. Which wasn't much anyway. The only thing he requested was that his paycheck be split in half. Half went to his sister and half went into a savings account.

Anger boiled beneath the surface. Why would Pete think Joe had the plates? Why would Kurt talk to Pete about giving the plates to Joe? That didn't make any sense.

Joe blew out a frustrated breath. He picked up the phone and dialed Cheryl's number. He'd called her the minute his plane landed, telling her he'd watch the kids for her while she had some much needed time to herself. And now he was going to have to renege. He hated it for her, but it couldn't be helped. The phone rang three times. "Hello?"

"Hey there, Princess, is your mom home?"

"Hey, Uncle Joe. She's here, but I want to talk to you first." His five-year-old niece loved talking on the phone. Joe closed his eyes. As much as he loved his sister's kids, he didn't have time to talk.

"Can't talk right now, kiddo, get me your mom."

"Say please."

"Please."

"Pretty please?"

Joe bit his tongue on the words he really wanted to say. "Pretty please, Gina. Now get your mom."

"Well, you don't have to be mean about it."

Joe winced and shook his head.

"Brat," he muttered, but couldn't help the smile. His sister and her kids were the only people on this earth that he cared about. And he needed money to take care of them.

"Hey. You're backing out on me, aren't you?" Cheryl sounded weary and run-down.

"Yeah. But when I'm done, I'll come spend the night and you can sleep in and get up and go do whatever you need to do."

"Okay, thanks, Joe." The relief in her voice hit him hard. "Thanks."

"Sure."

He hung up and rubbed his eyes. A rap on the side of his cubicle brought his head up. "Hey."

"Hey." Stuart slipped into the chair across from him. "Welcome back, partner."

"Yeah." Joe snorted. "Welcome back to me. It never stops, does it?"

"Nope."

Joe gave his eyes another scrub. "So, how's it going?"

"Got a lot to tell you about."

"Like?"

Stuart snickered. "Like the case that landed on my desk this morning."

"What case?"

"Some old woman thought her kid was growing pot in her basement, so she called us."

Joe rolled his eyes. "And?"

"I rode out there. He's not growing pot, he's growing a garden and selling the vegetables."

38

"Inside?"

"Yeah. It's like the perfect greenhouse down there. Said he was desperate to get out from under his mother and found he can do this and make pretty good money."

"How old's the kid?"

"Fifteen."

Joe snorted and Stuart laughed. "I know." He leaned forward, wondering if Stuart knew anything about the plates. "So, did Kurt ever talk to you about his cases?"

"Kurt?" Stuart shrugged. "No. We didn't talk if we could avoid it, you know that."

"Right. Right."

Stuart leaned back and crossed his arms. "Why would you even ask that? What are you after?"

Joe stood. "Nothing." If Stuart had the plates, he didn't want to press the issue. Not yet. He'd just wait and watch. "I've got to go. Catch you later."

Stuart frowned, suspicion glinting. Joe ignored it and left, feeling Stuart's gaze drilling holes in his back.

———

Not all plans worked out, the watcher knew that. In fact, most of the time, plans fell through because they weren't thought out to completion. The planner was too hasty in his need to put it into action.

However, the watcher had prepared for this. Planned, schemed, lied, and done whatever it took to make sure all the players were in place. Like chess pieces on the board, they only moved where the watcher guided them.

There were a good many players. Too many almost, but the plan would work. No doubt about that. It had to.

Ironically enough, the watcher had enjoyed putting the plan

together and manipulating the players in this deadly game. However, it was time for everything to come to a head.

Time for the pieces to take over and do their job.

Revenge was the ultimate goal and no one would stop the watcher from achieving it.

6

Stuart tossed the file onto his desk and sat with a thump on the faux leather chair. Saturday mornings at the office were usually slow. Normal business hours during the week were from 8:15 to 5:00, but no agent actually kept those hours, so when Stuart came in on Saturday, he usually had company. This morning seemed quieter than usual. Just the way he preferred it. But he couldn't concentrate on what he needed to get done.

All he could think about was Dani. And the fact that she wasn't cooperating with him at all. He wasn't sure what her problem was, but he'd about had enough of it.

He had to show her she needed him. It had been six months since Kurt's death. Long enough for her to grieve. Or at least put on the appearance of grieving. He wasn't sure she was actually sad Kurt was gone, but he'd allowed an appropriate amount of time to pass before suggesting they start dating.

And she'd turned him down flat.

He attributed that to the fact that she just didn't know what she wanted. After all, Kurt hadn't let her hardly think for the past twelve years.

41

A rap on the door brought his head up. Joseph Duncan, his partner. Stuart decided if he had someone to call a friend, it would be Joe—even if the man had also been friends with Kurt.

"Hey man, can I talk to you?" Joe asked.

"Yeah. Sure. Have a seat."

Joe settled himself into the chair opposite Stuart and leaned forward. "How's it going?"

"It's going. What are you doing here on a Saturday morning? Figured you'd be with your sister and her kids." Joe tried to reserve Saturdays for them. He couldn't do it every week, of course, but Stuart couldn't think of anything the man had to take care of that couldn't wait until Monday morning.

Joe waved a hand of dismissal. "I wanted to talk to you and make a few phone calls." He took a deep breath. "So . . . how are you handling Kurt's death?"

Stuart narrowed his eyes. "You know Kurt and I were never close. More competitive than anything."

"Yeah. I know."

"So I guess you could say I'm handling his death just fine."

"How about that pretty wife of his?"

Stuart's radar blipped. What was Joe up to? "Dani's doing all right too."

"Ralph said his wife stopped by the other day to check on her. Said she looked stressed."

Stuart leaned forward. "Stressed? About what?"

Joe shrugged. "Said you were harassing her."

Stuart stilled. "Harassing her?" He forced a laugh. "I don't think Dani would say that." His partner studied him and Stuart found he wanted to squirm under the stare. "What?" he demanded.

Joe shook his head. "I don't know. I always thought you and Dani would have made a good couple."

Not what he'd expected to come out of Joe's mouth, but the words punctured a hole in his defensiveness. "Excuse me?"

"I don't mean any disrespect to Kurt, but he didn't treat her right. I've seen how you looked at her. You're in love with her, aren't you?"

"Well," Stuart leaned back in his chair and crossed his arms. "This conversation certainly puts a new twist on the day."

"You're going to deny it?"

Stuart sighed. "I don't know if what I feel for Dani is love or not." He answered honestly because he saw no point in lying. He only lied when it was to his benefit. "I know that I want her, so I suppose that's enough, isn't it?"

Joe cocked his head. "That's a weird answer, dude."

Stuart shrugged. "It's the only one I've got." He stood and paced to the window. Shoving his hands into the front pockets of his neatly pressed khakis, he turned, debating whether or not to say anything further.

Before he could make up his mind, Joe said, "I was thinking about that."

"Why?"

"You're my partner, man. We look out for each other, right?"

"Of course."

"Then if you want Dani, you should do something to get her."

Stuart lifted a brow. "Like what?" He had his own ideas on that, but didn't figure it would hurt to hear what Joe had to say.

"Like I said, I've been thinking. I think you should come to her rescue and make her appreciate you."

"Come to her rescue? Make her appreciate me?" Stuart let out a little laugh. "Any ideas on how to arrange that?"

Joe snorted. "What? You want me to do all the work?"

Stuart stared and Joe shrugged. "Think about it. What woman can resist a man who fights for her?"

"Right." He gazed at his partner, whose words brought to mind another woman. One he'd fought for, killed for, and had the allegiance of. Joe's words were startling in their accuracy, and Stuart wondered why he hadn't thought of it himself. "I'll think about that. Thanks." He shoved the file that he needed to read to the side and studied Joe. "Why did you take that long undercover deal?"

Joe shrugged. "You know how it is, man. You do what you've got to do."

"But you pushed for that case."

Joe sighed and dropped his head. "Look, I have my reasons, all right? I had the opportunity and I took it."

"You seem to have a lot of those opportunities." Stuart rubbed his chin and stared at Joe. "You recovered a lot of missing guns. Arrested an entire fleet of gunrunners."

"Yeah. So?"

"So, I guess that makes you a hero around here now."

Joe sighed. He opened his mouth to say something and his phone vibrated an interruption. "I gotta take this. Good luck with the lady. I've got a few ideas on how to get her attention and make her look at you like you're her hero."

Stuart nodded. "I'm interested in hearing what you're thinking."

Joe waved his phone. "I'll catch up to you in a few. We've got cases to go over and a game plan to come up with."

"Right."

Joe left and Stuart stared at the computer, his mind whirling with ways to convince Dani he was all she needed. That he could be her hero.

Yeah. Maybe Joe was on to something.

Saturday midmorning, Dani looked around her kitchen and sighed. She loved her kitchen and was glad Kurt had allowed her to decorate it and stock it as she saw fit. He hadn't cared what she *did* with it as long as he liked what came *out* of it.

She straightened the candles along the windowsill. Black, red, and white, they went with her black and white décor. Although she didn't light them, she did appreciate the subtle scent they gave off. She smiled. Jenny brought her a candle every so often and Dani couldn't bear to stick them away in a drawer or a closet somewhere. Besides, when Jenny came over for coffee, she seemed to take delight in the fact that Dani displayed the candles so openly. She'd even arranged them. Five black ones, one red, and five white. All in a neat row. Dani smiled and shook her head. Jenny was a bit strange, but she liked the woman.

She took another look around and nodded. All was as it should be. She went upstairs and found Simon in the bonus room playing a video game. She got his attention and signed to him, "I'm going for my run."

"Is Jenny going with you?"

"Not this morning, she's not feeling well."

He frowned. "So you're going alone?"

"Yes, why?"

He shrugged and turned back to his game.

She flicked the light switch to get his attention again. He blew out a heavy sigh and looked at her. She signed, "What game are you playing?"

"The math one Mitchell and I compete with each other on."

Dani shook her head and smiled. "It's the weekend. Aren't you tired of math?"

He snorted. "I'm never tired of numbers. They're about the only thing in this world that makes any sense."

She'd never understand her son's fascination with digits, but understood his need for something to make sense. If that was math, so be it. "I'll be back in about thirty minutes, okay?"

"Fine." He frowned at her, worry in his eyes. "Be careful."

She walked over and planted a kiss on his head, then made sure he could see her lips. "I'll be careful. I love you."

"Love you too."

She knew he worried about her and she hated it, but she wasn't going to let fear rule their lives. Kurt was dead. He couldn't hurt them anymore.

Dani bounded down the steps, her ponytail swinging behind her. She'd dressed in her favorite pair of black-and-pink jogging pants with matching hoodie. Even in the South, December could be a cold month.

She opened the door and bit back a scream. Then groaned. "Stuart?" He gave her the once-over and she fought the urge to slam the door in his face. "What are you doing here?"

"I thought we'd talk."

"I thought I'd go for a jog."

"I'll go with you."

"Dressed like that? Pressed khakis, a hundred-dollar sweater, and leather dress shoes aren't going to get you very far."

"Look, could I just come in and—"

"No. Please, just stop. You've got to stop this." She moved out onto the front step with him and shut the door. And checked to make sure it was locked.

A familiar face coming her way made her breathe a sigh of relief. "Jenny?"

Jenny looked pale, her red nose attesting to her illness.

Dani frowned. "Are you okay? You need something?"

Jenny sniffed. "Yeah. Sorry. Chester got out and I was wondering if you'd seen him."

Chester, the little schnauzer Jenny loved like a child. "No, I'm sorry. I haven't been outside until now."

Tears welled. Jenny bit her lip and nodded. "Okay, thanks. Will you look for him while you're running?"

"Of course."

"Hey, let me just come help you look."

Dani realized Stuart was still standing behind her. She frowned at him over her shoulder. "Goodbye, Stuart."

"Give me five minutes, Dani."

Dani took a deep breath, closed her eyes, and gathered her strength. She spun around and faced her brother-in-law. From the corner of her eye, she could see Jenny watching them.

Dani realized she was going to have to talk to Stuart. "I'll just be a few minutes, Jenny. I promise."

"Sure. You need me to hang around?"

"No." She supposed she should introduce the two. "Stuart, this is my friend Jenny. Jenny, my brother-in-law Stuart."

Stuart nodded. "Hello."

Jenny gave him a weary smile, but even through her friend's tears, Dani could see the spark of interest in Jenny's eyes. "Hello."

"Nice to meet you."

"Yeah. You too. Come back when I don't look like I've been hit by a truck." She took a step back and waved a hand toward her house. "I've got to go look for my dog. Dani, you won't be long, will you?"

"No. No I won't."

"Okay, thanks." Jenny turned and headed back toward her house, which was four doors down.

Stuart didn't waste a blessed minute. "Come on, Dani, don't be like this. Kurt would want you taken care of. I've wanted to take care of you for twelve years now."

He what? Alarmed, she took a step back. He took one forward, so she stopped. "Stuart, he's only been dead six months—"

"Plenty of time to grieve and move on."

She stared at him, jaw hanging. She snapped it shut. He'd been bugging her about the two of them dating for the past two months. He took her hand and she swallowed a ball of nausea at his touch.

"I know Kurt wasn't the kind of man you need. He was cruel. Evil even."

Dani removed her hand from his and wiped it on her pants. "I won't argue with you there. Kurt was a psychopath. He had no conscience, he took pleasure in other people's pain. And yet he loved himself. Is there such a thing as a narcissistic psychopath?" She gave a humorless laugh.

"Probably." He waved a dismissive hand. "It doesn't matter now. He's dead and we can finally be together, can't you see that?"

Dani's mind spun as she tried to figure out what to say. She didn't want to make him mad—he might be like Kurt in his re-actions—but then again, apparently he'd waited twelve years to express his feelings, so maybe he had a little more self-control than his brother. *God, what do I do? What do I say?*

She felt frozen in indecision. Finally she decided to stall him. "Stuart, just let me think. This is all so crazy and I just need time to think." She glanced in the direction Jenny had taken and saw her friend watching. Probably wondering if she needed help.

She looked back at Stuart. A smile had blossomed across his face and her heart sank. Oh no. She'd led him on. Let him think time would make a difference in how she felt about him.

He leaned over and kissed her cheek. "All right, Dani, I'll give you some time, okay."

"Stuart, I didn't mean to make you think—"

He frowned and placed a finger against her lips. She jerked

her head from his touch and his frown deepened. "You've got some time, Dani. And don't worry, I'll be watching out for you. Like I always do."

"Don't you have to work?" she blurted.

"Of course, but I did just lose my brother, you know."

"Six months, you keep reminding me it's been six months."

"Yes, but everyone at the Bureau feels sorry for me."

"So you're milking it?"

"Of course."

He didn't bother to pretend with her. At least she knew where she stood with Stuart. Not that she liked it, but she was thankful there were no surprises with him. At least not yet.

She shook her head. "Go away, Stuart."

"Only for a little while."

Stuart left and Dani shuddered. He was driving her crazy. And starting to scare her. She jogged to catch up with Jenny. "How'd Chester get out?"

"I took the trash out and he barreled around me." She sniffed. "I'm just worried because we've only lived here about a year. He's only gotten out one other time."

Jenny had moved in six months before Kurt's death. Dani had been getting the mail when Jenny walked over to talk. Dani shuddered at the memory. Kurt had stood at the window and glowered until she'd come back in.

Jenny had apparently put two and two together very quickly, because the next day, as soon as Kurt left for work, she had come over and handed Dani a pamphlet on Winchester House. A shelter for abused women and their children.

Neither had mentioned it since and a fragile friendship had formed, then deepened over the past six months since Kurt's death.

"What did Stuart want?"

"Nothing."

"Looked like something to me."

"He's like Kurt, I'm afraid."

"How's that?"

"Mentally off."

Jenny frowned. "That's a pretty harsh judgment."

"I know. Believe me, I know." She took another deep breath. "But I don't want to talk about Stuart. Let's find poor Chester. Would he wander off toward the street?"

Jenny shook her head. "I don't think so. He's around here somewhere. Chester!" Jenny went left, so Dani went right with a glance over her shoulder. Stuart was in his car, the window rolled down.

"Chester!" For the next fifteen minutes, Dani searched for the little dog with no success. When she made her way back to her street, she noticed Stuart's car had disappeared. "And stay gone, please," she muttered.

Dani spotted Jenny's neighbor, Mr. Barnhill, getting ready to burn a pile of leaves. "Have you seen Chester?" she asked him. "Her little white-and-gray schnauzer?"

"No, sorry. I've been out here working in the yard and haven't seen the little guy."

"Thanks."

She moved on and found a woman sitting in her car, texting. Dani tapped on the window. The woman jerked and placed a hand against her chest, but rolled the window down. "Help you?"

"Have you seen a little white-and-gray schnauzer? He got away from his owner."

"No. Sorry." She lifted her phone. "I'm just looking at houses in the area and am waiting on my realtor."

"Okay. Thanks. Good luck with your house hunt." Dani left the woman and decided to head back toward Jenny's to see if her friend had any luck. She pulled her cell phone from the pocket of her pants and dialed her friend's number. "You find him?"

"No." Jenny's despondency tugged at her heart.

"I'm sorry, Jenny. I questioned everyone I saw and no one has seen Chester. Maybe he'll come back when he gets tired of exploring."

"Maybe. Will you come have a cup of tea with me?"

"Sure. I'll be there in a couple of minutes. Let me stop off and tell Simon where I'll be." She could go running a little later. Her friend needed her. Besides, she'd gotten a good workout just walking the neighborhood looking for Chester. And avoiding Stuart.

After a quick stop at her house to let Simon know she'd be at Jenny's, she walked over, rapped on the door, and stepped inside the kitchen. "Jenny?" No answer. "Jen? I'm here." Water boiled on the stove. Two tea bags sat next to the sink. Dani turned off the water and walked toward the den. "Jenny?"

A flash of movement in the mirror above the fireplace caught her eye. A masked figure with a gun and a silencer.

She screamed and ran for the French doors.

The gun barked.

Wood splintered next to her head. She twisted the knob.

Locked.

The gun spit again, the bullet hitting the wall and sending shards of drywall into her hair. She bolted through the second doorway that looped back to the kitchen. And came up short as he cut her off with a low laugh.

Dani's stomach twisted. He was playing with her. This was some sick, twisted game for him. Terror wanted to shut off her brain. She forced it to work. She'd been afraid before and had to think. Now was no different. At least that's what she told herself.

Her breath strained in her lungs as she tried to figure out what to do. She started to run back to the den and he darted to intercept her. She waited until he was out of sight, then raced into the kitchen for the back door she'd left open.

Another thwack hit the door above her. She gave another scream and froze.

"Stand still or the next one goes through your head."

She didn't move. He stepped closer, the gun held steady, almost relaxed. That sent chills racing through her. Killing her meant nothing to him.

The mask hid his features. Brown eyes glittered at her through the holes.

Her brain raced. "Please," she whispered. "I have a son."

"A shame to be sure. Sorry it has to be this way."

"Why do you want me dead?"

"I don't have time for explanations. The chase has been entertaining." The gun shifted. "Now we're going to walk out of here without any more trouble. Let's g—"

"I heard screams. Everything okay over here?" Mr. Barnhill at the screen door. His eyes landed on the man with the gun and he gasped.

Dani didn't hesitate. She grabbed the still hot water from the stove and flung it straight into her attacker's face. He screamed and she threw herself at the door. "Run!"

Mr. Barnhill grabbed her arm and they ran. Dani fumbled with her phone and managed to punch in 911.

7

Dani followed Mr. Barnhill into his home. There was no way she was going back to her house if the shooter was still following her. Not with Simon there. But she didn't want to put this sweet man at risk either. Her heart thudded as she wrestled with the fear skittering through her.

Jenny. Where was Jenny? Had he killed her? Shudders racked her. Sobs grabbed at her throat. No time for a breakdown.

Where were the cops?

"Ma'am?" The 911 operator.

Mr. Barnhill went from door to door, checking the locks. Dani positioned herself by the front door window so she could see if someone approached the house. "I'm here." She didn't recognize her own thin voice.

"Do you see the person shooting at you?"

"No. We're next door." She gave him the address. "But I don't know where my friend is." Dani sucked in a deep breath. "And my son is at home alone." She gave that address. "He's deaf."

Dani listened as the dispatcher requested officers to head to her home.

"Officers are on the way. Just stay on the phone with me."

Mr. Barnhill slipped up beside her. "You okay?"

His pale face and sweat-dotted brow worried her. "I'm all right. You?"

"I think so. Why's that guy shooting at you?"

"I wish I knew," she whispered. "Do you have any weapons?"

"No. I've never shot a gun in my life." He paused and swiped at the sweat on his brow. "You see him out there?"

"No. I think he left." She prayed he had.

Sirens sounded in the distance. *Please, Lord, let Simon stay put playing his video games.*

She desperately wanted to text him, but didn't want to worry him.

Police cruisers finally pulled in front of Jenny's house.

And then she spotted Jenny, Chester in her arms, hurrying toward the chaos, her brow knotted in a concerned frown.

Officers descended, motioning for Jenny to get behind cover. Jenny cowered under the arm of one uniformed policeman as he led her to his cruiser. Two officers approached Jenny's house, weapons in hand.

Dani opened the front door.

One officer held up his hand. "Stay in the house, ma'am, we have reports of a shooter in the area."

"I know, I'm the one that called 911."

"Then just stay there."

Dani hung back and the minutes passed.

Finally the officer waved her over. "Looks like it's all clear."

Dani ran to the cruiser. "Jenny!" She slipped into the seat beside her friend. "I'm so glad you're okay."

"What's going on?"

Dani gave a quick summary of the events and Jenny simply blinked, mouth gaping as she clutched Chester to her. The officer wrote down everything Dani said.

When she finished, she climbed out of the car. "I've got to check on Simon."

"Who's Simon?" the officer asked.

"My son."

The two officers who'd entered Jenny's house came out and Dani paused. The first one said, "Bullet holes are in the walls." He looked at Dani and Jenny. "Anyone get a good description of this guy?"

Dani shook her head. "Jenny wasn't there. It was just me. He had a mask on." She fought through the remembered terror. "He was tall, lean. And he enjoyed taunting me."

The officers exchanged a glance. "Taunting you?"

"It was like a game. Like he already knew the outcome and was just savoring my fear."

"Any idea why someone would want to shoot at you?"

"No," she snapped and glanced down the street toward her house. "Look, my son is at home alone. I want to see him."

She started walking toward her house. One of the officers fell into step beside her. "Do you have any enemies?"

"Not that I know of." Dani racked her brain trying to figure out why someone would want to kill her. "He didn't want to kill me, though."

"What?"

"He said something about me going with him. 'We're going to walk out of here without any trouble.' That's what he said."

"So he wasn't trying to kill you?"

She ran a hand over her ponytail. "I don't know. Not at the house. He wanted me scared for sure, but it sounded like he meant to take me somewhere before he—" she gulped—"killed me."

Had he mistaken her for Jenny? But what could Jenny have done to spark such evil in someone?

She ran up the porch steps and unlocked the front door to her house. She glanced at the officer's name tag. Officer T. Owens. "Wait here, please."

He nodded. She darted up the stairs and into the bonus room.

Simon looked up at her entrance. He smiled and signed, "You're back?"

He didn't know a thing. Her heart slowed its frantic pace. She signed, "Yes. Are you going to stay up here for a while?"

He shrugged and nodded.

Dani said, "I'll be downstairs."

She pulled the double doors shut behind her, closed her eyes, and drew in a deep breath. "Lord, give me strength, please," she whispered. Then headed back down to where Officer T. Owens waited in her foyer.

A half hour later, after checking on Jenny and Simon, she made her way to the laptop she rarely used. When Kurt was home, he had forbidden her to get on it. When he was gone, she was able to sneak and use it. She'd watched him type in the password often enough that she didn't have any trouble accessing the laptop.

Between her trips to the library computer lab and finally learning how to cover any obvious tracks that she'd been on his computer while he was gone, Kurt had never suspected the things she'd discovered online. The internet had been her doorway to the outside world. She'd even made some online friends in a linguistic group. But she never told anything too personal, although some of the others did.

Dani settled herself in the chair and typed in the password.

"What are you doing?"

She jumped and spun to find Simon watching her. He tilted his head and his hearing aid squealed.

Placing a hand over her racing heart, she said, "I'm going to figure out how to disappear."

"Why?"

Dani paused, not wanting to tell him the details of what had happened today, but knowing he had to be aware that they might be in danger. She signed and spoke at the same time. "Because someone tried to . . . hurt . . . me today and I think I need help figuring out who it was."

"Hurt you?" He frowned. "Why?"

"I don't know."

He blinked and rubbed his nose, then pressed his ear mold to stop the squealing hearing aid. "Who are you going to ask for help?"

She pointed to the website she'd found a couple of months before Kurt had been killed. "Operation Refuge."

8

Adam Buchanan read the email forwarded from Ron. "My name is Danielle Harding. I need help. My husband was killed six months ago. Someone just tried to kill me today. I can't go to the cops. I have a twelve-year-old son and I desperately want to protect him and don't even know how. If you can help me, please email me back or come to my house or call me. It doesn't matter, just hurry, I think I'm running out of time."

Adam stared at the name. Danielle Harding. What was it about that name that nagged at him? He'd been wrapping up another case and hadn't had a chance to do his homework. Now it was time to get to work on her.

She'd found the Operation Refuge website and placed the plea for help late yesterday evening. Ron had forwarded the email to Adam. He dragged a hand through his rumpled hair and glanced at the clock. Eleven in the morning. He hadn't been to bed yet but didn't let that faze him. He looked at the email again.

Danielle Harding.

With a grunt and a prayer, Adam went to Google and pulled

58

up everything he could find on the woman. Which wasn't much. An obituary on her husband, Kurt.

Who'd been an FBI agent.

That was interesting. Now he knew why her name sounded familiar. He remembered the story. An exemplary agent, killed when he confronted another agent about his illegal activities.

And now someone had tried to kill Harding's wife. Coincidence?

Probably not.

And so now he found himself pacing in front of the window. Ron had told him to stay put, he was bringing in a case for him. A knock on the door had him spinning. And blinking. "Sarah?"

"Hey."

"Are you okay? Mom? Dad?" His sister had never visited his office before. She only had his contact information for an emergency. For her to show up . . .

She waved a hand. "Dad's fine."

"Dad's fine? What about Mom?"

She sighed and slumped into the nearest chair. "I can't stand this."

"What?"

"This tension between you and Mom and Dad."

"It is what it is, Sarah. I can't change what Uncle Parker did and I can't change what I did." Parker Holland, his mother's brother, had been guilty of murder and an assortment of other crimes, including being in the pocket of organized crime leaders. Adam had helped stop the man's deadly activities, and as a result his uncle was now dead. A fact that his parents were having a hard time getting past. And forgiving.

"I know," she sighed. "But you could do wonders for your relationship with our parents if you would go back to the marshals."

Adam gave a mental groan. They'd been over this before. "What does it matter what I do?"

"Being with the marshals looks better."

"For who?"

"You know for who!" She stood, her agitation clear. "Can't you just, for once in your life, do something to make them happy?"

Adam gave a shout of laughter and she flinched at the harsh sound. He leaned forward. "I hate to tell you this, but no matter what I do, it will never be the right thing or make them happy."

"If you went into politics, it would." Her quiet answer took him by surprise.

"That's not even an option."

She sighed and rubbed her eyes. "Right."

"What's the real story behind your visit?"

"Are you coming tonight?"

He froze as he scrambled to remember what was happening tonight. The dinner for his cousin, Ian. Ian was running for the Senate. Frankly, Adam thought it would be a miracle if the man received even one vote after the stunt their Uncle Parker had pulled. "No."

"They want you there."

"I don't want to be there."

"Not even for Ian?"

"Look, Sarah, Ian's a great guy. I think he's honest and will do the best job he can if he wins the election, but I'm staying out of it. I don't want the publicity or the cameras in my face. With my job, it could make for a sticky situation."

"Then would you do it for Mom?"

"Mom? Why?"

He could almost hear Sarah grinding her teeth in frustration. He felt a pang of remorse, but nothing she said would get him to attend some stuffy political dinner.

"Mom's . . . sick."

Except maybe that. "Sick? Sick how?"

"She has breast cancer, Adam."

The words punctured his lungs. "I . . . see."

"I don't think you do."

"Then why don't you give me the full story?"

Dani had an appointment to meet with Ron. Ron who? She didn't know. Just Ron from Operation Refuge. Ron, who'd asked her numerous questions over the phone. Who was Stuart? Why was he after her? How had her husband been killed? What route would she be taking to the meeting? Did she think Stuart would follow her? Her heart thundered in her chest as her pulse pounded. Someone had tried to kill her yesterday. If it hadn't been for Mr. Barnhill, she'd be dead and Simon an orphan.

And now Stuart was giving her problems again. Constantly. Her nerves were just about shot when it came to that man. Kurt was bad, but she had a feeling Stuart could be worse. He simply wouldn't give up. "Yes, he'll follow me."

Now she bit her lip and held back a scream of frustration when Stuart's white Lexus came up behind her. So she'd been right. He planned to follow her. She couldn't even go to church without him showing up. In spite of the crazy events of yesterday, she hadn't wanted to stay home and hide. Some stubborn part of her wanted to fight back and prove she wasn't going to be a victim any longer.

"He's there again, Mom."

Simon's voice held fear. A fear that shouldn't be there. Her stomach clenched. "I know, hon, just ignore him."

No kid should have had to grow up and live with what he'd lived with for the past few years. Six months free of the constant worry had softened her edges. Feeling safe had made her stop looking over her shoulder. Only now Stuart was pressuring her.

Just last night, he'd said, "It's been six months, Dani, I've waited long enough so people won't talk if we start dating. And besides, it's my duty to make sure you and Simon are taken care of. Why won't you let me?"

"It's not your duty! Please, just leave me alone!" She'd resisted the urge to slam the door in his face, instead saying, "I'm done right now, Stuart. I'm closing the door. Please go away and think about what you're doing. Think about what you'd label this if it was anyone else doing what you're doing. It's called stalking. And I need you to stop."

And here he was behind her. Following her once again. She shuddered and wondered if she would ever be free of the Harding family. One thing she did know was that Stuart didn't like rejection. She had to admit the thought crossed her mind that it had been Stuart who'd tried to kill her. Or someone Stuart had hired.

But who? Who would be willing to do something like that for him?

She sighed and glanced in the mirror again. She wanted this to be over. She wanted her life back. Memories of her days before she'd met Kurt were the only reason she knew the way she'd lived the last twelve years was not normal.

Christmas was less than three weeks away. This year, she was going to give her son the kind of Christmas he deserved. One without fear, without worry, and without stress. Without Stuart and his grating presence.

She glanced in the mirror and chastised herself. First she had to get away from him—again. Lately, he'd followed her everywhere. It was getting old. Not to mention totally creepy and she was scared.

"Why does Uncle Stuart keep following us? He's starting to scare me, Mom. It's not normal."

Simon's voice cracked on the last word. Not because he was

getting to that age where his voice changed, but because he was doing his best not to give in to the fear she could see starting to consume him. The fact that he had voiced her thoughts told her how much Stuart was keeping them both on edge. But Simon was right. Nothing about Stuart was normal. And she and Simon seemed to be the only ones who could see it. Just like Kurt.

She bit her lip. Or was there something else behind Stuart's obsession with her?

She wondered if he was involved in Kurt's illegal activities. She didn't know. What she *did* know was she didn't want to be alone with Stuart. Ever. After the incident at Jenny's house yesterday, it was time to get some help. Help that she hoped lay just ahead.

"Where are we going?"

Driving with her left hand, she signed with her right, "To meet someone who's going to help us."

"Who?"

"His name is Ron." She spelled the name for him.

"How's he going to help us?" He checked the side mirror again.

"I'm not sure. But we're going to find out." Would he be there like he'd promised? And what was she going to do about Stuart? Pull over and tell him to leave her alone?

He drew closer and honked at her. Pulling over wasn't an option right now.

The road narrowed. Cars passed her on her left. The four-lane road would soon turn into a two-lane. For a brief moment, she thought about stopping anyway and demanding that he leave her alone, but a quick glance at Simon's white, pinched face told her she couldn't do that.

And the promise of help ahead kept her hopeful.

She came to a red light and stopped. Stuart stayed behind her. He flashed his lights indicating he wanted her to pull over.

Through the next traffic light, then the next. Until she hit the little two-lane road that would take her the back way into the neighboring city of Duncan. Up ahead, she saw a lone figure leaning against a dusty vehicle with the hood popped.

The rest of the stretch loomed empty.

A quick glance showed Stuart right on her tail. Closer, closer. What was he doing? Then she saw his expression in the mirror. Determination glittered.

Frustration filled her. Fine. He wanted her to stop, she'd stop. In pure fury she slammed on the brakes.

Only he was closer than she'd anticipated and he rammed the back of the Navigator. She shot forward. A scream welled, she bit it back. Her tires caught gravel. Simon hollered and grabbed the door.

The man leaning against his car straightened and looked back.

Her car swung around and she lost control. The vehicle lunged into the open field. Dani kept her foot on the brake, her only thought to bring the big car to a stop.

The wheels spun, Simon screamed, and Dani prayed.

When the car finally ground to a halt, she turned to Simon and grabbed his shoulder. He opened his eyes and stared at her, his terror striking a chord deep within her.

Panting, sweat pooling at her neck and running down her back, she signed, "Are you okay?"

"He wants to kill us." His hands trembled.

She signed, "No, he wasn't trying to kill us." At least she didn't think so. Dani searched for Stuart, her gaze darting from one mirror to the next. Had anyone seen the accident? "He was just trying to stop us." The white Lexus sat on the side of the road behind her.

Then Stuart's fist came down on the window. She flinched back and screamed. "Go away! What are you doing? Leave us alone!"

Stuart's dark eyes glittered with suppressed wrath. In that

moment, he looked so much like Kurt, Dani thought she might vomit. "Get out of the car, Dani."

"Stop! You're scaring us."

He flinched. "I don't want to scare you, I just want—"

A hand reached over and jerked Stuart from the window. Dani jumped and stared. The man with the broken-down car.

Stuart pulled his weapon and Dani opened the door to stumble from the vehicle. "Stuart! No!"

Her scream distracted him for a fraction of a second. Long enough for the stranger to bring a fist down on Stuart's forearm. The gun dropped, Stuart hollered and swiveled, but not fast enough. The man gave a solid punch to Stuart's chin and Dani saw Stuart drop like a rock.

9

Adam stared at the trio who'd just stepped into his office. His sister had left ten minutes ago and he hadn't quite recovered from her bombshell. He gave himself a mental shake and held out a hand. "Ron. It's been awhile."

Ron gave his hand a firm pump. "Couple of months since my last rescue."

Summer came into the room. "Ron. I thought I heard your voice." She gave him a quick hug, then turned her attention to the woman Adam couldn't seem to take his eyes from. Long blonde hair and eyes the color of a chocolate mocha, she was breathtaking.

"Who are your friends?" Summer asked the question Adam had stuck in his throat.

"Meet Dani Harding and her son, Simon," Ron said.

Dani and Summer exchanged greetings.

Dani Harding was undeniably a beautiful woman. However, Adam could see stress in her eyes. Her hands clutched a bag, and her son wore his backpack low on his back. The kid stared lasers at Adam, his distrust and suspicion speaking volumes. "I'm Adam Buchanan. Pleased to meet you." He offered his hand to Dani, who took it after a brief hesitation.

"Thank you. You too."

Adam let go of her soft hand and immediately missed her touch. He swallowed and wished he had time to mull over the spark of attraction he'd felt when he looked in her eyes. Eyes that made him want to know the woman behind them. Strange. Stunning, actually. He'd never reacted this way to a woman before.

He turned to Simon. "How are you?"

Simon simply leaned into his mother and kept up that unnerving stare. Dani placed a hand on her son's head and he transferred his look from Adam to his mother. She nodded.

Simon looked back at Adam. "I'm fine. Thanks."

His words sounded odd. Almost as though he had an accent.

"Can I get you two anything? A coke? Something to eat?"

"I'll take some food. What do you have?" Simon asked.

Adam realized the way to the kid's heart was through his stomach. He looked at Summer and lifted a brow. She nodded.

Dani turned to Ron. "Why did you bring us here?"

"Because you need more help than a shelter can offer. You're in a unique situation and these people specialize in that kind of thing. Especially Adam. It may be Sunday, but I knew exactly where he'd be." He snickered.

Adam scoffed. "Don't act like you have some special powers of knowing. You told me you were coming, remember?"

Ron waved a hand. "A minor detail."

Summer shifted and backed toward the door. "I'm going to go check on Riley." She looked at Dani. "Riley's my five-month-old daughter."

"How sweet. You're fortunate that you get to bring her to work with you."

"I am." Summer nodded toward Adam. "You're in good hands, I promise. I'll get Simon's drink and some crackers. Be right back."

At her departure, Adam found his footing. These people were

in trouble. He could deal with that much better than the riptide of attraction for the pretty woman. "I read the email you sent, but why don't you fill in the details?"

Ron motioned for Dani to sit. "Come on, tell him your story. He'll listen and help, I promise. Give him a chance."

Dani didn't look like she believed Ron, but took the seat anyway. Simon planted himself on the floor, his back against the wall, eyes darting between his mother and the men.

Ron backed toward the door. "I've got to go, but you tell him." And then he was gone.

Dani looked like she might be ready to bolt.

Adam sat back and tried to look as nonthreatening as possible. "Tell me."

She exchanged a look with Simon. The child nodded. Dani nodded. She took a deep breath. "Yesterday morning someone tried to kill me. I was at a friend's house and he shot at me."

Adam sat up straight, all pretense of relaxing gone. "Shot at you?"

"Yes."

"What about your friend?"

"She'd gone after her dog who'd gotten loose, she wasn't in the house. Thank goodness."

"So why would someone shoot at you?"

"I don't know that he meant to." Adam knew his confusion was reflected on his face. She sighed. "Like I said, I was at a friend's house. He found me there. I'm really not sure if he was after me or mistook me for my friend."

Summer delivered Simon's goodies, then disappeared again.

Adam picked up where he'd left off. "Who would want to kill your friend?"

"I have no idea. No one. I don't think. Maybe he got the wrong house all the way around."

"Possibly." He held up a finger and she paused. "What's your friend's name and address?"

Dani told him and he picked up the phone. "Hold on a sec." He dialed David's number. "Hey, I need you to run a background check on Jenny Cartee." He provided the information Dani had given him. He hung up. "David will get back to me after he checks her out." He spun his pen between his fingers. "So the person may not have been after you."

"Right. But—"

When she hesitated, he pushed. "But?"

"My husband was killed about six months ago," she blurted.

He remembered the email and nodded, brow creasing. "I know. I'm sorry."

"I am too. Not sorry that I'm free of him, but how it all came about."

So the marriage hadn't been a good one.

"When Ron came to the rescue, I was actually running from my brother-in-law, Stuart Harding. Stuart rammed my car because I didn't anticipate how close he was when I slammed on the brakes. Anyway, Ron rescued me and my son and brought us here."

"Why not go to the cops?"

She let out such a weary sigh. "Stuart *is* the cops. He's an FBI agent."

Adam blinked and leaned forward. "Okay then. Now I'm getting a better picture of why you're here."

"Exactly. If I made a complaint, as soon as Stuart flashed his badge, it would be hands off for them. Whether they believed me or not." Bitterness glinted at him. "Trust me, I've learned that the hard way."

"Depends on the cop," Adam said, "but I understand your concern about needing to trust the right one."

"Kurt, my husband, was an evil man." Dani shifted and narrowed her eyes. "He was evil and also corrupt. No one saw that side of him, though. Ever. Just me."

Adam leaned forward. "A dirty cop?"

She shot a look at her son. Adam realized he'd almost forgotten the kid was there. He looked back at Dani. "Should he wait outside while you tell me this?"

"No. He's not under any false illusions about who his father is. Was." Grief pinched her face and she moved hands, making different shapes with her fingers. He blinked. Looked at Simon. The kid responded in kind.

Adam blinked. "He's deaf?"

"Yes."

"I know most of the alphabet and a few words. What's he saying?"

"That he doesn't want to leave, he's staying right here. That he knows his dad was a bad guy—" Her voice choked. "And that everyone is better off with his father dead." She lifted watery eyes to his. "He wants to know if you'll put his uncle in jail so he and I will finally be safe."

Adam's heart jolted at the pain on mother's and son's faces. He picked up a pen. "Let's see what we can do about that." Her hesitation told him she wasn't finished. "What is it?"

"I . . . saw something eight months ago. Something that has plagued me ever since and I need to tell someone about it or go crazy. Only I wasn't sure who to trust, who to tell, but I think you're the right person."

Adam lifted a brow. "Okay. What did you see?"

"A murder."

10

Dani stared at the man who had his complete attention centered on her. She squirmed. She'd never had that before. At least not in a good way. Her father had died before she knew him and her mother had never dated or remarried.

Which was probably one reason Dani had been so susceptible to Kurt's smarmy charms.

Adam stilled. "You saw a murder?"

"About two months before Kurt was killed."

"And you never reported it."

She glanced at Simon. He was now bent over the electronic video game Stuart had given him as a gift shortly after Kurt's death. "No. Kurt knew I saw what happened, but no one else did." She shuddered at the memory of his ballistic rage once everyone had left the house.

"How was he involved?"

She rubbed her eyes, taking a moment. "Let me start at the beginning."

"Good idea."

"I married Kurt when I was nineteen. I got pregnant on our

71

honeymoon. Kurt was thrilled. When Simon was born, he was Kurt's trophy, his son, his legacy. Until it became obvious that little boys don't always do exactly what their father says." She slid another glance at her son and tried to make sure she had her face angled away from him. He wasn't paying any attention to her, totally engrossed in his game. How he'd longed for the Nintendo 3DS. Kurt had refused his every request, saying that he had a Wii, he should be happy with that. And Kurt only agreed to the Wii because it kept Simon out of his hair and occupied when he was home.

She pulled herself back. "After Simon was born, Kurt was gone for long stretches of time. At first, I missed him, but then he started with the verbal abuse, then one day things escalated and he hit me. I was stunned. I think Kurt was too. Then it became a regular thing. When Simon was five, he tried to intervene and help me." Tears welled and she blinked them away. "Kurt knocked him into the wall and he hit his head. I managed to call 911. An ambulance and police arrived. Simon was unconscious. I rode to the hospital with him and filed a report with the officers who followed."

"If you filed a domestic abuse report, Kurt should have spent some time in jail."

She snorted. "Not when you're an FBI agent and the apple of your boss's eye. Strings were pulled, the charges were dropped, and—" she pulled in a deep breath—"Kurt said that if I ever said another word about his abuse and threatened to leave, he would kill Simon and make me watch." Dani cleared her throat to loosen the tightness. "When Simon woke up, we discovered he was deaf. I was furious—and consumed with guilt. When Simon was released from the hospital, a nurse tried to help me leave Kurt, but he found us and broke two of Simon's fingers, saying next time it would be his neck." Her lips trembled. "The nurse was found dead two days later. Her death was ruled a suicide and I never ran again. Until the day of Kurt's death."

The pen snapped under the pressure of Adam's fingers. He jerked and tossed it in the trash, realizing he'd been so caught up in her story, he hadn't written a word. People like Kurt were why his services were necessary and it sickened him. But Kurt was dead and someone was still threatening Dani and Simon.

"You think he killed the nurse?"

"I don't know." Dani pressed the tips of her fingers to her lips and he could tell she was having a hard time getting the words out. "I don't know for sure, but I . . . I think so. Anyone who offered to help me would be in danger if Kurt found out, so I didn't dare do anything that might cause someone else's death."

Adam drew in a deep breath. "Who did you see killed?"

Simon's bent head reassured Adam he wasn't listening.

"A man who had crossed Kurt and whoever else was working with him. I didn't know his name at the time, but then his body was found and the newspaper said it was a man by the name of Trennan Eisenberg. He had some connection with organized crime and the FBI was all over it, of course. Only they never found who killed him because my husband and others working with him covered up the evidence."

"What evidence?"

"The evidence in my house, the fact that they were even there. The fact that they knew Mr. Eisenberg and were associated with him. I'm sure if there was a paper or electronic trail, they erased it." She shrugged. "I don't know what all the cover-up entailed, I just know they did it." She swallowed hard. "I started eavesdropping whenever I could. I figured the more I knew, the more I'd be able to protect myself and Simon."

"And did you learn anything more?"

"No, not really." She fiddled with the strap on her purse.

"And no one else knew you'd seen this."

"Right. At least I don't think so."

"Is there something else?"

"About a month ago, Simon and I left for a short weekend to go to the beach with Jenny."

"The Jenny Cartee that David is checking up on?"

"Yes."

"Okay. What happened?"

"When we got home, my house felt . . . strange." Adam lifted a brow and she sighed. "I know it sounds crazy and maybe it is. But it felt like someone had been there. It even smelled different. I found some dirt on the carpet on the stairs that I would have sworn wasn't there when I left." She shrugged. "It bothered me for a while, but nothing else happened so I just let it go."

"And then yesterday happened."

"Yes."

"And you think the two things are related?"

"I have no idea. I'm just trying to tell you everything so you can piece it together. If there's anything to piece together."

He nodded. "That's good." When he finished writing, he looked up. "And then there's your brother-in-law. The man Ron pulled away from you today. Do you think he's the one that shot at you?"

"I can't believe he'd follow me to a friend's house and try to kill me, but he'd just been at my house not too long before everything happened, so it's hard not to think—" She shrugged again and looked away.

"Tell me more about him."

Adam listened as she explained her brother-in-law's obsession. She shuddered. "He's as bad as Kurt and I just want him to leave us alone."

Adam leaned back, his blood still boiling at all she'd suffered over the last twelve years. And she still wasn't free to live her life like any other normal person. "First, I think we need to make sure you and Simon are safe. That's our priority."

"Okay."

"I think what we'll do is set up round-the-clock protection for you at your house. You'll have someone with you wherever you go."

"You mean like a bodyguard?" She wrinkled her nose.

"Yes, something like that. We're not a bodyguard service, but we've all trained to do that kind of work should we need to do it. I'm just trying to think of the least invasive way of keeping you safe."

When David and Summer decided to set up Operation Refuge, they went to the governor to get her support. When they presented their reasons for establishing the company, the governor decided to back it. It had taken awhile, but they'd gone against the norms and been granted all the powers bestowed upon any other law enforcement agency. Not only did they have permits to carry weapons and were licensed to investigate and provide protection, they also had arrest powers and the authority to submit evidence to state labs. The attorney general even threw in his support. With state and federal liaisons, they had all of the tools—and more—that they needed.

She took in a deep breath. "All right. We could do that. But for how long? I mean, all Stuart has to do is wait for you to leave."

"True, but it may be that every time he comes over and you have someone with you and you're telling him to leave you alone, he'll be more open to the fact that you seriously don't want to see him."

"Do you think it'll work?"

"It has before."

She looked uncertain. "I guess we can try it."

"All right. Hold on a second." He picked up the phone. Summer answered. "What can I do for you?"

"I've got a previous engagement for tonight. David's busy and I need someone to do some protection duty for Dani and her son."

"All right, let me check."

"What about Tabitha or Isaac? Or maybe Janessa?" If he couldn't have David, the six-foot-two-inch Janessa Glenn would be the next best thing. Her rich ebony skin would blend in with the night. Her self-defense skills would give him much comfort in knowing she could fight whatever came her way.

"Janessa's available. I'll call her."

"Thanks." He hung up. "Janessa is going to be with you tonight. We'll take shifts for the next week to see how things progress. We'll see how determined Stuart is and do our best to persuade him that he needs to leave you alone."

She nodded, still not looking convinced. And frankly Adam wasn't either. If it came down to it, he would make Dani and Simon disappear. He was hoping it wouldn't have to come to that. "All right then." He picked up his keys and looked at Dani. "I'll take you home and make sure you're settled. Janessa will meet us there. Let's go."

11

Dani liked Janessa. She was intimidating and beautiful. And very kind.

They sat at her kitchen table, each of them nursing a cup of coffee. "Simon's a great kid."

"Yes, he is. He's always hungry, though. I'm surprised he's not down here."

Janessa smiled. "So, tell me about your husband's family."

Dani lifted a brow. "Oh goodness. That's a topic."

"Sorry, didn't mean to pry."

"No, it's okay." She set her cup on the table. "Kurt's family is wealthy. And distant. I don't see them. Have actually only met them a handful of times. They came to the wedding and stopped by to see Simon after he was born. And then again about five years later."

"Wow. They don't see their grandson? That's a shame."

Dani shrugged. "I'm not sure it is. Kurt and Stuart grew up with nannies. A different one every few months or so."

Janessa winced. "Why have kids if you're not going to raise them?"

"Good question." She shook her head. "I don't know what I'd do without my son. Simon is everything to me."

"I can tell." She smiled. "So they grew up with nannies. I find it strange they'd both end up in law enforcement. It's not exactly an executive's salary kind of job."

Dani sighed. "I think Kurt chose to become a cop because of the power trip. Respect was very important to him. And he liked it when people were afraid of him."

Janessa frowned. "And Stuart?"

"He hated Kurt. I think their rivalry started out as a bid for attention from their parents. You know, whoever got the better grades got the most praise, whoever scored the most points in the basketball game or got the biggest trophy got the most attention." She waved a hand. "I don't know. But at some point, the childhood competition morphed into a rivalry that I was afraid might be deadly."

"Really?"

"It didn't have a chance to come to that, but I really think it could have. Kurt liked to play practical jokes on people. Mean ones. He would figure out your weakness, then turn it into a joke. Only it wasn't ever really funny. Stuart was the brunt of Kurt's jokes more than once." She swallowed hard and picked up her mug. More to give her hands something to do than out of a desire for a sip.

Janessa sighed. "It's a shame people feel like they have to do things like that to build themselves up or hurt others to fill an emptiness inside them. If they only understood they were created for greater things than those of this world. That they have a unique and special purpose for being put on this earth. It would make a world of difference if they knew that."

Dani gave a soft smile. "I agree."

Janessa pushed away from the table. "I'm just going to check in with Adam and scan the perimeter."

Dani nodded. "Okay. I'll check on Simon, then I think I'll watch some television and try to unwind."

"Sounds good. I'll be back soon."

Janessa left and Dani found Simon in his bed staring at the ceiling. She caught his attention. Her hands moved in the signs that had become second nature to her. "What are you thinking about?"

"I was wondering what it was like to live that normal life you're always talking about."

Her heart ached for him. For both of them. "I'm sorry. I know it's hard right now, but it'll get better, you'll see."

"That's what you keep saying."

"It will. Don't lose faith, don't lose hope. Not now. Not when we're so close." She sat next to him and stroked his hair. "I love you, Simon. Very much."

He smiled and sat up to hug her. "I love you too, Mom."

He leaned back and she made sure he could see her lips. "We'll get through this together."

"Just like we always do, right?"

Tears threatened to choke her. She cleared her throat. "Yeah, just like we always do. Now get some sleep."

He flopped back onto the pillows and she pulled the covers up to his chin. She kissed his cheek and turned off the light.

Weariness invaded her, but the thought of crawling in bed made her restless. She walked downstairs and made her way to the couch. She picked up the remote and clicked the television on. Found an old rerun of Andy Griffith and closed her eyes. *Oh Lord, keep your hand on us. Keep your protection around us. And Lord, give us a much needed break, please.*

Adam drove toward the hotel downtown. Even as he scanned the streets and watched for pedestrians, he let his thoughts go to

Dani Harding. Ever since she'd walked into the Operation Refuge headquarters, she'd stayed in his mind, her image refusing to leave him alone. Her story touched him, made him angry on her behalf.

He dialed her number.

"Hello?"

"Hi, it's Adam."

"I recognized the number." He thought he could hear a smile in her voice.

"How is everything?"

"Quiet. Thank goodness."

"Good. Good."

An awkward silence fell between them and he cleared his throat. "Well, I really didn't have anything to say, just wanted to make sure you had everything you needed. And that you felt safe."

"I do feel safe. Thank you."

"I'm sorry I couldn't be there tonight. I have a . . . thing."

"A thing?"

"A dinner. One of those black-tie deals that keep you uncomfortable until it's all over."

"Ah. I understand. *That* kind of thing."

"Yeah."

"Why are you going if you're going to be so uncomfortable?"

Adam blew out a sigh. Did he want to get into that with her? He'd just met her a few hours ago. But he found himself wanting to explain a little. "My relationship with my parents has been on rocky ground for the past year. Going to this dinner will make them happy, so I'm doing it." He paused. "At least my sister says it will. I'm not so sure, but a fellow can hope."

"Then you're right. It's worth a try."

"I suppose."

Adam vaguely wondered what he was doing making small talk with her, but realized he liked it. He'd felt a connection with her

80

that hadn't happened to him in a long time. If ever. It made him wary, yet curious too.

"Do you mind me asking what happened with your parents?"

Okay, so maybe small talk was a bad idea. This kind of small talk anyway. "It's not a pretty story."

"And mine was?"

"Touché." The hotel lights beckoned. "But it looks like my story will have to wait. I'm here."

"Hm. How convenient." She gave a small laugh. "All right. Have a good time."

"That probably would take an act of God."

Dani gave another small chuckle. "Then it could happen."

Adam found himself smiling. "I suppose it could. I'll talk to you later."

"Goodbye, Adam."

He hung up and let her melodic voice ring through his mind. He decided he really liked Danielle Harding.

Thwack, thwack.

Dani's eyes popped open. A soft thud from upstairs reached her ears and she stilled, listening. Simon? Janessa?

Dani rose from the couch and padded on silent feet to the bottom of the stairs.

All was still.

Just as she started to relax and decide it was just the house settling, she heard another quiet hiss. A snick. Like a latch catching. Or a door closing?

What was Simon doing?

Where was Janessa?

Dani hurried up the stairs. At the top, she turned left, her bare feet silent on the hall-length carpet runner. The blackness pressed in on her and she thought about flipping the light switch, but hesitated.

She stepped into the first door on the right. Simon's dark room greeted her. The faint nightlight provided enough of a glow to see his still form curled under the covers.

She frowned. Her pulse sped up a notch. Simon was asleep.

So who was making the noise? Janessa? What would she be doing?

Her stomach tightened. She backed out of his room and went for the guest room. Inside, she stopped. The open blinds allowed the moonlight to filter through. Janessa's still form stretched across the bed, her head on the pillow, face turned away from the door.

Anger surged. Janessa was supposed to be making rounds, keeping her and Simon safe and she was sleeping? What kind of agency had she hired? Had she put her trust in the wrong people?

With a quick glance back down the hall, Dani stepped into the room and placed a hand on the woman's shoulder. She shook her.

No response.

A coldness settled in the pit of her stomach. She trailed her fingers down the woman's arm to her wrist. Felt for a pulse.

She thought she felt something, but wasn't sure.

Terror swept through her. Janessa wasn't sleeping, she was unconscious. Dani's brain clicked with panic. She pulled in a deep breath and forced herself to think. She had to get Simon to safety and help for Janessa.

Another sound. A rustling in the hall, a light footstep.

Dani's heartbeat sped up and her hands went clammy. She glanced back at the woman on the bed and knew she wasn't going to be able to offer any help. Dani just prayed she wasn't dead.

She walked to the door and peered out. Trying to keep her panicked breaths silent, she noted the empty hallway and headed for her bedroom to get to the nearest telephone. She'd left her newly acquired cell phone downstairs. Her bare foot stepped in something warm. Slick.

Then she noticed the coppery metallic smell.

Blood. Most likely Janessa's blood. She'd been taken by surprise in the hall and moved? Dani didn't know what had happened and right now details didn't matter.

Simon did. Nausea churned.

Simon. Think about his safety. Get help.

At the door to her bedroom, she froze. Movement sliced the air within. Soft, quiet. A dark figure near the bed. A low curse when he realized she wasn't there.

She spun, and darted silently down the hall to Simon's room. Who was he? Why was he here?

Stuart? He'd come by earlier, apologizing profusely, trying to explain away his crazy actions, and she'd refused to talk to him. She just couldn't. Not yet. She was still furious with him for scaring her like he had. Janessa had intervened and sent Stuart on his way, cursing them, but at least leaving.

Had he come back and slipped into the house?

Another whisper of sound from down the hall.

He was still in her bedroom. Probably checking out her bathroom.

She slipped into Simon's room, touched his shoulder, and gave him a small shake. He stirred, blinked up at her. She made sure she stood in the glow of the nightlight and lifted a finger to her lips. Between the nightlight and the moonlight filtering through the blinds, she knew he could see her. She quickly signed, "Someone's in the house. Come with me."

His eyes flared with panic and she hated it. Her own fear threatened to consume her, but she had to keep Simon safe. He threw back the covers and grabbed his T-shirt from the floor. Dani gripped his hand and pulled him behind her. She walked to the door and glanced out into the hallway, then pulled back when the shadowy figure stepped out of her bedroom and headed toward them. Would he search the house until he found them? Was he even looking for them or something else? One thing for sure, he didn't hesitate to remove anyone who got in his way. Her heart cramped at the thought of Janessa. She still felt the sticky substance on the bottom of her foot.

She didn't need to be a genius to figure out the intruder had surprised Janessa and removed her from the equation. Guilt wanted to consume her, but she shoved it off for now.

Indecision warred within her as fear threatened to strangle her. What to do?

Simon stared at her, blinking fast, the big question in his eyes. How was she going to save him this time?

She bit her lip and peeked into the hall.

The figure was gone.

But where?

Did they dare make a run for it? Was he alone?

A floorboard squeaked and she pulled back, heart beating. She signed, "Get in the closet."

Simon didn't hesitate. His complete trust brought tears to her eyes.

She blinked them gone. She could cry later. She moved to his bed and arranged his pillows and cover to look as though he were still sleeping. She just prayed the person glanced in and kept going. If not—

She moved to the corner of the bedroom and removed Simon's prize baseball bat from its perch on the wall. Sweat slicked her palms. She slipped into the closet beside Simon and pulled the door closed, leaving only a slight crack. She could feel Simon's terrified shudders. Anger, swift and hot, burned through her. Kurt was dead. They shouldn't still be scared to death.

84

Her grip tightened around the handle of the bat. Softball had been her game in high school and the years hadn't dimmed her memory on how to swing. She just prayed she wouldn't have to. Dani rested her left hand on Simon's shoulder, trying to convey comfort with her touch.

Light footsteps sounded. Paused at the door.

Dani breathed through barely parted lips. Her heart beat so loud, she was sure the intruder could hear it.

Her ears strained to hear. Was he coming in? She didn't dare push the closet door open farther to see. From her position directly across from the entrance to the room, he would come right into her line of sight if he moved two steps more. She prayed he didn't take those two steps.

He did.

Simon gasped.

The figure froze.

12

Adam couldn't raise Janessa on her earpiece. He frowned. That wasn't like her. He'd finished up his family obligation and decided to ride over and check on Dani and Janessa.

His gut had hurt all evening as he'd tried to focus on the dinner and the conversation at the table. He'd hoped showing up would help speed up the process when it came to mending fences with his family.

Especially his mother. He hadn't mentioned her illness and she hadn't brought up the topic either. He wondered if she even knew Sarah had told him.

Unfortunately, the whole time he'd been eating prime rib and asparagus, he'd been itching to bolt to Dani's house while wanting to hug his mother and apologize for his uncle's death. Apologize that it had come to that, not necessarily for his part in exposing the man's crimes.

"Are you all right, Adam?" his mother had asked. She sat to his left.

"Of course, Mom, I'm fine. Are you all right?"

She lifted a brow and her lips tightened. He'd thought she might say something. Instead, she simply nodded. "Good. Good. I'm fine." She'd returned to her meal with a quick look at his father, as though expecting him to reprimand her for speaking to him.

Although Adam had to admit, when he'd first walked in, his mother had looked pleased to see him. For a brief moment, he let himself believe she'd forgiven him for being a part of his uncle's—her brother's—death.

Adam's father had given him a tight smile and short nod. It was more than he'd expected and raised his hopes. Friends of his parents stopped by the table to chat and shake hands. Some of the well wishes were genuine, others not so much. Adam couldn't stand the fakeness but was relieved no one seemed to want to point out his shortcomings.

It appeared his family had accepted him back into the fold. Not that he was terribly concerned about it for himself, but he was glad to see his parents smiling and relaxing.

He just wished he could have given the dinner and his family his full attention.

Instead, Dani and Simon took over his thoughts.

He couldn't help the feeling that they just needed more security coverage than they'd been assigned. Someone had broken into a neighbor's house and tried to shoot Dani. However, did that make her the target? Or just in the wrong place at the wrong time?

He'd been sitting in the car in front of Dani's house since he'd pulled to the curb, thinking about the situation and the best way to handle it.

From his position in the car on the curb, the house looked peaceful. Still.

Maybe too still. Just thirty minutes ago, Janessa had checked in with him to let him know everything was fine.

"Janessa, come on, speak to me. If you can't talk, tap the piece. Let me know you're there."

Still nothing. He tried Dani's cell phone.

No answer.

And the landline just rang. No voice mail, nothing.

Adam checked his Glock and climbed from the vehicle.

———

Don't move, Dani silently begged Simon. *Please, don't move.* The nearest phone was in her bedroom. Her cell phone was in the bottom of her purse.

The figure stood in the doorway, listening. Dani shifted her gaze so she wasn't looking directly at him. How many times had she overheard Kurt, once on the sniper team, talk about how he never looked directly at the enemy. "People can feel you looking at them, Dani."

So now she used her peripheral vision to keep him in her sights. The ski mask hid his features, but she took note of his height, his build, the way he stood quietly and cocked his head. He took two more steps into the room and Dani's blood pressure ratcheted up to the point she felt like she might explode. Simon stood rigid just behind her to the left.

And then the figure turned and left the room. She didn't bother relaxing. With her right hand, Dani kept a tight grip on the baseball bat and counted to thirty. When the intruder didn't return, she pushed the closet door open. Slowly. So slowly.

The well-oiled hinges didn't creak. She wrapped her hand around Simon's sweaty one and gave him a gentle tug, silently telling him to follow her. Pulse pounding, blood rushing, she stepped out of the closet, Simon on her heels.

At the door, she stopped, listened.

Heard nothing.

She peeked around the corner.

Saw nothing.

Dani pulled Simon with her and made a beeline for the steps.

Together, they raced down.

She reached for the front doorknob.

A hard band wrapped around her throat from behind.

Dani cried out and Simon gave a harsh scream.

"Where is it?" the voice hissed in her ear.

She tried to swallow, but he held her too tight. He gave her a shake and she gasped, remembered the bat and swung it back-handed.

A sharp crack and a cry of pain greeted her. She broke loose from his hold and whirled to see Simon swinging the brass lamp from the dining room end table.

The figure ducked and knocked the lamp aside. He planted a fist in Simon's chest and shoved. Simon screamed and fell back, crashing into the piano.

Discordant notes jangled and sheer desperation swept through her. A wild cry ripped from her throat and she swung the bat again, catching her intruder in the left shoulder. He gave a pained grunt, went to his knees, then recovered. She met his gaze as he came to his feet.

Dani backed up, kept her grip on the bat, and wished she could yell at Simon to run. Everything in her wanted to make sure her son was all right. And that meant keeping this attacker's attention on her. Dark eyes glittered. "Where is it, Dani?"

She didn't recognize the voice. Her heart pounded.

"What?" she gasped. "Where is what?"

The door crashed in and Adam, weapon in hand, yelled, "Freeze!"

The intruder moved fast. Before Dani could blink, he'd yanked the bat from her hand and shoved her aside with one hand while bringing the bat around with the other. The wood connected with Adam's forearm and his gun flew from his fingers.

Adam leapt forward and tackled the man. Both hit the tile floor with harsh grunts. A fist connected with Adam's jaw. His head snapped back against the floor. The masked attacker jumped up and raced through the open front door.

Dani bolted to Simon, who sat on the floor, hands gripping Adam's gun. She placed her hand over his and took the weapon from him. He flung himself into her arms. The gun was snatched from her hands and she turned to see Adam's back as he charged after the escaping intruder.

She moved toward the kitchen, Simon attached to her side like a leech.

Dani snatched the phone handset from the base and dialed 911.

"Are you okay?" Her pulse spiked as she spun to see Adam standing in the doorway of her kitchen. The 911 operator said something, but Dani missed it. Sweat stood out on his face. He dragged a sleeve across his forehead and said, "He got away."

Dani nodded.

Adam moved closer. "What was he after?"

"I don't know." She lifted the phone to her ear and told the dispatcher what had happened. "He's gone now, but there's a woman who's been hurt. Send an ambulance."

"Where's Janessa?" Adam demanded.

"Upstairs. I think he shot her," she whispered.

Adam raced for the stairs.

Simon wilted into the nearest chair at the kitchen table.

Within seconds, Adam was back, his white face and tense jaw said it wasn't good. "She's dead."

Tears flooded Dani's eyes. "I'm so sorry."

"I am too. I have to call Summer and David. They'll contact her family."

"We should have left here. We never should have come back. I'm sorry, I didn't know, I never dreamed—"

He placed a hand on her shoulder. "Don't. It's not your fault."

"But—"

"Janessa knew the risks." He paused. "And we underestimated the danger level." His jaw hardened. "We won't make that mistake twice."

A knock sounded and he turned to answer it. Dani spoke into the phone. "They're here." She hung up and went to meet the officers. Simon followed, staying close enough to see her.

Two uniformed officers stepped into her foyer, and when Adam took the lead, Dani let him, grateful to him and yet, at the same time, irritated. She was going to have to learn to handle things by herself now. No more letting a man tell her what to do or push her around.

Then she told herself to stop. This was serious and Adam knew what he was doing. She had enough sense to know he wasn't being a macho jerk. He'd just saved her life and he was concerned.

Dani swiped the tears still dripping, squared her shoulders, and firmed her jaw. She refused to let her life with Kurt color her perspective of men or cause her to doubt her judgment. Her gut told her Adam was a good man. Nothing like the one she'd been married to. In the end, Kurt had been more of a warden than a husband.

With a heavy heart, she watched the EMTs head up the stairs. *Oh Janessa, I'm so sorry.*

She looked at the officer nearest her and said, "He was wearing gloves and a mask."

The officers exchanged a glance. "No sense in checking for prints then."

"No," she murmured. "Probably not."

"Did he speak?"

"Yes, but I didn't recognize his voice." She paused. "I don't think."

"What do you mean?" Adam asked. He'd come up behind them, silent, watchful.

"He may have sounded a bit like the guy who tried to kill me at Jenny's house."

"May have?"

"I don't know. I was scared and I just . . . I don't know."

"It's all right, just think about it," Adam said. "I know one thing. He's skilled at self-defense. He met me move for move." Adam rubbed the back of his head. "In fact, he might know a few moves I don't."

An officer tapped Adam on the arm and he followed him into the kitchen. Dani let out a breath and signed to Simon to follow him.

"Dani?"

She froze, then turned to see Stuart standing in the open front door. "What are you doing here?"

He entered the foyer. "I had about five agents call me and ask me if I knew what was going on here at your house." He flipped the cover on his badge closed and stuck it in his pocket. No doubt he'd used it to gain access to the scene. Anger stirred. He held his hands out. "I came to help. To be here for you." He reached to take her into his arms.

Dani suppressed her nausea and dodged him. She stared at him, wishing she had the words to tell him to get out of her life and stay out.

But she couldn't. Fear of what he might do held her quiet. Dani squared her shoulders. "Stuart, go home. This doesn't concern you and I don't need you here."

His brows drew together in a thunderous frown. "Dani, Kurt would want me to do whatever I could to help. Let me take you up to the lake house. It's quiet, peaceful, and no one knows about it. You can stay there and be safe."

Dani shook her head. Did he really think she would go with him after the incident on the road? He may not have meant for the accident to happen, but he sure was the one who caused it. She didn't trust him any farther than she could throw him.

"You can help by leaving, Stuart." She softened her tone. "Please. There's nothing you can do here. Go home. We'll . . . talk . . . another time."

She saw the protest forming on his lips and simply stared at him, willing him to leave before Simon came out of the kitchen and saw him. If he refused to leave, she'd have to make a scene and get one of the officers or Adam to help send him on his way. She didn't want to do that at all.

Stuart's jaw tightened. He blew out a breath through his nose, flaring his nostrils. "Fine," he finally said. "But I'll be back tomorrow to check on you."

Dani didn't bother to tell him not to, she simply ushered him from the foyer onto the front porch. "Bye, Stuart."

She shut the door.

"Ma'am?"

Dani turned, pushing aside the weariness and grief that threatened to turn her into a puddle on the floor. One of the officers—she couldn't remember his name and her eyes wouldn't focus on his badge—stood just outside her kitchen tapping his notebook with his pen. "Yes?"

"If you don't have anything to add, I think we're done down here."

Once the officers were satisfied she had nothing else to say, they moved upstairs where other law enforcement personnel had secured the scene.

They were still waiting on the crime scene unit and the ME.

Adam returned to the foyer, causing her to put aside her suspicion that Stuart had been her intruder. "While we're waiting for the medical examiner and the homicide detectives, I'm going to call David and Summer."

"Sure."

Adam looked at her. "You realize they may never catch him."

"I know."

"Ma'am?" She turned to see one of the officers at the top of the stairs looking down on her. "Your safe is open. Did you open it?"

"No. I mean it was empty to begin with, but I didn't have it open earlier." She stared at Adam. "He wanted the stuff from the safe," she whispered.

"What stuff?"

"The stuff I cleaned out the day I was going to run from Kurt. The day he died."

"What was in the safe?"

"I'm not sure. Papers and—" she shrugged. "Stuff. And money."

"It's been six months since Kurt's death. You haven't gone through the contents?"

She shook her head and pressed her fingertips against her lips to keep them from quivering. "I couldn't. I didn't want to. I took the money and the will from the bag and put everything else in my end table drawer, intending to put it back in the safe, I just . . . never did. I really haven't thought of it until now."

"How much money are we talking about?"

"Several thousand."

He lifted a brow and made a note of it.

For the next two hours, law enforcement came and went. The crime scene unit arrived and Janessa's body was finally removed. Dani answered question after question until everyone seemed satisfied with the answers.

Her house was now empty with the exception of Adam and her son.

Adam said, "Pack what you need, including the items from the safe. We're getting out of here."

Dani looked at Simon.

He nodded and with fingers splayed like the number five, he tapped his thumb against his chest. Then placed his palm against his chest and moved it in a circular motion.

"What did that mean?" Adam asked.

"They're the signs for 'fine' and 'please.'"

Adam copied the movement and said, "Fine. Please. Got it."

Her heart warmed. Kurt hadn't learned the first sign. Not willingly. He'd picked up a few over the years, but—

Dani cut off the thought and gave a small smile. "Right."

"What do you think about disappearing?" Adam asked.

She tilted her head and shot a glance at Simon. "As in changing our identities?"

"Yes."

"I'm very good at being invisible," she whispered.

Adam flinched, and a look of compassion skittered across his features before he replied. "All right. Then let me get you new IDs, new names, and a new place to live. You'll go straight there from here and start on your new life. While you're working on that, we'll be working on who broke into your house tonight."

She blinked. "You mean like the Witness Protection Program?"

"Yes. Exactly like that, just not with that title."

"Oh me. I . . . don't know . . . I mean, Simon—"

"I know it seems a bit much, but it's very obvious that someone is after you. There's no way we can properly do our job until we know what we're up against. Keeping you safe in your home is not an option now. What if the man who shot at you didn't make a mistake? What if you were actually the target? After all, you did see a murder. While you say no one knows you saw it except a man who's dead, how do you know he didn't tell someone? What if Stuart is going to new lengths to get to you?"

Dani chewed on her lip. "We're in trouble, aren't we?"

"I hate to say it, but yes, looks like you've got big trouble. Are you ready to disappear yet?"

Dani hesitated, battling their options. One person had already lost her life over whatever reason someone was after her.

Simon said, "Yes, she is. We are."

Dani blinked to find Simon watching them, his gaze jumping from her to Adam. His hearing aid whistled. She tapped her ear to let him know. He didn't even roll his eyes this time, simply pressed his mold tighter and the whistling stopped. The brief thought that she really needed to make an appointment with the audiologist fluttered through her mind.

She took a deep breath. "Fine." She was weary. Beyond exhausted. And grieving for a woman she'd only known a few hours. The audiologist would have to wait. She looked at Adam. "Yes. We're ready to disappear."

Simon's relieved sigh made her heart clench. "Can we get something to eat on the way to disappearing? I'm starving."

He sounded bone weary and sad. Dani wrapped her arms around him and hugged him. Then she signed, "Go pack. We'll get some food."

He nodded and trudged upstairs.

Adam looked at her. "Cheeseburger or chicken?"

13

She'd sent him home. Disbelief filled Stuart. Restraining himself from giving in to the urge to smash something, Stuart walked into his house and went straight to his office.

He opened his laptop and clicked on the software that would allow him to watch Dani's every move. It had taken him awhile, but he'd managed to install cameras in almost every room. Except the bathroom. He would allow her to have that one room for privacy.

For now.

However, everything else was fair game. He watched her while she slept, while she fixed dinner, while she paced in front of the window that overlooked her backyard, while she helped Simon with his homework.

Over the last six months, Stuart had even found himself picking up some sign language without even realizing it. Not that he planned on needing it. He was still debating what to do about his nephew. Send him to boarding school or arrange for a convenient accident? The thought of raising Kurt's son didn't exactly appeal to him. Once he and Dani had their own children, she'd forget about Simon. Or at least not fawn over him as much. He rubbed his chin as he thought about it.

Finally, he brushed the decision aside. It wasn't one he had to make right away.

He clicked from room to room and frowned when he couldn't find her. Where was she?

The master bedroom was empty. He panned the guest room and paused. He recognized the Tyvek suits. Crime scene cleanup. A woman had died tonight. In Dani's house.

That had been unexpected.

In fact, the whole thing at Dani's house had been a surprise. Breaking in to scare her hadn't been part of the plan, but the more Stuart thought about it, the more he liked it. Or he *would* have liked it had it worked. He'd have to talk to Joe about it tomorrow. Frustration had him curling his hands into fists.

Someone had broken into her house and attacked her, had even killed a woman, and still Dani hadn't called him. Of course she would have called 911 first, but then she should have called *him*.

Who were all these people that she suddenly had at her beck and call? The man who'd rescued her on the side of the road? Where had Dani found him?

More obstacles. More unexpected annoyances.

His jaw tightened. He shouldn't have gone to her, but he'd waited as long as he could before giving in to the need to see her. He'd really expected her to call and ask him to help her out. The fact that she hadn't burned a hole in his gut. The fact that she'd shooed him away like a bothersome child sent tremors of vexation racing through him. "You're mine, Dani. The sooner you learn that, the better off you'll be."

One thing did worry him. Slightly. Had Joe left any way to trace the intruder back to Stuart?

His cell phone rang and he snatched it. "Hello?"

"Hey." The person Stuart had hired to watch Dani when he couldn't.

"Did you see what happened tonight?"

"No. I got here after most of the excitement died down."

Stuart blew out a breath. "Great."

"Well, your sister-in-law took off."

"Took off? What do you mean took off?"

"She and the kid left with some guy."

"What guy?" Jealousy simmered. Was it the same person who'd taken her from him just yesterday? He knew he'd acted impulsively and scared Dani to death. He hadn't meant to, really he hadn't. It's just that he'd already waited so long and she'd been giving him the brush-off, distancing herself from him. It had scared him. And made him mad. Like tonight.

A flash of uneasiness shot through him. He didn't know who the man had been, but he'd handled Stuart like a pro. Who had Dani hooked up with?

"I've got his picture but I'm not sure who he is. I'm following them now."

"Send me the picture. I want to know what he looks like."

Within seconds, his phone chirped to let him know the photo had arrived. "Where are they going?"

"I don't know. I'll let you know when we get there."

Early Monday morning, hours before the sun would put in an appearance, Adam led Dani and Simon into the house.

David greeted them with a smile. "We've been busy while you've been traveling."

Simon signed something to Dani and Adam caught the word "we." He looked at Dani with a raised brow. She said, "He wants to know where we are."

Adam looked at Simon. "Near the beach."

Simon said, "I thought so. I can smell it." His words sounded slurred.

Dani said, "When he's tired, his speech gets lazy."

David said, "Why don't I show him his room and Adam can acquaint you with the house?"

"All right." Dani signed David's suggestion to Simon, who shrugged and nodded. His full backpack had to be a heavy burden and he was probably ready to shuck it.

David held out a hand toward Simon, who flinched and took up a defensive stance, fists raised like a boxer. Dani moved fast, catching his hands. When she had his attention, she signed something, her fingers flying, expression earnest.

Adam felt his anger rise up hot and boiling once again. If Kurt hadn't already been dead, Adam might be tempted to take care of it himself. Or at least put a serious hurting on the man.

David caught his eye and he could see the same emotion mirrored on his friend's face.

Simon relaxed and looked at David. "Sorry, I'll follow you."

David nodded, but Adam noticed he held his hands to his side and walked four steps in front of the boy. "What did you tell him?" he asked Dani.

Weariness mixed with grief played across her features. "Just that you guys were here to help us and that you weren't anything like his father. Neither one of you would raise a hand to him in anything except friendship and an offer to help."

"Did he believe you?"

"No. He said he'd believe it when he saw it."

Adam nodded. "His trust meter is shot."

"Yes," she whispered and he watched her blink back tears.

Adam wanted to hold her, to comfort her. But he wasn't sure how she would take his gesture, so he resisted. "It's okay. He'll be fine, you'll see. It'll just take time."

"Time. Yes. Time is something we both will have now."

He lifted a hand and ran it over her new haircut. He saw her swallow, but she didn't pull away. Instead, she kept her eyes on his and a warmth settled itself around his heart. She was willing to trust him. "You look good. Different, but good."

"I feel very self-conscious. It's definitely not a style I would have chosen."

He smiled. "All the better."

She returned the smile, hers shaky and tremulous. She clasped her hands together, then released them. A nervous gesture that endeared her to him. He took her right hand in his left and gave a reassuring squeeze.

She drew in a deep breath. "So . . . when do Simon and I get pushed from the nest?"

"When I'm sure you're safe."

Dani sat on the bed and stared at the far wall. Adam had called this place a safe house. A place where she didn't have to look over her shoulder or wonder who was watching her. She looked at the new cell phone Adam had given her with her new number.

Adam. A very attractive man with a gentleness to him that made her long to curl up in his arms and just be. She had a sense that, with his arms around her, she'd always feel safe.

She hardened her heart. No. While it would be a relief to shrug off the burden of going it alone, she wasn't ready to team up with a man again. She'd been afraid for so long. Mentally, she knew why Adam was so attractive to her. He could be a safe place. He could be her comfort zone. But she needed to spread her wings a little, become comfortable with herself before she would be ready for another relationship. Maybe one day. But not yet. No, not just yet.

She flipped her wallet open and her new driver's license stared back at her. Sofia Lansing. She now sported short black hair and red secretary glasses with clear glass lenses.

Simon's shaggy blond hair was now a crisp auburn, cut military style. He thought it was cool. She thought he looked too grown up.

But that was the whole point, wasn't it? To look like anybody but themselves.

Be anyone but themselves. Sofia and Ricky Lansing.

She sighed and ran a hand through her hair. Then looked down at her fingers. The bandless ring finger of her left hand glared up at her.

Her husband was dead. Had been dead for six months. Still, it seemed like she should feel something more than just relief.

Before they'd left the house tonight, she'd grabbed the bag from the safe. Now she stared at it, wondering if she should have gone through it a lot more carefully long ago. Stuart had been coming over to get something from the safe for Kurt. Then Kurt had been killed and she'd basically shoved the bag aside and forgotten about it. She'd kept out a stack of twenties to have some cash on hand, but hadn't needed much of anything else, thanks to Kurt's FBI widow's benefits. Dani knew that an agent's widow would only get benefits if he had agreed to a portion of his pension being designated for survivor benefits. She'd been blown away when she'd learned Kurt had done this. But the more she thought about it, the more she knew it was for bragging rights. Kurt never expected to die before her. He never thought she'd actually get the money. But he'd died and she got it. She wouldn't dwell on the fact her husband had put that in there only to make himself look good.

Gerald Peabody, Kurt's lawyer, had expertly executed the will and now Dani wondered about the rest of the contents of the bag. She reached for it and paused when the door opened and Simon signed, "Can I come in?"

"May I," she automatically corrected.

Simon rolled his eyes. "No one says that."

"Then 'no one' needs to study the rules of grammar," she signed back.

"Exactly." Simon walked in and sat on the bed beside her. He fidgeted with the bedspread.

"What is it, Son?"

"Do you miss Dad?" he blurted.

She flinched at the question and debated how to answer. His gaze drilled her and she knew she had to be honest. He was too sharp and would see straight through a pat answer. Or a lie.

Dani sighed and signed, "I miss what could have been, Simon. I miss the man I thought he was. I miss a lot of things, but no, I don't miss who your father turned into." She didn't drop her eyes. "Do you understand what I mean?"

Simon's lip quivered and he gave a slow nod. "I think that's what I'm feeling too. I was trying to figure out why I was feeling bad that he was dead and—" his thin shoulder lifted in a shrug— "glad at the same time."

Regret and self hate filled her. She curled her hand into a fist and put it against her heart. Then she moved it in a slow circle. "I'm sorry," she whispered. He started to say something and she stopped him. "I'm sorry he wasn't the kind of dad you deserved. The kind you needed. I'm sorry I didn't take you and try to leave again a long time ago." She placed her hands over his ears and closed her eyes. She whispered, "I'm sorry I wasn't the kind of mother I should have been and protected you." Her voice broke on the last word. That last sentence wasn't for him, but for her.

Simon hurled himself into her arms and she held him close. His thin frame shook with sobs and Dani bit her lip to keep hers from erupting. Not over Kurt. Never again over Kurt. Her heart broke only for the fact that he was a lost soul, never to know redemption.

As much as she'd wanted to escape him, as much as she hated him, she still wished he would have changed, that she could have reached him and pulled him from whatever dark pit he'd allowed himself to sink into.

Simon finally drew in a deep breath and let it out on a long sigh. She kissed the top of his head and lifted his chin so he could see her lips. "We're going to have to figure out how to forgive him, you know."

His brow furrowed and anger blazed, chasing his sorrow away. "No way."

"Yes. We are. Otherwise the anger and bitterness are going to destroy us. I don't want to give him that satisfaction."

"I don't want to give him my forgiveness. He doesn't deserve it." He pulled away from her and scrubbed his eyes with his palms.

"Forgiveness isn't given because it's deserved. Do you understand what I mean?" He didn't answer. When he met her gaze again, she said, "We've had a long couple of days. Why don't you try to get some sleep?" She couldn't push the forgiveness issue when she was struggling with it so much herself.

Simon nodded. "After I get something to eat. I'm starving." He slipped out the door and left her alone. She wondered if he would find his way back to her later, during the night. Over the past six months he'd had more nightmares than he'd ever had when Kurt had been living.

Dani pulled her Bible from the backpack on the floor and held it in her lap. She hadn't been a Christian all that long, but she'd read the Bible cover to cover. Not all of it made sense. A lot of it did. The forgiveness part had hit her hard and wouldn't let go.

Dani lay on her side and curled into a ball, holding the Bible against her stomach. She wondered if she would ever be free to live her life as a normal person. She wondered if forgiving Kurt would be a step in the right direction.

Adam stepped into the smoky bar and paused, allowing his eyes to adjust to the darkness. When he could see, he let his gaze roam the occupants. Sadness curled through him. What did people think they'd find at the bottom of a glass or in the arms of a stranger they'd just met?

On a purely logical level, he supposed he understood. Loneliness, emptiness, made people act in ways they might never otherwise consider.

He had to fight that particular emotion on a regular basis, but he refused to make choices that would compromise his standards. He wanted the real thing, not phoniness wrapped in a pretty package.

His mind immediately went to Dani. Now she was the real deal as far as he could tell. She was also off-limits for now. Getting emotionally involved with someone he had to protect would not be a good thing. He would do his job and keep his emotions at a distance.

Right after he handed out a little warning.

The man he'd come looking for sat about ten feet to his left.

14

Stuart sat at the table with three of his fellow agents. He didn't particularly like the smoky atmosphere, but the bar provided obscurity. Something he and his buddies needed right now. He knew to anyone from the outside, they looked like any other partiers on a Monday night. They didn't look like cops, they didn't look like agents, they looked like four guys hanging out, living it up. Which fit in with their plans.

"Was it you last night?"

The low whisper caught him by surprise and he turned to see a familiar face. One he'd seen on his phone. "What?"

"You're Stuart Harding, right?"

"Yes."

"I'm Adam Buchanan."

Stuart stared at the man. Adam's narrowed green eyes glittered with suspicion and Stuart's guard went up. "Is that name supposed to mean something to me?" The name didn't, but the face did. Stuart trembled with the desire to plant his fist on Adam's arrogant nose.

"No, not right now." Adam stepped back and Stuart stood. They shared the same height.

106

Ignoring the questions on the other three faces, he followed Adam, intrigued by the man's boldness.

And by the fact that Adam seemed to have the ability to see beneath the surface. He didn't like that he was suddenly uneasy. Fresh anger rushed through him. He squinted. "What about last night?"

"Did you break into Dani's house? Did you kill the woman who was there?"

Stuart drew in a hissing breath. "Of course not, are you crazy? Why would I do that?"

"Because you can't seem to stay away from her. Because every time she turns around, you're there. Because you have some sort of sick obsession with her. It's called stalking."

Stuart went cold. His friends read his body language. Hands covered their hidden weapons, ready to draw them on his behalf. He kept his voice low. "I knew someone broke in, obviously. I went over last night to see if I could help, but she said there wasn't anything I could do and we'd talk later. So you tell me, pretty boy, if she has a state-of-the-art alarm system, how did her intruder get past it?" Stuart let his skepticism show.

"We haven't figured that out yet. But I'm willing to bet you have the code to that alarm system."

Stuart gave a soft snort. Of course he had the code. "So what if I do? I didn't use it to break in and scare Dani. I don't have to." He stared at this new threat. "I just ring the bell and walk in when she opens the door. So don't try to intimidate me. I know where I stand with Dani."

Adam didn't drop his gaze. A fact that made Stuart frown.

"You see," Adam said, "that's it. I don't think you *do* get it. She doesn't want you around. Stay away from her and stop harassing her or I'll have to make a report to the OPR."

Stuart flinched and hated himself for it. Office of Professional Responsibility and the FBI equivalent of Internal Affairs.

Adam leaned in. "And then I'll go over your boss's head. Might even name your boss as having excused prior unlawful acts. Want me to do that?"

Stuart felt the flush of rage begin at the base of his neck. But a twinge of fear had him hesitating. "Who are you and what makes you think you have the right to tell me to stay away from my dead brother's wife?"

"Dani gave me that right when you tried to chase her down and attack her."

Stuart blinked. "That was an accident. I wasn't going to hurt her. I wanted to stop her from running."

Adam looked surprised at his admission. "So you weren't interested in the contents of the safe?"

"The what? No." Stuart breathed a small laugh. "Why would I be interested in that?"

"Because Dani said you came over the day Kurt was killed to get something from the safe. She'd cleaned it out by the time you got there."

Stuart frowned. "Kurt asked me to stop by and pick up something for him. I don't even know what it was he wanted. Said he needed a small locked box and to just bring him the whole thing."

"From what I understand, you and Kurt weren't exactly best friends."

"Couldn't stand each other."

"And yet you were willing to do his bidding?"

Stuart shrugged. "Sure. It gave me a reason to see Dani." He saw no reason to keep his attraction for his sister-in-law a secret anymore.

Adam's brow lifted. "I see."

Stuart offered the man a small smirk. "I'm sure you do." He let the smile slide from his lips. "So I suggest you just keep your distance from Dani and Simon. They're mine."

"I mean it, Harding, leave Dani and Simon alone. They have help now."

Stuart curled his fingers into a fist, his anger still roiling within as he watched Adam turn and leave without a backward glance.

The man had no right to tell him what Dani wanted or didn't want. Dani didn't know what she wanted or needed. That's why it was up to Stuart to take care of her.

His phone rang and he let out a slow breath as he realized who was calling. He kept his voice low and controlled. "What do you have?"

"I almost lost them, but managed to keep up."

"And?"

"They're at a safe house. One of them left. Adam, I think. I don't know where he went, but everyone else is inside."

"I know where Adam went," Stuart muttered. "Don't worry about him."

"Fine. As soon as I dismantle the security system we'll be in."

Stuart thought for a few moments. "Don't do anything yet. Just watch them. Tell me how many people are there besides Dani and Simon."

"Just watch them?"

"Yes."

"I can do that." A pause.

"What is it?"

"Do you have someone watching me?"

"What?" Stuart frowned. "What kind of question is that?"

"So you don't."

"No," Stuart said. "I don't."

"Okay, but I could have sworn while I was following Dani and the others, someone was following me."

Stuart snorted. "Who would be following you? Don't get paranoid on me. Just stay on Dani and wait for further instructions."

"Right."

15

Later that night, Dani looked in on Simon. He lay curled up on his side, his ever-present Nintendo game clutched in his hand. Against her better judgment she'd allowed him to keep the gift that had come from his uncle Stuart. Two months ago when Stuart had stopped by with the game, Simon had looked at it with such longing. And yet she'd seen the fear in his eyes too. On impulse, she'd taken the toy from Stuart and given it to Simon.

Maybe she shouldn't have.

She sighed and stepped back, shutting the door. There were a lot of things she shouldn't have done. Letting her child find some joy in a simple game wasn't one of them.

Setting her shoulders, she turned and gasped. Adam stood there, watching her. "You scared me."

"I didn't mean to."

"Where did you come from?"

She caught the smile that crinkled the corners of his eyes in the dim hall light. He said, "I was walking the perimeter."

"Oh. Is there trouble?"

"Not so far. Blake's taking his turn."

She nodded.

"We're going to take care of you and Simon, Dani."

"I appreciate it."

His phone rang and he looked at the screen. With a sigh he stepped back. "I need to take this. When I'm done, we'd like to go through the bag from the safe. Do you mind?"

"Of course not." She stepped into the room, grabbed it from the bed, and handed it to him. "Let me have a few minutes and I'll be right there. It won't take me long."

"Okay." He pressed his screen and held the phone to his ear. "Mom? Oh. Sarah. What are you doing on Mom's phone?"

Dani watched him walk down the hall, then she closed her door, wondering about Adam's personal life. She shook her head. She had no business thinking of him as anything more than a professional, the man who was keeping them safe. She didn't need to be wondering about such personal things like his family. She needed to focus on getting away from Stuart and keeping Simon safe. Those were her immediate goals. Feelings for Adam weren't an option.

The fact that she wanted to ask him about his family mocked her as she stepped into the bathroom.

Five minutes later, when she walked into the kitchen, the bag lay on the floor next to David, the contents spread over the table.

At the conference-sized table that seated twelve, David sat next to Summer. A man Dani had never seen before sat next to David. He held out a hand. "Blake Wyatt."

Dani shook the offered hand. "Nice to meet you." Blake looked like he belonged on the cover of a military magazine. "Which branch?"

He lifted a brow. A glimmer of respect and dimple in his left cheek peeked at her. "Army."

She took the chair next to Summer. "Where's your daughter?"

"With my sister and mother. I wanted to be in on helping you as much as possible." She ran a hand through her hair. "I'll have to leave soon though. I mostly handle the office stuff, but your case is special."

"Special?"

"It kind of reminds me of what I went through last year."

"It was because of me," David said quietly. "It was my fault she was almost killed."

Summer hushed him. "Stop it. We're past all that, but knowing someone is after you and you're on the run for your life—well, I just want to be a part of helping you."

"I understand. And thank you for that." Dani decided she liked this woman and thought that under different circumstances they could have been good friends.

Her eyes fell on the objects from the safe. Adam slipped into the chair next to her and his shoulder brushed hers. Warmth traveled along her arm to the tips of her fingers. She felt a flush begin to rise and did her best to clamp down on the attraction.

It bothered her that she could be so drawn to another man so soon after Kurt's death. Then again, it wasn't *that* soon after. But was she really that needy? Was she so brainwashed that she was actually afraid to be on her own? Determined not to be, she reached for the nearest item. An envelope. "What's this?"

"It's got your name on it," David said. "So we didn't open it."

"It was in the bag?"

"Yes, mixed in amongst the papers." He lifted a brow. "You haven't seen it?"

She shook her head. "I didn't go through the bag very carefully. I just needed the money and the will. I didn't care about the other stuff." She studied the envelope, then slipped her fingernail under the flap. "But I don't remember seeing this." How had she missed it? The envelope contained one sheet: a letter. Typed in the same font as her name. She took a deep breath and scanned the words.

The more she read, the more she paled. Adam wondered at the contents and had to refrain from snatching it from her now trembling fingers. "What does it say, Dani?"

Adam exchanged a look with the other three at the table. Each face held concern. And each person didn't want to butt in until she was finished.

She ignored his question for the next two minutes. Then she handed him the letter. "You can read it out loud. I don't think I can."

Adam glanced at the print. "'My dear Danielle, I hope you never have to read this, but just in case I die, I wanted to let you know that you won't have to grieve long.'" Adam stopped and glanced up at her. She stared at the table, her expression stoic, blank.

He continued. "'You know my job is dangerous, it's never safe. I take risks every day. Risks that ensure I'm making huge deposits in the bank for our future. They're risks you'll never know about, of course, but one day those risks might get me killed. Naturally, I'm not planning on it, but you never know. One other thing. You may think I'm not aware of Stuart's obsession with you, but I am. Let me make myself clear, Dani. Only you hold the key to my heart. There's no one else for me and there's no one else for you. He will never have you. Once Stuart finally realizes that, he will understand that I will always win and he will always lose. I'll see you soon, my darling. Kurt.'"

The silence echoed around the table.

Finally Blake spoke. "Sounds like he didn't have all of his marbles in the circle."

Adam placed the letter on the table. "Dani? What are your thoughts?"

She looked up, her face pale, eyes conflicted. "It's a very oddly worded letter."

"What do you mean?"

Her frown deepened. "Just the words. They don't sound like him, his speech pattern, if that makes any sense. For example, he would never say I hold the key to his heart. Why would he write that?"

Adam rubbed a hand down the side of his face, thinking. "There are two lines in there that bother me the most. The ones where he says 'you won't have to grieve long.' And then the last one. 'I'll see you soon, my darling.' Kurt was abusive, we know that." She flinched and nodded, and his heart ached in a strange way he didn't have time to examine. "But it sounds like he might have arranged to have someone kill you in the event of his death. Would he do something like that?"

It wasn't a question he really needed to ask. He already figured he knew the answer to it. But he did wonder what Dani would say.

She raised a hand to rake it through her shortened hair. For a moment she didn't answer. Then she stood and walked over to the water pitcher on the counter. After filling a glass, she turned. Her pale, pinched features worried him, but she simply took a sip of the water and said, "Yes."

Adam nodded.

David raised a brow and looked at Summer, who blew out a breath.

"All right, then. Who?" Adam asked.

"I have no idea." Dani came back to the table and took her chair. "I can't believe this. I thought . . . when I heard Kurt was dead, I—" She cut off her words with a shudder. "I didn't want him to die, I just wanted to be free of him, but when I was told that he'd been killed, I know it was wrong, but the first emotion

I felt was—" She bit off the words and her pleading gaze angered Adam.

Not anger with her, of course, but with the whole situation that selfish, arrogant—

He stopped his thoughts and took a deep breath. "Relief, right?"

Agony in her eyes, she nodded.

"You don't have to explain anything, Dani." Adam reached over to squeeze her fingers. "He was a monster. And while you might not have wanted him dead, you had every right to want to be free of him."

"But he is dead and I'm still being held prisoner by him."

"Then we'll have to come up with a way to figure out who Kurt would have hired to carry out his wishes," Summer said. She shot a concerned glance at Dani.

Dani looked back down at the table, then lifted her gaze to meet the eyes of each of them. She said, "He didn't have many friends. At least not true friends. He had people who were afraid of him and would do things for him because of that. But someone who would kill for him?" She shook her head. "I have no idea. I truly believe Kurt was mentally ill. He wouldn't admit it, of course, and I couldn't encourage him to get help without getting a fist in the face. So I stopped trying. Instead, I plotted and planned and scraped together funds that would enable me to leave him. And then he died and Stuart started in with his craziness." She pulled in a deep breath. "And now my dead husband is still trying to control me from the grave." She stood and paced from one end of the kitchen to the other. "But why wait six months?"

"Good question," Blake said.

"So we have more questions than answers right now," David said. "The letter explains a lot, like the fact that Dani's truly in danger. We'll keep her under wraps while we investigate who would be willing to carry out a hit for Kurt."

"Someone who owes Kurt a favor and would want to follow through with paying him back even if Kurt were dead," Summer murmured.

Blake said, "I'll check into that." He stood and pulled out his phone. "As soon as I'm done with that, I'll check the perimeter again."

"Thanks," Adam said. He looked at Dani. "What about Stuart? Would he be willing to do that for Kurt?"

Dani snorted. "No. They got along all right on the surface for professional reasons, but Kurt hated Stuart and the feeling was mutual. Everything Kurt did, Stuart wanted to do better. It was like there was this constant competition between the two. Kurt became a cop, Stuart became a cop. Kurt joined the FBI and then Stuart joined the next year. Whenever Kurt received a promotion, Stuart busted his tail to get one too. It was exhausting watching the two of them sometimes."

Adam studied her. "And does Stuart want Kurt's wife like Kurt indicated in the letter?"

She stilled and stared at him. "Yes. He does."

Adam nodded. "It's fairly obvious that Stuart's been stalking you. He even chased you until you wrecked your car. Not normal behavior by any stretch of the imagination." He steepled his fingers. "I wanted to meet this guy myself, to get a read on him, so I went and found him tonight and he warned me away from you. Said you and Simon were his."

Dani paled even further. He wouldn't have thought it possible. She sank back into the chair. "You saw him? He said that?"

"He did."

She covered her face with her hands and let out a shuddering breath. "Yes." She closed her eyes, then opened them. The anguish there cracked the hard walls around his heart. "He wanted— wants—me. I'd have to be blind not to see it. But I ignored it.

After Kurt died, Stuart's stalking intensified. That's when I turned to Ron."

"It definitely could have been Stuart who broke into your house last night."

She swallowed. "Why do you say that?"

"I can't say for sure, of course. I confronted him about it. You said he showed up during all of the chaos."

"Yes."

"He could have run off, ditched his clothes, and circled back very easily."

"He could have."

"And I don't necessarily believe him just because he said it wasn't him. Stalkers are some of the best liars out there."

She nodded.

Adam leaned forward. "Whoever got in your house knew your alarm code and the combination to the safe. Does Stuart know those?"

"Yes, I'm sure he does."

"I thought so. So really, Dani, what does your gut say about it being Stuart?"

"I can't say with a hundred percent certainty one way or the other. I wondered if it was him, but his voice—" She shook her head. "I just don't know."

"From what you've said, Kurt and Stuart are a lot alike in personality," Adam said. "Stuart wants people to think well of him, right?"

"Yes. He and Kurt were very much alike in that regard." She pursed her lips. "But I think Kurt had more people fooled. I think Kurt was able to keep up the façade better than Stuart. Stuart doesn't have as much control as Kurt."

"Control?"

"Over his emotions. He's more easily angered."

"I don't know, Dani. If he's been obsessed with you for a long time, he's shown remarkable restraint."

"That's because Kurt was alive."

Adam drew in a deep breath. "And Stuart was afraid of Kurt."

"Very much so. He wouldn't admit it, of course, and he put up a pretty good front of bravado, but yes, he was."

"Okay then. As for someone breaking in your house. It could be he didn't want to get his hands dirty and hired someone to snatch you."

She pressed both palms to her eyes. "If he just wanted to take me, why open the safe, why kill Janessa?"

"To make it look like a robbery gone wrong?" David said. "And he wasn't expecting Janessa to be there. She might have taken him by surprise? He may not have even meant to kill her."

"Maybe." Adam narrowed his eyes. "Whoever it was, the fact remains that Stuart thinks you're his and I don't think he's used to not getting what he wants."

"You're right. He's not." Dani stood, grabbed the letter, and stared at it as she paced to the door and back. "Then Stuart's not out to kill me, he's just out to get me."

16

In a nervous habit he'd thought he'd kicked, Stuart snapped his fingers as he paced his home office. He wasn't worried about finding Dani. He'd made sure he could find her whenever he wanted, but he didn't want to move too soon. He had to think things through, figure out who he could trust to help him get Dani to see the light.

He just didn't understand why she was running from him. He didn't want to hurt her, he just wanted her to understand her place was with him.

But what if she never understood that? What if she kept pushing him away?

He shuddered. No, that wouldn't happen. It couldn't.

But what if it did?

Stuart wanted to shut the taunting inner voice up. Unfortunately, he couldn't help wondering. He pictured Dani and tried to imagine his life without her, but couldn't do it. He'd built this house for her, he'd saved almost every penny he could so he could take her to exotic locations and buy her fine jewelry.

But what if she continued to defy him? Reject him? What if she refused to see things his way?

Stunned, he considered the questions. The thought that he wouldn't eventually wind up with Dani had never crossed his mind. It had never occurred to him that she would refuse him.

A coldness settled around him and he knew exactly what would have to happen if Dani continued to push him away.

A knock on the door pulled him from his thoughts. He placed Dani's picture back on the mantel and went to look through the window.

Her.

He opened the door. "Hello, Butterfly." Not her real name, of course, but it suited her. "You're early."

She pushed her bottom lip out in a pout. "I wanted to see you."

He sighed and let her in. She went straight to his favorite chair and made herself comfortable. "Have you found Dani yet?"

"No, she's off the grid for now, but I'm watching and will snag her when she comes back on. Are you still setting yourself up to be her hero?"

Stuart frowned. He never should have said anything to her about his plan. "Why do you care?"

Butterfly got up and walked over to him to wind her arms around his neck and place a kiss on his lips. "You know I'm here for you. Why do you insist on chasing a woman who keeps running from you?"

Stuart bit down on his tongue hard enough to draw blood. He wanted to push her away. Far, far away. But he still needed her, so he reined in his ire. "It's not your business."

Butterfly sighed and dropped her arms. "Why did you pull me from the gang, Stuart? Why didn't you let me be taken in the raid? Why did you warn me if you weren't going to keep me for your own?"

"Because I couldn't leave you there." She needed to hear the words. "Because there was something about you that I just couldn't bear to see rot in a prison cell." He gave her the answer she wanted. They both knew he never would have taken her in if she hadn't been willing to be used by him. He needed her loyalty, her willingness to do whatever he asked. Right now he had that. He also couldn't afford for her to suddenly turn on him.

"And yet you don't want me." She pouted.

He pulled her to him and kissed her. Hard. Then pushed her away. "Of course I do. And I need you." Needed her to get to Dani. "Now stop this nonsense. We have work to do."

"So you're set on this?"

"Of course. And you said you'd help me."

"And I did! I followed them to that place. I took a picture of the guy she left with. What else do you want me to do?"

"Set up the next thing. And I need it set up so I come out the hero."

Butterfly scowled at him for a moment. He could see her hurt, her frustration. But she owed him. She'd never refuse him anything.

"What if she never comes around? What if she doesn't want to be with you? Ever?"

He paused and stared at her. Hadn't he just asked himself those very same questions minutes before? Only now, the answer was so simple, so clear. He sank into the leather chair and pulled up his favorite picture of Dani that he'd taken with his phone last Christmas. She had a smile on her face and the usual tension around her eyes had disappeared for a brief moment. He couldn't remember what had made her laugh, but he'd snapped the picture and kept it. Only right now, it made him sad.

Because if Dani continued to defy him, she'd simply have to die.

Dani stared at the ceiling. She knew it was Tuesday and it was morning. And yet she couldn't bring herself to crawl out of bed. The sheets felt wonderful, but the feeling of safety felt even better.

Then she remembered why she was there and frowned.

She couldn't believe the turn her life had taken. Yes, she'd been an abused wife. Yes, she'd lived in fear for twelve years. But even then, at some point, the fear had become the norm. Now Kurt was dead and before she could even regain her footing or find some kind of routine, she'd been knocked for another loop.

The letter had been enough to send Dani skating too close to the edge of insanity. She'd crumpled the note on the table and walked to her room, slipped between the sheets, and promptly fallen asleep.

She couldn't believe she'd actually slept, but supposed her body had said "enough." Or maybe she just felt safe for the first time in a long time. No Kurt, no Stuart . . . she didn't know. But whatever the reason, she was grateful for the rest.

She didn't want to move but felt the need to check on Simon. He hadn't disturbed her during the night, so she hoped that meant he'd slept well too.

Dani sat up and swung her legs over the side of the bed. She padded down the hall and stopped when she spotted Simon's empty bed. Her pulse rate shot up. "Simon?"

He wouldn't hear her, of course, but saying his name aloud helped for some strange reason. Where was he? The bathroom?

She checked. Empty.

Dani hurried into the kitchen to find Simon munching on a bowl of cereal and laughing in between bites. Her fear drained away and she stared. Laughing? When was the last time she'd seen Simon laugh? Sorrow gripped her and with supreme effort she pushed it away. She wouldn't dwell on that.

Adam lifted his hand and made another sign. Dani blinked. She didn't recognize it. Again Simon laughed. He put down his spoon and shook his head. "No, like this." He shaped his small hand into the letter A. Then D. Then another A. And finally an M.

Adam copied him and did it well this time.

Simon offered a high five. "Good job." As Simon brought his arm down, his elbow caught the edge of the bowl. Milk and cereal went flying. Simon shot to his feet, face pale, hands trembling. "I . . . I'm sorry."

Dani moved farther into the room, ready to rush to her son's defense. But she stopped, rooted by the look on Adam's face.

Complete and utter compassion. "It's okay. It's fine." He placed his thumb against his chest, five fingers spread, pointed upward. "Really, it's not a problem."

Simon blinked as though shocked Adam wasn't angry.

Adam saw her watching. "Can you help me let him know it's all right?"

She glanced between Simon and Adam. "I think he got the message."

Adam grabbed a hand towel from the counter and handed it to Simon. Simon took it and began to clean up the mess. Adam pulled some paper towels from the roll and went to help him. Dani simply watched.

Watched them clean and watched her son let down his guard a fraction as he shot wondering looks at Adam in between his swipes. *Thank you, Lord, for spilled milk.*

When they finished cleaning it up, Simon looked at her, then Adam. To Adam, he said, "You didn't get mad."

Adam shrugged. "It was an accident."

"But—" Simon took a deep breath. "Yes. It was. Thanks for helping me clean it up."

Adam smiled. "Anytime you need help, you just ask, all right?"

Dani signed the words to make sure Simon understood. He nodded, then slipped past her and down the hall.

"Is he going to be all right?"

She watched her son, then turned to Adam. "He's probably processing everything. He'll be fine."

"Kurt would have yelled?"

"Kurt would have hit."

Adam's jaw tightened and a muscle jumped underneath his left eye. "I wish Kurt was still alive."

She jerked. "What?"

"Yeah. So I could pound on him for a while."

Dani let out a humorless laugh. "Don't. It's not worth it."

"I know." He sighed. "So—" he smiled—"good morning."

"Good morning."

"Are you ready for some more news?"

"Good or bad?"

"It depends on how you look at it."

She blew out a sigh. "Sure. Bring it on."

Adam led the way into the kitchen. David sat at the table, studying a computer. He looked up when she entered. "Hey there, how are you doing?"

"Hanging in there, thanks." She shot him a smile that eased some of the worry he felt.

Next to David were the letter and the other items from the safe. "In the past six months that you've had this stuff, Stuart's never asked for it?"

"No."

"But he went to your house the day Kurt was killed to get something from the safe."

"Yes."

"And he was angry enough to chase you down for it."

Dani sat down and studied the items. "I thought so at the time, but now I'm not so sure he was chasing me down for the contents of the safe. He may have been chasing me for other reasons. Like to simply stop me from running."

"What makes you think that?" Adam took a chair next to Dani. He had his own thoughts, but wanted to hear hers.

"Kurt and Stuart worked together, but didn't like each other. Kurt was with the FBI division that works with gun trafficking. Stuart is with the gang unit. Kurt used Stuart whenever it suited his purposes, but I don't think he would have given Stuart anything that could be used against him later."

"Like evidence of something illegal?"

"Yes."

Adam scooted his chair closer. "So, we've got a stack of money."

"Yes. I used a little, but not much."

"And Kurt left everything to you?"

She cleared her throat. "Yes. Which I find very strange. I thought he'd leave me destitute and out on the street. Just when I think I understand him, he does something like this."

"It might not be so strange. Was Kurt's reputation important to him?"

She gave a harsh laugh. "It was everything. That's why on the outside we looked like the perfect family."

"Then he wouldn't want that reputation ruined after his death. If he hadn't made sure you were taken care of in the event that he died, people would have talked about that."

She frowned. "True. Which is the conclusion I came to about why he left me survivor benefits in his pension plan."

"And it sounds like he didn't plan on you being around long enough to use the money anyway."

"Right," she muttered.

"Take a look at this." David turned the laptop he'd been studying.

Dani leaned in and Adam got a whiff of her unique scent. He liked it. *Focus, man.*

"A video."

"Yeah. Dani, you want to take a look and tell us anything you can about it?"

Dani stared at the video playing out on the laptop screen.

Adam paused the video. "Who are those guys?"

Dani ran a trembling hand through her hair. "The one in the chair is the one they killed."

"Trennan Eisenberg."

"Yes."

"What about the others?"

She pointed to the man on the left. "That's Peter Hastings. He was at the house a lot. If Kurt was able to have a close friend, that's who it would be."

Adam nodded. "Blake checked to see if there's anyone who might owe Kurt a favor or who might feel obligated to do something above and beyond for Kurt."

"Did he find anyone?"

"Just Peter Hastings and a guy named Joseph Duncan."

"Joe. He and Kurt weren't that close, I don't believe, but I think they worked together sometimes," Dani said. "Hastings and Kurt worked together a lot. Joe works more with Stuart—I think they're partners. I've never met him. And Kurt saved Joe's life twice."

Adam gave a low whistle. "That would inspire some loyalty in a fellow."

David nodded. "Enough to commit murder for him?"

"Maybe." Adam said.

David let the video play, and Hastings answered his cell phone, leaned over and grabbed keys from the table, then left. Not more than ten seconds later, one of the men pulled out his gun and aimed it at Eisenberg.

Adam reached over to pause the video again. "Who's the guy holding the gun on Mr. Eisenberg?"

"He's another FBI agent, Ryan Blanchard." She paused and shook her head. "His wife brought me a chicken casserole after Kurt was killed."

"And the guy by the door?" Adam asked.

Dani shook her head. "I never saw him."

"And we can't either," David said.

Adam zoomed in. "His face is in the shadows. Can anyone make out anything about him?"

"Looks tall. See where he hits the doorframe?"

"Hair color?"

"No. The video's not exactly topnotch. Who was taking it anyway?"

Dani shrugged. "I don't know. I never saw anyone filming. I was at the door. I peered in and saw Ryan holding the gun. They were arguing and then Ryan shot him. I must have made some sound. Kurt was right next to the door. He turned and saw me. None of the others noticed."

"Was Stuart there?"

"No, I don't think so. Unless he's by the door. They're about the same build."

Adam narrowed his eyes. "So, we've got the guy who was murdered, the guy who murdered him, Kurt to the right watching what's going on, the guy by the door on the left."

"And whoever was filming," Dani whispered. "I didn't even think about him until just now."

Adam blew out a breath. "I want to get this video to the FBI ASAP."

"But which FBI agents can we trust?" Dani asked.

"Good question," David murmured. He tapped the table. "So, do we get a restraining order against Stuart?"

"You think it would help?" Summer asked.

"It can make things a little difficult for him if he approaches Dani or Simon again," David said.

"We could try it." Adam shrugged. "See what happens. I'm hoping we can just help them disappear and start living their lives."

"Yeah."

Blake came into the room, his tension visible.

Adam immediately felt his guard come up. "What is it?"

"We're being watched."

Adam stood. "How did you figure that out?"

"I've been scoping around the house. We've got trees straight out behind us, houses to the left and the right. I saw a flash of something. Like the sun off glass."

Binoculars? "Where's the watcher?"

Blake frowned. "The flash came from the trees to the side, but now, I think he's moved directly behind the house."

"We need to know for sure," David said. "Any suspicious activity around the neighbors'?"

"Not that I can tell." He paced to one end of the room and back. "I think we need to go on the offensive."

"Absolutely." Adam ran a hand down his face. "We need to get a closer look."

"How close?" Blake lifted a brow.

Adam narrowed his eyes. "Real close."

17

Dani crossed her arms and sucked in a breath. "What do we do?"

"Get Simon and be prepared to run. I'm not saying we'll have to, but be ready."

Without another word, she headed down the hall to find Simon munching on a protein bar and engrossed in his video game. She tapped his shoulder and waited for him to pause the game. When he looked up and caught the expression on her face, his own features tightened. "What?"

"They think someone is watching us." She signed and spoke at the same time.

"Who? Stuart?"

"They're not sure, but we need to be ready to leave if they tell us to."

His lips tightened and anger glinted in his blue eyes. "Why can't they just put Stuart in jail and leave us alone?"

Dani's throat tightened. This was so hard on him. She'd give her right arm to make him feel safe and secure. "Because I'm afraid it's not that easy." Dani would keep Simon in the loop about some things, but there was no way she was going to tell him his father had possibly arranged to have her killed in the event of his own death. Simon just didn't need to know that.

Her tension level threatened to take the top of her head off, and she drew in a deep breath even as she offered up a prayer for everyone's safety.

Adam appeared in the doorway. "Stay down and stay low. Away from the windows. They're wired and bulletproof, but they're not impenetrable."

Dani nodded. "Fine." She knew about weapons and bullets that pierced body armor. She figured there was ammunition that went through supposedly bulletproof glass too.

Adam left and she signed the instructions to Simon, who set his jaw and squared his shoulders. "I thought we would be safe here."

"Come on, Simon. I'm sorry about all this, but if we're not safe, we're not safe."

Defiance glittered in his eyes and for a second he looked so much like Kurt, she gasped. He frowned and the look faded. "What is it?"

"Please, Simon, let's listen to these people. They're risking their lives for us and we need to do whatever they want us to do to help. One woman's already died trying to help us, I don't want anyone else to get hurt."

His shoulders dropped. "Fine."

She blew out a relieved breath. "Good."

Adam pressed the piece a little tighter against his eardrum. "You copy me?"

"Loud and clear," Blake said.

"David?"

"Copy. Mama bear and cub are hibernating."

Good. They were all ready. Someone was watching. Adam wanted to know who it was. David would stay behind while Adam and Blake worked the perimeter doing their best to stay out of sight.

And avoid getting shot.

Reinforcements were on the way. Tabitha Young and Isaac Hart, more Operation Refuge associates. "How far away are Tabitha and Isaac?"

"Six minutes out," David reported.

Sit tight and wait? Or go ahead and move and hope for the element of surprise? He looked back at Blake. "Where did you see the flash of light?"

"Up on that hill. From the shelter of the trees."

"Then we need a plan to come in behind them."

"That's what I was thinking." Blake checked his Glock and slid two extra clips into the pocket of his jacket. Adam did the same. They'd gone over the emergency evacuation plan upon arrival at the safe house, but he wanted whoever was watching in custody.

His lips tightened. If it was Stuart . . .

Single file, they slipped out the front door. Adam pointed. "Go down four houses and cut through to the back. We'll work our way back toward the center behind the house."

"Got it."

"Stay in touch. If you can't talk, tap your mic."

Blake nodded and started down the street at a trot. Adam went the other way. Midmorning on a Tuesday and most everyone was at work. A few stay-at-home mothers and maybe a few of the unemployed might be around, but no one was on the street as of right now. He kept his weapon hidden as he darted between cars, doing his best to keep from looking suspicious. No telling who had her nose to the window.

"Coming up the side of the fourth house," Adam said. "There's a fence I'm going to have to get around."

"Same here. Going up to the next house. There's no fence."

"There're fences all the way down to the end of the block, I'm going to have to go over."

Adam scanned the house. No cars in the drive. He went up to the front door and rang the bell. No sense in having someone see him in the backyard and call the cops. A dog yapped in triple time but no footsteps sounded. He rang again.

Nothing.

Adam stepped off the porch and walked to the side of the house once again and slipped through the gate into the backyard. Scanned the back of the tall wooden fence. He could easily haul himself over, but wanted to see what was waiting for him on the other side before he made an appearance. Sturdy patio furniture graced the large concrete area. He grabbed the small glass-topped end table and carried it to the back of the fence.

A quick scan said he was clear.

Within seconds he was over.

Carefully, he made his way toward the back of the safe house. He spoke into his mic. "See anything?"

"Nope. Getting close though."

Adam let his eyes roam the area. Nothing behind him. Nothing alarming in front of him. "I'm closing in too."

He dodged trees and limbs, his steps crunching on the frozen ground and underbrush. He stopped. "I'm making too much noise."

"Having the same problem." Blake spoke in almost a whisper.

"Hold still, I'm going to take a look." Adam whipped out his Steiner binoculars and focused in on the safe house. All looked quiet. He moved the view to the area Blake said the person was watching from.

"I don't see anyone."

"I'm going to move in a little closer."

David's voice came through the earpiece. "Tabitha and Isaac are ready to move when you need them."

"Good."

Adam kept the binoculars to his eyes. Blake stepped into sight, hunkered low, caution in every line of his form. "I see you."

Blake kept moving and Adam kept scanning, searching for any hint of danger. The vest Blake wore wouldn't protect him from a head shot. Adam moved closer, ready to shoot anything that threatened.

Blake reached the area, and after several seconds of scanning, he stood and pointed. "Footprints, crushed leaves. This whole area's disturbed. He's gone, but he was here."

Dani stepped into the hallway. David stood by the door. Simon had his bag ready, as did Dani. "Anything?"

David shook his head. "They're at the site, but didn't find anyone there."

"You think Blake was wrong?"

"I don't know. They're checking it out now. Something just . . ."

". . . doesn't feel right?" she finished it for him.

He lifted a brow. "Yeah."

The doorbell rang and Dani froze. David sucked in a breath and said, "Stay here." He bolted down the hall toward the door.

Simon clutched her hand. "What happened?"

"Someone's at the door."

"Who?"

Fear settled cold and heavy in her belly. "I don't know." She looked at her son, so lost and confused, his world turned upside down. "Stay here."

She followed in David's footsteps, slow and steady. Kurt's weapon rested between the small of her back and her waistband. She pulled it out.

"Who is it?" David's voice carried to her.

She paused at the end of the hallway. Two more steps and she could see the front door.

"It's Stuart Harding, I'm here for Dani and Simon."

Her knees went weak. Nausea threatened. How had he found them? "Don't open the door," she gasped.

David shot her a frown. "Get in the back. I'm going to see what this joker wants."

"He'll shoot first and ask questions later," she hissed. "Please! Don't." She gulped. "Just don't."

David's frown turned to compassion. "I can handle this, Dani. Just go back and stay out of sight with Simon."

"What if he's not alone?"

"I've already thought of that. Tabitha and Isaac are on the way over." He pressed a finger against his ear. "We've got company."

"Open up! Dani! I know you're in there."

"How far away are Blake and Adam?" she asked.

"Almost here."

Adam rushed to the fence and opened the gate that had been installed when the house was chosen to hide away victims. He could feel Blake on his heels. "You take the left, I'll go right."

Blake veered off and Adam did the same. They exited the gates on either side of the house. Adam held his weapon ready. He rounded the house. "What do you want, Harding?"

Stuart jerked and spun, dropping to one knee, his right hand reaching under his jacket.

"Don't do it!" Blake hollered.

Stuart hesitated and Adam prayed he'd listen. They didn't need the headache of an investigation right now. Then again, with Stuart dead, Dani would breathe easier. But Stuart held his hands above

134

his head. Blake moved in to remove his weapon. Tabitha and Isaac closed in from across the street.

Hostility glittered in Stuart's eyes as his gaze bounced from person to person, finally landing on Adam. "You have no right to keep my family from me."

Blake stepped back, Stuart's weapon held firmly in his left hand. With his right, he kept his gun on the man.

Adam said, "They're not your family. Not anymore."

"Of course they are," Stuart scoffed. "Dani!"

The door flung open and Dani stood there, eyes blazing. "Go away! Leave us alone!"

Stuart flinched. "What are you saying?" He blinked and stared. "What have you done to yourself?"

She stomped her foot. "I'm saying I don't want anything to do with you or your crazy family. I'm sorry, but I can't deal with you too. Kurt nearly killed me and Simon. And you're just like him. Now leave us alone." She stepped back.

Before she could close the door, Simon hurled himself through the opening and slammed into his uncle. Stuart went down with a grunt. Simon fell too, but quickly rebounded. Back on his feet, he pointed a finger at a stunned Stuart. In his slightly nasal fashion he spit his words like bullets. "You stay away from us. You leave my mom alone or I'll kill you myself." He spun on his heel and went to Dani. Taking her hand, he pulled her inside.

A sharp crack.

Splintering wood.

Dani pulled Simon to the floor.

18

Adam fell to the ground and rolled. He came up firing back at the car. His bullets slammed into the side as tires squealed. Burnt rubber assailed his nostrils and he noticed Blake rushing after the vehicle. Tabitha lay on the ground, hand against her chest, face twisted into a grimace.

Isaac's weapon blasted bullet after bullet. Glass shattered, but the car never slowed.

Adam grabbed the binoculars from his pocket and tried to zoom in on the plate. "AIE5 something." He rolled to his feet to train his weapon on Stuart.

Who was nowhere to be found. "Where'd he go?" Adam itched to go in search, but instead turned his attention to the others. "Tabitha!"

Isaac knelt beside her. "She's all right. Two bullets hit her vest. Just got the breath knocked out of her."

David raised up from the porch floor. Adam spun back to Blake, who held a hand to a bleeding shoulder. "Blake? How bad is it?"

"Nothing a Band-Aid won't take care of." His gruff voice held no hint of the pain he must be in.

"Where are Dani and Simon?" Adam asked.

David opened the bullet-riddled door and Adam's stomach

twisted. Had they been hit? He raced up the front porch, confident the shooter was gone. He also knew Tabitha and Isaac would take care of the cops, who were no doubt on the way. "Dani! Simon!"

Stuart clutched a hand to his wounded side and bit out curses like they were the only words available. "Stupid, stupid, stupid."

His phone rang and he glanced at the caller ID as he pulled his car to the curb. His partner, Joe Duncan, tracking him down.

Stuart shot a glance at the rearview mirror and wondered if they'd try to give chase. Probably not for him. They'd go after the shooters.

His phone rang again. Dani would have to wait. "Yeah?"

"Where are you? You get your personal errand taken care of?"

"Not quite. What's up?" Pain radiated through him and he did his best to cut off the gasp that ruptured through his lips.

"You know that body that turned up in the Reedy River yesterday?"

"Yeah."

"Coroner thinks it's gang related."

"Which one?" he panted. He rummaged through the glove compartment looking for anything he could use as a compress. He grabbed a handful of napkins and pressed it against the wound. Stars exploded in his head and the world quivered as though it might fade away at any moment.

"Yours." Joe's voice came through the line, sounding faint and far away.

Stuart blinked through the pain and focused on how he needed to respond. Infiltrating the Bloods had taken time and patience. Kurt had sneered and told him he wouldn't last a month. That had been a year ago. "I haven't heard anything. I'll see what I can find out."

"You okay? You sound weird."

"I'm fine for now. I might need your help a little later."

"What's up?"

"I'll call you after I see what I can find from the Bloods." He hung up, then dialed another number. "Butterfly? I need you. Meet me at Barney's, will you?"

"What's wrong?"

"Just meet me there."

He'd head to Barney's Bar where the Bloods hung out. Butterfly would dig the bullet out of him and patch him up. If she was too squeamish, he'd do it himself.

If he had to get shot, he might as well use it to his advantage and gain some status in the Bloods' eyes.

Dani huddled over Simon just inside the door. Bullets had come too close and she trembled with a sick fear. First Stuart finding them, now this? And if Stuart wasn't shooting at them, who was? Someone he'd hired?

"Dani!"

Adam's shout pierced her haze of terror and she slowly stood, Simon clutching at her hands. "We're fine." They were, weren't they? She ran her hands over Simon's newly cropped hair and pale face. She signed, "Are you hurt?"

He shook his head.

The relief in Adam's eyes touched her. Sparked something in her she hadn't realized she could still feel. He was worried about them.

Adam looked at David. "Blake and Tabitha were hit, but it doesn't look bad."

Blake's grunt came from the front porch. "When you take a bullet, you can decide how bad it is."

"I took one not too long ago, you big baby. Wasn't any worse than getting stung by a bee," he deadpanned. "You need medical attention?"

"Unfortunately, I think so. The bullet's in there."

"Get to the car," Adam told Blake. He frowned at Dani. "I'm sorry, but we're going to have to move."

"Where to?"

"Someplace a lot safer than this 'safe' house."

He bolted back outside and Dani gathered her wits even as she ushered Simon into the bedroom. "Get your stuff."

He grabbed his backpack and slung it over his shoulder. The Nintendo DS lay on the bed. Simon stared at it for about ten seconds, then turned on his heel and walked out of the room.

Dani swiped a stray tear and sniffed as her heart broke once again for her child. All the emotions that must be going through her son's heart, the thoughts in his mind. She could imagine. Probably the same ones that were going through hers. She snagged the game and dropped it into the side pocket of her bag. Just because it came from the man who was stalking her didn't mean Simon should forgo the only entertainment that might be available.

She walked back into the den to find Simon standing with his back against the wall watching the activity around him.

She placed a hand on his shoulder and looked at Adam. "What now?"

"We go through the kitchen and into the garage. Get in the car and get out of here."

Simon was scared. Flat-out terrified. Not just for himself, but for his mother. He'd seen how close the bullets had come and he knew one of them had been meant for his mom. A lump lodged in his throat too big to swallow.

139

He knew he was only twelve years old, but there had to be something he could do to keep his mom safe. But what?

Not being able to hear didn't bother him much. He remembered some sounds. Like speech and the way some words were formed. He remembered the sound of his mother's voice when she told him she loved him. And he remembered the scorn in his father's voice when he did something wrong.

That was one sound he was willing to forget.

He watched them talk. Read their lips.

And headed for the garage.

With each step, he thought about praying, but wasn't sure God was listening. Then again, none of the bullets had hit him or his mother, so maybe God was there after all.

He wanted things to go back to normal.

The last six months of normal anyway. Minus Stuart.

When his uncle wasn't being so creepy over his mom, life had been pretty good. Now that the threat of his father wasn't hanging over his head, Simon had finally started to understand what it was like to live without that constant ball of dread in his belly.

And now this. It wasn't fair.

But he was mature enough to understand that life wasn't fair and it wasn't just picking on him. It picked on everyone. And at least they had people willing to help them.

But he sure missed his friends at the school. Especially Mitchell Lee.

His mother handed him the Nintendo game over the back of the seat. He sighed and took it from her. Every time he played it, he felt almost guilty for accepting the gift from his uncle. But not guilty enough to give it back.

———

Stuart groaned as he slid into the passenger seat of Joe's truck. He'd abandoned his car in a parking lot nearby and walked the rest of the way to find Butterfly at Barney's Bar. There was no way he could show up in his Lexus.

Joe eyed him with a raised brow. "What happened to you?"

"I was in the wrong place at the wrong time."

"Obviously." He leaned closer. "Man, you're going to bleed all over my truck. What happened?"

"I got shot."

"Did Dani shoot you?"

Stuart shot the man an irritated look. "No, she didn't shoot me." He clamped his lips on the fiery pain radiating through his ribs and into his gut. It hurt to breathe, but at least Butterfly had gotten the bullet out. As long as he didn't develop some sort of raging infection, he'd be all right. He had a bottle of antibiotics at home. Hopefully they'd be strong enough. "You change out the plates on this thing?"

"Yeah. If any of your brilliant gang members decide to trace it, they'll find it's a stolen vehicle."

"Good."

"Will that elevate your status?"

"Of course." He panted and leaned his head against the headrest. All he wanted to do was get home. "I'm going to have to take a few days off."

"Yeah, I think that might be a good idea. What are you going to tell the SAC?"

"That I'm sick with the flu. Half the building has it. He won't question it."

"Does that wound have anything to do with Dani?"

"It does."

"You found her."

"I did, but I didn't plan on this happening."

"Was this your way of rescuing her?"

"Well, yeah, but I sure didn't plan on being shot in the process.

They were just supposed to shoot in her direction." He bit his lip. Nothing had gone according to plan. Dani hadn't played the role he'd assigned to her. She was supposed to walk out to talk to him. The drive-by was supposed to shoot in her direction and Stuart was supposed to tackle her to the ground, roll, and shoot back, "scaring" the shooters into submission. Instead, Adam Buchanan had come out looking like the hero and Stuart had had to limp away with a bullet in his side because there's no way he could afford to wind up in a hospital. That would generate way too many questions.

Then again, he wondered if he should have let them take him in. Dani might have felt sympathy for him and stayed by his side.

Rage burned in his gut, adding to the fire in his side. He was making all kinds of wrong decisions. He had to start thinking and thinking smart.

"Who'd you pay to pull that off?" Joe asked.

"The wrong people." He studied Joe. "You willing to help me again?"

"Depends on how much you're willing to pay."

Adam glanced in the rearview mirror for the umpteenth time since they'd left the safe house. David had taken Blake to the hospital and would report in when he knew something.

Tabitha claimed she was fine and insisted she could handle the cleanup at the house and deal with the questions from the cops.

Adam had no doubt she could.

"Where are we going?"

Dani spoke for the first time since sliding into the passenger seat after the latest restroom break an hour ago.

"Do you or Simon get seasick?"

"No." He heard her confusion.

"How do you feel about living on a houseboat for a while?"

"Isn't that kind of confining?" In other words, if they were found again, how would they escape?

"A little. But no one can get close without us seeing."

"And Stuart can't walk up and ring the bell," she murmured.

"Exactly."

She shot a glance in the backseat and his eyes followed hers. Simon had his head against the window watching the world go by. He hadn't said a word since they left.

They'd been driving for hours with only two stops for food and restroom facilities.

But Adam wasn't taking any chances.

"You keep watching the mirrors," Dani said. "Have we been followed?"

"No."

"How can you be so sure?"

He shrugged. "Nothing is a hundred percent, of course, but I'm as certain as I can possibly be."

"How?"

"Because I've had Operation Refuge employees following, doubling back, tracking and watching our tail."

She lifted a brow. "You have?"

He gave her a half smile. "Yes."

"Oh."

"So while it's not out of the realm of possibility that we were followed, it's extremely unlikely."

She closed her eyes and blew out a breath. "Good. That's good."

His phone rang. "Hello?"

"Blake's going to be fine," David reported. "The bullet's out and he's getting patched up."

"Good, thanks for keeping me updated."

"Sure thing. I'm letting Tabitha and Isaac handle the questions from the cops about the shooting. Dani and Simon were never there."

"Excellent. What about Stuart?"

"He's disappeared. I'd put a BOLO out on him, but he hasn't done anything we can arrest him for."

"Yet."

"Yes. Yet."

"Keep your phone on. This isn't over."

"Ten-four."

Adam drove the last leg of the trip in relative comfort, but refused to lower his guard. He'd been honest with Dani when he said he didn't think they'd been followed.

All of Operation Refuge's employees had stellar skills, either from a military or law enforcement background. Operation Refuge had exploded into a full-fledged protection agency shortly after David and Summer Hackett had birthed the idea and taken it to the governor. She'd immediately given her stamp of approval.

With fourteen operatives, there was always help to go around. Granted, Dani and Simon's case seemed to be a bit extreme. He had to admit all of the other cases bored him in comparison. Except when David and Summer had been on the run.

Yeah, on the run, lied to by family, and getting shot were enough excitement for the next hundred years or so. He'd take boring.

He slid a sidelong glance at Dani, then turned his attention back to the road. Something told him boring wasn't going to be in his future anytime soon.

19

When Dani stepped out of the car, a frigid breeze off the nearby lake froze the air in her lungs. She pulled her scarf across her mouth and nose and turned to make sure Simon had his hood up. Of course he didn't. She signed for him to do so. With a roll of his eyes, he snapped the hood over his head.

She tapped the tips of her fingers to her lips and pulled them down, palm facing up.

"What does that mean?"

Adam had a bag slung over his shoulder. She grabbed her small carry-on and said, "It means 'thank you.'"

"I see he's got the eye roll down pat."

"Oh yeah."

Adam shook his head and stepped closer, his eyes roaming behind her. "Is it okay if I act like we're a couple and put my arm around you when we start walking to the boat?"

"A couple?"

"Yeah. Just to be on the safe side. I don't think anyone followed us, but appearances can be everything if someone starts asking questions."

"Um . . . okay."

Dani made sure Simon had his things and told him what Adam was going to do.

"Pretend?" he signed.

She snagged his fingers. "Maybe we shouldn't sign when we're in the open. I wouldn't put it past Stuart to hire someone who knows sign language to report back to him what we're talking about."

Simon's jaw tightened and he looked at Adam.

Adam lifted a brow and said, "I'm impressed. Good thinking. Like I said, I don't think we were followed, but that's a good precaution to take."

He settled an arm around her shoulder and reached out to ruffle Simon's hair. "Come on."

When Simon didn't pull away or frown at the familiar touch, Dani felt a catch in her heart. *Oh Lord, continue to heal us.*

They started toward the marina, Adam's arm a welcome weight. She felt . . .

. . . safe.

Settling on that word jolted her and she sucked in a deep breath. Safe with him, yes, but not safe in general. "When I walk out in the open like this, I feel like I have a target on my back."

"I know." He hugged her closer and Dani finally had to admit his nearness took her breath away. She clearly had some kind of crazy attraction for this man. An attraction she had to let go, get over, move past, or something.

"Where am I going?" she asked.

"To the houseboat down there. The white one."

To distract herself from the way her heart seemed to change rhythm and the way she wanted to lean into him and give in to the desire to let him help shoulder her heavy burden, she looked back to find Simon walking four steps behind, his eyes glued on the arm around her.

Dani couldn't identify the emotions she saw flickering in his eyes, but wondered if he didn't like seeing her so cozy with Adam. She held out her right hand to him and he lifted a brow as if to say, "Really?"

Right. He wasn't her baby boy anymore. Holding her hand had become a thing of the past. Unless he was scared or hurt.

"Is anyone watching?" she asked.

"No."

From the corner of her eye, she could see the earpiece buried in his ear. "You're keeping in touch with other—" She paused. "What do you call yourselves? Agents? Operatives?"

"We're not law enforcement. I suppose you would call us employees. Friends."

"So are your friends listening?"

"Yes." His head tilted toward her, a smile on his lips, but his eyes never landing, always watching. "On the way here, my friends were also following. If they'd seen anyone, they would have warned me."

Dani stepped out onto the wooden dock. As they approached the houseboat, a young woman appeared on the deck. Dani stopped. Adam gave her shoulder a squeeze, then stepped forward to greet the woman. "Hi, Tori."

Tori waited for them to board the boat, then flung herself into his arms. Adam laughed and gave her a quick hug, then set her from him.

Tall, a natural blonde with pouty lips and brown eyes, Tori was a natural beauty. Dani felt a pang of jealousy at her easy familiarity with Adam and wondered at the history between the two.

"This is Victoria Holland, my cousin. Better known as Tori. She's also with the US Marshals. She just transferred back to the East Coast. Some people catch a plane. Tori bought a boat."

His cousin. Dani relaxed a fraction and held out a hand. Tori shook it and gave her a sweet smile. "Come on aboard."

"This belongs to you?"

"Sure does."

Simon hopped on deck and looked at Dani, a question in his eyes. She held up a finger and he fidgeted.

Tori caught the unspoken exchange. "He can look around all he wants. It's pretty kidproof."

Simon signed, "You live here?"

Tori signed back, "Yes. This is my home."

Simon's left brow rose and his eyes lit up. Adam smiled. "Another reason she might come in handy."

"Cool," Simon said. "Can I raid your refrigerator?"

Tori giggled. "Of course."

Simon grinned. "I'm going to like this place."

"But won't we be putting you out by staying here?" Dani asked, shooting her son a warning frown.

"Not at all. I'm not here much thanks to work. And even if I was here, I have four bedrooms." She waved them in. "Come on. Let's go inside and get out of the cold." Tori opened the sliding glass doors off the deck, and Dani followed her into a spacious living area with an L-shaped leather sofa. "We'll keep the curtains closed over the doors so no one can see in."

Just beyond the living area was an open-concept kitchen. The bar-height table was built into the wall and sported four high-backed bar stools. Above the table, a large flat-screen TV hung on the wall.

Simon's head swiveled on his neck as he took it all in.

"It's lovely," Dani said.

"Thanks," Tori smiled and moved to close the curtains. "I got a sweet deal on it from a friend who was having some financial problems and needed out from under it. I needed a place to live, so . . ." She pointed at a doorway. "If you keep going through here, there're the stairs to the next level, a bedroom on the right and a bathroom on the left." A short hallway connected everything with the outside once again. "The master is upstairs, and down below are two more bedrooms. Take whichever rooms you like."

Simon thundered down the steps and Dani let him go. He must have been paying more attention than she thought and been reading lips. She looked at Tori. "I'll take the bedroom downstairs near Simon. Unless we need to share one?"

"Nope, you can have your own." She gave her cousin a light punch on the arm. "Guess that leaves you with the bedroom off the kitchen."

"That's the one I wanted anyway."

"Kinda figured that." Tori smiled. "Y'all make yourselves at home."

"I think my son already has," Dani muttered with an exasperated roll of her eyes.

Tori laughed and Dani decided she liked this woman.

Adam tossed his bag onto the bed and looked around. Small, compact, and perfect for his needs, the bedroom was tastefully decorated in golds and browns. All Adam really cared about was the fact that the bed was comfortable and the bathroom was across the narrow hall.

And he was right next to the entrance to the boat and whoever boarded would have to go through him to get to the occupants below. He'd make sure the other end of the craft was secured. And with the sliding glass doors, a broom handle would take care of that. Someone might get on the boat, but they wouldn't get *in* without him knowing about it.

Not the best circumstances, he thought, but they had to work with what they had. And he knew they weren't followed.

The boat rocked with a barely noticeable sway and he hoped

the slight movement didn't bother Dani or Simon. Adam loved it and always enjoyed visiting Tori when he could. They'd had great fun as kids. Family reunions at the lake had birthed their love for all things water.

"Hey, cuz."

He turned to see Tori in the doorway. "Hey."

"Sarah told me about your mom."

A pang hit him. "Yeah."

"She's having surgery on Thursday afternoon."

His head snapped up. "I didn't know."

"Sarah just called me."

Concerned, he frowned. "On a secure line, I hope."

"Of course."

Adam sighed. "I knew she was diagnosed, but Sarah didn't mention the surgery."

"I don't know why she didn't mention it. I suppose you may still get a call from her."

"Yeah." He wondered if she really would call or if his mother would have gone through surgery without him ever knowing. "Thanks for telling me."

"Of course." She paused. "So. What are you going to do?" she finally asked.

Conflicted, he didn't answer right away. He unzipped his bag then stopped. "I don't know. I suppose it would depend on if she even wants me there."

"She wants you there, Adam, but would understand if you couldn't be."

"And yet Sarah hasn't called me." He sighed. "And she probably won't." He shrugged. "Maybe this will all be finished by the time she has the surgery and it won't be an issue."

"And if it's not finished?"

"Then I'll have to figure something out. I want to be there

150

for her, but my parents still haven't forgiven me for my part in bringing down your father."

"Actually, I think they have."

He snorted. "If they have, they haven't shared that with me." He narrowed his eyes. "So how did you manage to get out of going to that stuffy dinner the other night?"

"I pretended I didn't get the text. Or the email. Or the voice mail."

"That's just not right."

She grimaced. "No, but it worked."

Adam opened a drawer. "Did you ever wonder how we ended up in a family of politicians?"

"Of course." She shrugged. "I guess God put us here for a reason. We just have to figure out what that is and work with it."

He stared at her. "Since when did you care what God thought?"

"Since I almost died about three months ago," she said softly. "It sort of changes your perspective on things. Like where you'll spend eternity."

He blinked. "You almost died?"

She shrugged again. "Long story. I'll tell you about it sometime when we have more time." She glanced at her watch. "Bypass Sarah and call your mom."

Adam nodded and she turned away. Still thinking about the conversation, he pulled out the bag that contained the contents of the safe and walked into the kitchen to spread the items on the table.

In all the craziness, they still hadn't had time to fully analyze everything. He planned to get that done today. And of course, David and Summer were working behind the scenes trying to find who Kurt might have hired to kill Dani.

So far they must have come up empty, as he hadn't had a text or call yet. He returned to his bedroom to finish unpacking. He set his Glock on the bed and stacked his three shirts and two pairs of jeans on the dresser.

A high-pitched whistle behind him made Adam pause. He glanced up in the mirror then turned, catching Simon's eye. "Hi."

"Hi." Simon eyed the weapon on the bed. Adam tapped his ear like he'd seen Dani do. Simon reached up and pressed his mold tighter into his ear and the whistling stopped. Adam picked up the gun. "Your dad ever show you how this works?"

"No sir."

"You want to know?"

A hesitant nod accompanied an excited gleam in the boy's eyes. Along with a touch of fear. Simon firmed his jaw and the fear faded. "Yes, I want to know."

"Go ask your mom if it's all right," Adam said.

Simon's shoulders drooped. "She'll say it's too dangerous."

Adam gave a thoughtful nod. "Guns can be dangerous. But they can be used for protection too. You just have to know how to handle them and treat them with respect."

Simon bit his lip. "I don't think my dad was very respectful of his gun."

"Why's that?"

"Because I saw him hold it to my mom's head one time and—" he gulped and looked away. Then squared his shoulders and looked Adam in the eye. "I read his lips. He told her if she ever tried to leave him again, he'd—"

Adam's heart threatened to beat out of his chest as fury swelled inside him. But he kept his expression neutral, his face relaxed. "He'd kill her?"

Simon shook his head. "No. Me. He'd kill me and make her watch."

20

Dani placed a hand over her racing heart and clenched her teeth against the violence racing through her. Not at Adam or Simon but at Kurt. She remembered the day Kurt had held his weapon against her head and threatened to kill Simon should she take it upon herself to try to leave again.

She hadn't known Simon had witnessed the event.

Oh my baby boy . . .

She stepped into the doorway. Adam's eyes met hers and she knew *he knew* she'd heard every word. She tapped Simon's shoulder. "Adam can show you how the gun works, but you can't ever touch it unless he gives you permission."

Simon blinked and Dani bit her lip on a smile. Poor thing, she'd shocked him with her easy acquiescence. He gave a slow nod. "Okay. I can promise that."

Dani met Adam's gaze. "I don't expect you to . . ." She wasn't sure what she was trying to say, but Adam seemed to understand.

"No worries. I'd love to spend some time with him."

Dani relaxed. "All right then." Having a positive male influence would do wonders for Simon. Learning how to properly handle a weapon would be good for him too. Kurt had instilled such terror with his gun, having Simon develop a healthy respect would at least allow him to conquer one fear. It would be a start.

She returned to the kitchen to find Tori at the sink. "Want some help?"

"Sure." Tori handed her the knife and picked up the remote to power on the flat-screen television on the wall. The news played quietly in the background while Dani helped chop vegetables for the evening meal. "Have you always wanted to work for the marshals?"

Tori glanced at her and ran the water to wash away the remains of the food. "Not always."

"So how did you wind up doing it?"

"My family's always been in politics. My dad was a judge and had several death threats over the life of his career. We had marshals in our home more than once." She rinsed her hands and dried them, the look on her face thoughtful. And a bit sad. "My dad was a dirty judge," she admitted softly.

Dani felt her brows raise. "What?"

"He was on the take from an organized crime family, the Raimondis. Adam helped put the family out of commission and uncovered my father's dirty deeds, so to speak."

Dani gaped. "I'm so sorry."

Tori shrugged. "I am too. It's been a year and it feels like a lifetime."

"Poor Adam."

"He was devastated. My father set him up. With his position as a US Marshal, he had access to a lot of inside info. My dad used him, used his loyalty to the family to convince him that he should get information. Adam went along with it for a while until he realized what he was doing was putting the very people he was guarding in danger. Adam would never have jeopardized his career if he'd known my father was one of the bad guys. He thought he was just helping out his uncle, a man who'd put a ton of criminals behind bars. He never realized Dad was using him as a patsy."

"Wow."

"Adam was almost killed. My father put a hit on him. His own nephew." She shook her head and blinked back the tears that had surfaced.

Dani didn't know what to do.

Tori sniffed and gave a small laugh. "I guess you didn't need to know all that."

"No, it's fine. Adam said he'd tell me the story, he just hasn't had a chance to do it yet." She studied her new friend. "And besides, I think you needed to tell me."

Tori shrugged. "Maybe. But I think it's only fair you know what kind of family we are."

Dani stared into Tori's glistening eyes and thought about the man who'd risked his life to help her. Who continued to do his best to keep her and Simon safe. "You and your family are my heroes."

***

THURSDAY
DECEMBER 11

Simon stood at the rail of the houseboat and stared out across the water. A frigid wind blew off the water, but he didn't care. He pulled his hoodie tighter and studied the area around him.

A lone fisherman cast his line as the small dingy rocked beneath him. A motorboat zipped past and Simon felt the houseboat shift slightly as the waves hit against the sides.

He hadn't been bored the past two days, that was for sure. Adam had kept him pretty busy. It was too cold to swim, of course, but he'd learned how to fish. Not only catch them, but clean and cook them too. He'd learned how to take Adam's Glock apart and clean it and then put it back together. Maybe one day he'd even get to shoot it.

Simon had had more fun in the last couple of days than he'd had in his entire life. Even the threat of someone after them hadn't kept him from enjoying himself. And his mother was losing that pinched look around her lips.

Two days had passed without another incident and he felt like he could almost breathe again. Like he had some time to figure out his feelings, process his thoughts. He'd spent a lot of time with Adam, unsure at first about the man, but Adam didn't appear to be anything like his father.

Which made him like Adam. A lot. He wanted to trust him, but he kept waiting for the man to do something to show his true colors. His dad could be all nice and smiley, then lash out with a hard fist before you could blink. But it hadn't happened with Adam. Yet.

Simon took in a deep breath, inhaling the smells around him. Someone was cooking steak. The scent made his stomach rumble. Boredom was beginning to officially set in, but he didn't want to complain. He even missed school and his friends, especially Mitchell Lee. Blowing out a disgusted sigh, Simon pulled his Nintendo DS game from the back pocket of his jeans and turned it on.

Dani took a break from helping in the kitchen and watched her son hunch over the game. She monitored the games he played and refused to allow him to play the more violent ones. He was fine with that, thank goodness, preferring to solve mysteries and do puzzles.

Tori had arrived this morning with bags of groceries and a lot of chocolate. Dani liked her more and more each day.

"How's he doing?" Adam asked.

She took the can of soda he offered. "He's all right. I think he's a little bored, but if it wasn't for your care and attention, he'd be climbing the walls by now. As it is, he hasn't played that game since we've been here." She slid her eyes to him. "Which is a great thing in my book."

Adam smiled. "He's an awesome kid. You've done a good job in spite of what you've had to live with."

"Thanks." She sipped on the cola. "How much longer do we need to stay here?"

"Getting tired of us?"

"Not at all," she protested, then relaxed when she caught the twinkle in his eye. "No, I've just got to figure out how to have a normal life with my son and get started on it as soon as possible."

"That's understandable, but we don't want you leaving until we've figured out why someone broke into your home."

She nodded. "I've been thinking about that."

"Have you come up with any idea of who it might have been?"

"The only person I can think of is Stuart. He had the combination to the safe, the alarm code, but . . ." She shrugged. "Something bothers me about that."

"What?"

"Stuart knew the safe was empty. I cleared it out the day Kurt died. Why would he go looking there?"

"It's six months later. Maybe he figured you put everything back."

"Hmm. Maybe. You're probably right." But she couldn't help wondering if she'd missed something. "What have you guys been up to?"

"We finished going through the contents of the bag."

Adam and David had been in the kitchen at the table working and muttering between themselves while Dani and Tori were cleaning up breakfast dishes. She thought that bag might have had something to do with all the discussing. "And?"

"There are a couple of interesting things in there. Starting with this." He pulled his hand from his pocket and held up a small key.

"What's it go to?"

"I don't know. We were hoping you might have an idea."

She held it in the palm of her hand and studied it. "It looks like a locker key or something. Maybe a key to a padlock."

"Any thoughts on places where Kurt might have a locker?"

"Not really. He didn't share that kind of thing with me." She couldn't help the bitterness that leaked out. Dani drew in a deep breath and let it out slowly. "He went to the gym a lot."

"The one in his office building?"

"Yes. And he also used to go to the one at the country club occasionally." She pursed her lips. "That was one place he didn't mind me going."

"Why not?"

"Because it was exercise, keeping my body in shape. He used to taunt me about getting fat. I finally pointed out that he wouldn't let me do anything or go anywhere. If I did nothing but stay at home, then yes, I would probably get fat."

"What a—"

"I know."

"So he let you go to the gym?"

"The exclusive one with the country club and it had to be with a personal trainer. One that would report in to Kurt." She appreciated the outrage she saw flickering in the depths of his eyes. She gave a small shrug. "Brianna was a good woman. She helped me work out my anger and frustration and even taught me a few self-defense moves during some kickboxing workouts." Not that she'd ever dared use them on Kurt. He had the gun. "I don't think she really liked him."

"Then I think I like Brianna." Adam took the key from her. "All right. I think we'll see if this fits anything at the FBI office gym and then try the country club one."

"You might ask some of the agents he worked with about a storage unit or locker or something, but if they're in on the illegal activities Kurt was in on, then . . ." She shrugged.

"Yeah. I thought about that too. I'm also checking into any property he or your in-laws might have owned where he could store things." He sighed. "I'll get someone to pull his bank records and credit card statements to see if he was making regular payments on any storage facilities."

She nodded. "Okay."

"For now, though, is there anyone you met that Kurt worked with that you believe was a straight arrow?"

Dani tilted her head and stared off into the distance. "Maybe Ralph Thorn?"

"Why him?"

"He just seems like a good man. I met him several times. At a family cookout one time. He was at all of the holiday dinners and parties held at the office. Last year at the Christmas party, he came over and talked to me before Kurt interrupted." She shook her head. "I got the feeling Kurt didn't like him."

"And that's enough for you to trust him?"

She felt a flush creep into her cheeks. "It sounds stupid, I know, but . . ." She shook her head. "After Kurt was killed, there were so many people who came by my house. It seemed like swarms of people stopped by. I vaguely remember a few of them, but Ralph and his wife stand out in my mind."

"Why's that?"

"He and his wife came by the house the day after Kurt was killed. They asked me if I needed anything and were very kind.

159

They prayed with me. Being in their company just gave me a sense of . . . comfort. A sense of peace."

Adam nodded. "Okay, I'll check him out." He looked at Tori. "What's your partner doing these days?"

"Working just like the rest of us."

"Would he have some time to come over and keep you company?"

"I can ask him."

"If you don't mind."

"Not at all." Tori pulled her phone from the pocket of her jeans and stepped aside to make the call.

Dani frowned. "What are you going to do?"

"I'm going to see Ralph Thorn." He paused. "And my mother. She's having surgery today."

"Oh! I didn't know. I'm so sorry."

He gave her a slight smile. "I didn't tell you. I'm still processing the information myself. My sister told me that Mom has breast cancer. She's having a mastectomy."

"And you should be there with her. If you don't go, this may be one bridge you'll never be able to rebuild."

Adam swallowed and looked away, but not before she thought she saw a sheen of tears in his eyes. He cleared his throat. "I won't leave you unprotected."

"And I won't let you throw away your family," she whispered. "Go."

He nodded. "I'll go, but first I need to make some phone calls to make it happen."

While Adam made arrangements, Tori finished her call to her partner. "Nate says he can be here within the hour."

"Good." Adam tucked his phone into his pocket. "Kade said he could take me. I'm going to meet him now."

"Who's Kade?" Dani asked.

"Kade Garrison," he said. "Tori's boyfriend and owner of Garrison Flight Services. Kade provides transportation for anyone who needs it." He paused. "And right now, I need it."

Leaving Dani and Simon in Tori's and her partner's capable hands made Adam feel a bit better as he walked to his car. He was grateful for friends he could call on when he needed them, but he wanted to make this trip as quick as possible. The flight would only be about thirty minutes. Basically up then down as opposed to a three-hour drive each way.

And he didn't plan on staying long at the hospital. Just long enough to make sure his mother was going to be okay and let her know he loved her. She would understand. She'd have to. As mad as she might be with him for taking down her brother, she had a loving heart and she'd never want Dani to be in danger because Adam stayed with her. She had others she could count on. Dani and Simon didn't.

His mom would understand. What Dani said about not being able to rebuild the bridge with his mother if he didn't show up wasn't necessarily true. With his father? Yes. If Adam didn't come to his mother's bedside, his father would probably have nothing else to do with him. But his mother would understand. He repeated the phrase until he almost believed it.

Kade slid the headset on. "Might be a bad storm coming up. You sure you want to do this?"

Adam paused. "A storm? How bad?"

"Doesn't look too serious, but you never know."

"I need to do it if you can keep us in the air and land us safely."

"Right now that isn't an issue."

"I've got to get back too."

Kade pursed his lips and nodded. "Then let's go. The storm's not set to hit for another three hours or so."

Adam blew out a breath. "That'll be cutting it close, but I've got to chance it. I need to talk to this guy and see my mom."

Adam watched the darkening sky and wondered if he'd make it back before the storm broke.

He had to. While he felt pretty confident that no one had any way of knowing where they were, and he knew Tori and Nate could handle anything that popped up, he didn't want to risk leaving them alone too long.

Ten minutes later, Kade had them in the air.

His phone vibrated and he snagged it from his pocket. Tori. "Hey. What's up?"

"Nate can't make it after all. He got called in to help transport two prisoners."

"What about you?"

"I'm good. I already asked for the week off."

"I owe you."

"I'll collect."

Adam gave a short laugh. "I know you will." His other line beeped in. He hung up with Tori and answered. "Buchanan here."

"Hey, it's David. We traced the license plate of the car carrying the shooters."

"Great. Stolen?"

"You get the gold star."

"I figured."

"Let me know if you need anything else."

"Will do." He dialed his sister, who answered on the third ring. "How is she?"

She didn't bother with mundane pleasantries either. "She's in surgery. She asked about you before she went back, though."

"I'm on the way."

A pause. "Are you really?"

"I really am. How long will she be in surgery?"

"The doctor said two to three hours. They're not doing the reconstruction part yet. That'll come later."

Adam rubbed his eyes and mentally calculated how long he had. "I'll try to be there in about two hours."

"She should be waking up about that time."

"All right. See you soon."

He hung up and felt uneasiness run through him. He didn't like leaving Dani and Simon as long as he was going to have to. He thought about asking David for backup out at the houseboat, but figured by the time he got someone out there, Adam would be close to being back.

It was just a couple of hours. Tori could handle it.

21

Just as he was about to exit the building, Joe Duncan did a double take when Adam Buchanan stepped inside. His curiosity piqued, he stopped and turned to follow Adam to the elevator. Joe snagged his phone from his pocket and dialed Stuart's number.

"What?"

Did the man have no manners at all? "I spotted your target."

"Dani?"

"No, the other one. The guy you said she ran off with."

"Adam Buchanan."

"Yeah. He just walked into the FBI building."

"No kidding. So Dani wasn't with him?"

The man was obsessed. "Nope."

"Thanks."

Joe hung up and shook his head. One night on a stakeout, Stuart had confessed his interest in his sister-in-law. When Joe asked him what he planned to do about it, the man laughed and said, "Nothing. Not while Kurt's still alive. He'd kill me if I ever tried anything with Dani."

True enough. It was common knowledge around the bureau that Kurt was not a man to be messed with. And that included his family. Joe had met Dani a handful of times and never had she given the impression that she thought of Stuart as anything more than a brother.

Either Joe had lost his touch on reading people or Stuart was delusional. He figured it was probably the latter. But whatever. As long as he could use Stuart's obsession to his advantage, he would.

He stepped onto the elevator with Adam. They exchanged nods and Joe remained quiet, checking his email on his phone, acting oblivious to Adam's presence. The doors opened with a quiet whoosh and Adam exited without a backward glance. Joe flashed his badge and walked in the opposite direction. He knew Adam would have a slight delay while security cleared him. But where was he going? Who was he here to see?

Joe found a spot along the wall and leaned against it, once again using his phone to look as though he were involved in the device. His gaze, however, was fixed on the door Adam would come through.

Two minutes later, his patience paid off and Joe saw Adam head straight to Ralph Thorn's office. One of the few people to actually have an office.

Joe pushed off from the wall and frowned. He ignored the activity around him and made his way toward Ralph's door, wishing he had some way to listen in without being obvious.

Adam rapped his knuckles against the open door. The man behind the desk looked up. The woman in the chair across from him turned and stood. The agent waved him in. "You're Adam Buchanan?"

"I am."

"Come on in. I'm just finishing up here."

"I can wait outside. I didn't mean to interrupt."

"It's all right. This is Julie Faraday. She's the daughter of my former partner."

Julie offered him a weak smile, then turned back to the man Adam had come to meet with. "Thanks, Ralph. I appreciate all your help."

"No problem. Thanks for stopping by, Julie. Tell your mother hello for me."

"Of course."

Adam stepped aside and let the woman pass him. About his age, she had dark circles under her eyes and a tightness to her lips that said she was under stress. She gave him a short nod and disappeared around the corner.

"You mind if I close the door?" Adam asked.

"Not at all." Adam did, then slipped into the nearest chair, noting the clean desk and organized office. Pictures of family lined the credenza behind Thorn and a plaque quoting 1 Corinthians 13 hung on the wall. Adam nodded toward it. "The love chapter from the Bible. You don't get a lot of grief having that hanging there?"

Special Agent Ralph Thorn shrugged. "Some. But I don't let that bother me. It's something I try to live by and hope I can influence others to do the same. Way I figure it, if everyone lived by it, there wouldn't be any need for this office."

"True."

Ralph linked his hands on the desk and studied him. Adam shifted, not uncomfortable, just trying to buy some time while he figured the man out.

"What can I do for you?" Ralph asked. "Sounded rather urgent."

Time was up. Adam pursed his lips. "Are you aware Kurt Harding was a dirty agent?"

Ralph blinked and stood. "Okay, you can stop right there. I don't believe it, never will. You can leave now."

"Will you hear me out?"

"Nope."

He held up a finger indicating Adam should wait. Adam immediately understood. The man didn't want to talk in case his office was bugged.

Adam stood too. Kept up a conversation about nothing while the man pulled out a bug-detecting device and swept his office. A few minutes later he pronounced it clean. "I can't be too careful these days."

Adam got straight to the point. "Look, I'm part of an organization that helps people. Dani came to us because someone tried to kill her."

Ralph shot him a sharp look and Adam nodded that the man had heard right. Ralph dropped into his chair.

Adam leaned forward. "So, tell me about Kurt. Please."

"Tell me why you think Kurt was dirty."

Adam told him about Dani, and little by little, Adam could see the man starting to believe him. "I need you to trust me and tell me what you know."

"Trust isn't an easy thing for me right now."

"Please . . ."

Ralph took a deep breath and rubbed a hand across his wrinkled forehead. "Kurt was an enigma."

"How so?"

"He always knew the right thing to say, the right thing to do to make himself look good. But he had another side. One that didn't show itself often, but I was around him enough to catch a glimpse of it every once in a while."

"Such as?"

"He liked practical jokes. But not in a fun way. In a way I thought was cruel."

Adam lifted a brow. "Like what?"

"That young lady you just met? Julie Faraday?"

"Yeah, what about her?"

"Her father was Gordon Faraday. Kurt put about three hundred snakes in a box and when Gordon opened it up at his fifty-sixth birthday party, they popped out all over him."

"So?"

"So it was pretty well-known that Gordon was deathly afraid of snakes. To the point that he was getting counseling about it. He saw it as a weakness and wanted to beat it. But that night—" Ralph shook his head and blew out a breath. "It was pretty tragic. The snakes flew out and Gordon had a heart attack and died right there."

"Whoa." Adam leaned back. "If Kurt did that on purpose, that's almost like premeditated murder."

Ralph cleared his throat and blinked away what Adam thought might be a sheen of tears. "No 'almost' about it. Gordon was my partner. My friend. I can't prove it was Kurt who did it, but I was watching him that night and I swear he smiled when Gordon hit the ground." He nodded to the door. "Julie's like a daughter to me as well." He shook his head. "She's crazy smart. A borderline genius. She's the department sweetheart and everyone here loves her." He gave a small smile. "I have four boys. I've known Julie since she was born. Even after six months, she's having a real hard time with Gordon's death. She keeps coming in and wanting to talk about it, so I let her. We all do. I think it's therapeutic for her in some way. She's not coming as often, so maybe time is easing some of the pain."

"I'm so sorry."

"I am too."

The more Adam heard about Kurt Harding, the more he despised the man. "What did you think about him as an agent?"

"Excellent reputation, excellent agent. He was smart, determined, and was headed for the supervisory desk in Houston. But I think he died before he ever told Dani because she didn't mention it when I saw her last."

"He ever do anything to bring suspicion on himself?"

Ralph shrugged. "No. Never. At least not from the people that mattered most."

"What about the people that didn't matter?"

Ralph smiled. "Now you're catching on. He'd miss a meeting every once in a while with some lame excuse or he'd talk about how sick Dani was and he was the only one who could take care of her. Stuff like that. I didn't really buy it after a while."

"Why not?"

"I don't live too far from them. One day Kurt missed a meeting, said his wife was sick. I drove past their house and she was out in the drive shooting baskets with Simon."

"Maybe she felt better."

He shrugged. "Maybe. But like I said, I started noticing things."

"Tell me."

"There was some on-the-job stuff. We busted a drug ring about a year ago. Some of them had gang ties and Kurt wanted the top guy. He nearly killed a man trying to get a name." Ralph shook his head. "I'm not into that kind of thing. I'm not averse to a little necessary roughness occasionally, but what Kurt did . . . well, that was just wrong."

"So you saw some things that didn't line up with Kurt's excellent reputation."

"I did."

"Did he know you saw them?"

"He knew."

"And Alan James? Did he and Kurt get along?"

"Not really. Alan saw some of the same things I did. He couldn't stand Kurt and didn't bother hiding his distaste for the man."

"What was Alan like?"

"As straight as they come. There's no way he was dirty like Joe Duncan has said. Peter was singing Kurt's praises and destroying Alan's reputation every time he opened his mouth. I knew that wasn't right and that Peter was up to something. Joe was the only witness to the shooting." Ralph shook his head. "I don't know what happened in that room, but it's not what Joe says."

"Why haven't you said something?"

"Because I didn't want to end up like Alan James."

Adam sat back and pulled at his lower lip as he studied the man across from him. "What are you not telling me?"

A hint of a smile curved Ralph's lips. "I don't believe Alan was dirty. I believe Joe Duncan might be."

"And?"

Ralph clasped his hands together again. "Look, I don't know you, I don't know anything about you. I'm not spilling my guts to you. What I've said so far can't come back to bite me too hard, but if I keep going . . ."

Adam leaned forward. "I want to help you figure out what happened the day Kurt was killed. I want to know everything about Kurt Harding. Who he hung out with when he wasn't working. Where he went when he *was* working. I want to know what he ate for breakfast and everything else there is to know."

Ralph's stare turned intense. Adam met him stare for stare, his jaw tight, hands clenched. He needed an inside person. He understood why Dani felt she could trust Ralph. Even Adam got a sense of the man's integrity and he'd only just met him.

Ralph shook his head. "I think you're being straight with me. I think you care about Dani and want to help her. But I'm not ready to put myself out there yet. Give me twenty-four hours and a phone number where I can reach you. I'll let you know my decision then."

Adam sighed and rubbed his head, trying to decide what to do. If he made the wrong choice. *A little guidance please, Lord . . . just because the man has a passage of Scripture on his wall, it doesn't mean he's trustworthy.* Adam debated until Ralph glanced at his watch.

"Look—"

"No. I get it. Maybe this will help." Adam passed the recording of the Eisenburg murder to the man. "Play that on your computer and tell me what to do next."

With a puzzled look, Ralph took the flash drive and inserted it in the port. Thirty seconds later, he lost all color in his face. While he was silent, Adam figured his brain was going at warp speed.

When the video was over, Ralph removed the flash drive and took a deep breath. "Did I just see what I saw?"

"Yes."

"I know those men," he said.

Adam had to lean forward to understand the quiet words. "Will you help me now?"

Ralph rubbed a hand down his pale face. Adam could still see the shock in his eyes. Then Ralph shook his head. "Give me twenty-four hours."

Impatience ate at him, but he understood the man's reluctance to trust him any further. He'd met Ralph in the man's office on purpose. He could have called and had him meet him somewhere. Probably would have been safer considering there was no way to tell who was playing nice in this building and who was willing to kill a woman who'd seen them kill someone. But he'd wanted to catch Ralph before he had a chance to prepare for the visit.

"Fine. Check me out, then give me a call. I'll be waiting, but I'm keeping this." He waved the flash drive. "If you decide to trust me, come up with someone we can give this to. Someone who won't kill us and bury this video."

"Yeah. Yeah, I'll do that."

"One more thing. You guys have a gym in this building?"

"We do. We're one of the lucky ones. This is one of the newer facilities."

He passed Ralph the key. "Would this go to any of the lockers?"

Ralph picked it up and shook his head. "Nope." He rummaged in his pocket and pulled out a set of keys. He separated one from the other. "This is my locker key." It looked similar, but was shorter.

Adam pocketed the one from Dani's bag and stood. "I'll be waiting for your call." He left Ralph's office and made his way toward the exit. With his phone in camera mode, he held it angled enough to see the agent who'd been on the elevator with him. The man followed him with his narrowed gaze, watchful, intense.

Adam snapped the picture and tucked the phone away. He'd figure out who the agent was in about twenty-four hours.

Because he had no doubt Ralph Thorn would be calling him for a meeting. He glanced at his watch. And now it was time to go see his mother.

He lowered the binoculars. How lucky could a guy get? Adam Buchanan takes off and the kids play their games, hooking into the internet and becoming a nice big target on his computer screen.

Simon stood at the rail of the boat staring out at the lake. Three hours north of Greenville, South Carolina, they hadn't run far.

His phone rang and he answered on the first ring. "I've got them."

"Then you'll have her today?"

"Yes."

"Good."

Click.

He hung up and shook his head.

It surprised him that his conscience pricked him slightly. He hadn't been sure he still had one. And yet, he found himself reluctant to kill a kid. Which was why he found himself sitting there trying to figure a way around it.

One reason he hadn't struck yet.

Unfortunately nothing came to mind and he was running out of time.

22

The sky darkened and Simon glanced up to see gray clouds billowing overhead, chasing the sun into submission. The wind continued to pick up and the water churned, rocking the boat harder. He gripped the rail and wondered how much longer before the worst of the storm hit. Tori had driven the boat away from the dock and shown Simon how to beach the craft.

"Shouldn't we just get a hotel room?" he'd asked with a worried glance at the darkening sky.

Tori had laughed. "Nope. We're perfectly safe on the boat. We just have to get it ready for the storm." She shook her head. "We're in the South. We're not supposed to have thunderstorms in the South in December."

Not sure he believed her, he nevertheless did as she instructed and helped her tie the ropes at a forty-five degree angle to the side of the boat. Then they'd disembarked and pounded stakes into the ground until only about a foot of the stake showed.

When they were finished, Tori had said, "Now we just have to get back on the boat and ride it out."

"Ride it out? What if there's a hurricane? Or a tornado?"

"Then the weather channel would have warned us. Besides, those happen in the summertime. Not December."

"Thought you said we didn't have thunderstorms in December either."

Tori placed her hands on her hips and gave him a mock glare. "I'm not God, Simon, I don't control the weather. But trust me when I say, it's not a hurricane or a tornado, just a thunderstorm. A weird, freak, December thunderstorm." She'd signed as many words as she could and Simon appreciated her effort. He liked talking to Tori. He didn't have any trouble understanding her—or helping her. When they'd finished, she'd given his arm a light punch. "Thanks." When Tori went inside, Simon went to the deck.

He shifted and lifted his face to the wind. His cheeks had gone numb about five minutes before and he was sure his nose would fall off if he rubbed it.

But the cold felt good.

The man who'd been fishing earlier was gone. After tying up the boat with Tori, Simon had grabbed his Nintendo and had been playing for the last two hours. His mom had checked on him periodically and offered to play cards with him, but he'd shaken his head. He didn't want to play cards, he didn't want to watch television. He wanted to go home.

He missed his bedroom and his friends at school. Especially Mitchell.

He wanted to figure out what having a normal life was like and start having it. Running from someone who wanted to kill his mother wasn't part of that. The anger that boiled so close to the surface threatened to bubble over whenever he thought about anything too long.

Adam had been gone forever. Simon wondered when he'd be back. He could see his mother and Tori in the kitchen cooking dinner and talking. The two of them had become fast friends and Simon was glad to see it. Loneliness used to seep off her in waves. Of course she had Jenny, but even then they didn't get to hang out together too much since Jenny was always working.

A dark shadow passed under the part of the boat not beached on shore. The lights from the deck shone down into the water, illuminating the area. Simon blinked and looked again.

It was gone.

Simon raced to the other side and waited to see it again. He knew there weren't sharks or whales in a lake, but whatever kind of fish he'd just seen wasn't a catfish either.

He waited.

Nothing.

Weird.

He went into the kitchen. "Mom?" He snitched a carrot from the bowl.

She turned with a smile on her face. "Hey, we're almost ready to eat. You're hungry, I'm guessing?"

"Yes, but I also saw something in the water."

Tori straightened from where she'd been bent over the sink. "What'd you see?"

He liked that she signed and spoke at the same time. It made it easier to understand her. "I don't know. It was long and black. Like a huge fish."

Tori's eyes narrowed and Simon's stomach dropped. She placed her spoon in the sink and pulled her weapon. She said something to his mother, who nodded.

His mom signed, "Let's go below, down to your room."

"Why?"

"Because Tori asked us to."

Tori grunted and said something under her breath, but Simon didn't catch it. His mom looked at her. "What is it?"

Simon swiveled his attention back to Tori. He watched her lips carefully. "The boat is shifting. One of the moorings must have come loose. I'll have to go tighten it back down or we'll be in trouble."

"What if it's a trick?" Simon asked.

"What?" His mother stared at him like he'd grown two heads.

"A trick," he said again, wondering if his fear was making his words less understandable, so he signed while he explained. "You know, like in the movies. You go out there to fix that and the bad guy is waiting?"

Simon appreciated the fact that Tori seemed to consider the possibility and didn't just shake off his suggestion. "You could be right. I'll be careful."

His mother, on the other hand, frowned. "We don't know anyone is here. I think Tori is just taking some precautions."

Tori nodded. "Exactly." She lifted her phone and dialed Adam's number.

He shivered even with the drysuit on. Lurking in the water for much longer and he'd be an ice cube. But he couldn't move too fast or too soon. This was a one-shot deal and impatience would get him nowhere fast. He'd wait and watch. He had decided on a plan of action. Grab the kid and the mother would do whatever was asked of her. Only the kid was no longer standing at the rail of the boat.

Which meant more waiting. But he wasn't in a hurry. He'd take his time and do the job right. He moved so he could see the railing. Where had the kid gone? A quick kick of his flipper-clad foot propelled him to the other side of the boat. No kid. He moved around the other end of the boat. Aft? Stern? Port? Whichever. He never had any interest in boats, just diving. And money. Lots and lots of money. And as soon as he got his hands on Dani and Simon, he would have the latter. He swam back to where he'd seen Simon at the railing and waited, hoping he wouldn't have to board the boat, but getting ready to do so just in case.

* * *

Adam leaned forward to look out of the plane's window. Tori's call had come in exactly twenty minutes ago. It had taken him ten minutes to get to the airport and another ten to get in the air. She'd told him to hold off on calling in the local cops, she'd check it out and get back to him.

He'd called Kade and the man had the plane ready to go as soon as Adam climbed out of his rental car, flashed his badge, and threw himself into the seat. Adam decided the time it had taken him to get to the airport and in the air was a new record. Having a pilot who knew his stuff and a high-ranking official like the governor go before him had sped things up to warp speed. He shifted in the seat, his mind clicking along, anxious for Tori to get back to him.

She'd simply said Simon had seen something in the water. Something that sounded suspiciously like a man in a wetsuit. Or probably a drysuit considering how cold the water temperature was.

He was another twenty minutes away from setting foot on the boat. He gripped his phone. Call for backup? Call the cops? Tori had asked him not to, but she wasn't answering his calls and he needed to know Dani had help on the way.

He had to do it. "Sorry, Tori, but help's coming."

If she had things under control, great. If she didn't—

He had to trust that the good guys would get there first, even if the bad guys were monitoring police frequencies. Then again, if Simon had seen someone in a drysuit swim under the boat, the bad guys were already there. Time to even the playing field.

He called the local law enforcement and got help on the way to the boat.

Although the way Kade was flying, Adam might actually make it there before the cops.

Rain lashed the glass and turbulence rocked the small four-passenger aircraft while he watched the clock tick away the minutes. He tried Dani's phone and she didn't answer.

Neither did Tori.

Five minutes and he'd be on the ground and then it was just another five minutes to the marina. One of the reasons he'd chosen Tori's boat as a hideout. Having his own personal landing strip available was a plus.

The fact that Kade Garrison was not only Tori's boyfriend, but also had a pilot's license and could make himself available at the drop of a hat . . . well, Adam wasn't going to thumb his nose at what he considered God's provision. Some people would snort and shake their heads at that last thought, but Adam knew God worked in crazy ways, so he'd just give him the credit for it and be done with it.

And now . . . his family.

He called Sarah and told her the new development.

Her silence on the other end of the phone shouted louder than if she'd railed at him.

The quiet click brought tears to his eyes.

But he had no choice.

He had to keep Dani and Simon safe. And Tori. She was alone with two people someone wanted to either kidnap or kill. If something happened to them while he was gone, he'd never recover. He texted Sarah.

My client is in danger, I have to get to her. Text me when Mom's awake and I'll call her. Please Sarah.

He held the phone and waited for her to answer. While he waited, he prayed for their safety and let his thoughts go back to Ralph. His gut said the man would call him, but his gut also said it would be a full twenty-four hours before that happened.

He'd been gone for about three hours. And while he knew Tori was more than capable of taking care of most anything that popped up, he itched to get back. Especially after the conversation with Tori. She didn't sound too concerned, just that she was taking extra precautions and checking the area.

Kade said, "We'll be landing shortly. Gotta circle again while they clear the runway. This rain is crazy."

Adam bit back his impatience and nodded. He glanced at his phone. Tori hadn't called him back and Sarah hadn't texted him either. He dialed Tori's number.

She didn't answer and he frowned. That wasn't like her. He tried Dani's number. Again no answer. He sent another text to his sister and waited.

Now he was officially worried.

Thunder boomed in the distance, lightning flashed, and rain beat down as though seeking vengeance for some perceived wrong. The boat rocked with a surprisingly gentle sway.

In the bedroom at the bottom of the stairs, Dani gestured for Simon to get into the small closet. He protested, but she insisted. "And don't come out until I come get you," she signed. She glanced at the clock. It had been thirty minutes since Tori had called Adam and nothing had happened, but she was uneasy and wanted Simon tucked away somewhere. Now Tori wasn't answering her calls and Dani needed to find her. "Promise me."

Fear glittered in his eyes. "Where are you going?"

"I'm going to see if Tori needs help." Images of Janessa's dead body floated at the forefront of her mind. There was no way she was going to cower behind a closed door while Tori faced whatever possible danger lurked. Whether it was from nature or was man-made, Dani wasn't leaving Tori alone.

Apparently, Janessa was also on her son's mind. He grabbed her hand and held on tight.

Her heart thudded, a heavy beat in her chest that echoed in her head. With her free hand, she signed, "I have to go, Simon. Let me go."

He shook his head. Frustration filled her. She didn't want to fuss at Simon, but she had to go up to check on Tori. It was awfully quiet up there.

Dani pulled away from Simon and with a firm look, signed, "Now. Do it. I mean it."

Simon hesitated but it had been ingrained in him by Kurt that he was to obey her at all costs. Especially when she took that tone with him.

Probably the one thing she and her husband agreed on. She, to keep Simon safe. Kurt, because it would make him look bad if their son disobeyed his mother. Dani wasn't concerned about the reason, she was just grateful when Simon released her and sank to the floor of the closet, his gaze pleading and defiant at the same time.

With a prayer on her lips, she signed, "I love you." She handed him her cell phone. He looked at it, then held it back to her. "Adam called."

Dani grabbed it back and dialed Adam's number. "Dani?" She flinched at his frantic shout.

"Yes."

"Are you okay?" Relief filled his voice.

"Yes, for now, but I'm not sure about Tori. I'm going to see if she needs help."

"The cops are on the way and so am I. Just stay on the phone with me."

"I can't, Adam. I need to check on Tori."

He paused. "Okay, but call me back."

She promised she would and hung up. She handed the phone to Simon. He might need it more than she.

Dani shut the door on her terrified son, grabbed Kurt's Glock from her purse, and walked up the steps.

Cautious, she stopped at the top and peered around the door into the den area.

Empty.

The kitchen loomed vacant, the twin lamps on the wall above the table staring back at her.

All seemed fine. She held the weapon at her side, feeling her palm start to sweat. She knew how to use the gun when it came to aiming at paper targets. Could she actually point it at a human being and pull the trigger? She shivered at the thought but knew instantly that she could in defense of her child.

Had Simon really seen something or were her dry mouth and pounding heart all for nothing?

Dani wished Adam were there. But he was on the way and he'd alerted the cops there might be trouble. They were on the way too.

Now she pulled in a deep breath and wondered where Tori was. Dani glanced back toward where she'd left Simon and saw the closet door still closed. She didn't want to call out. Dread and fear coiled together in her gut. The storm rolled outside. The boat rocked and swayed. Nausea churned in her stomach.

No time to get sick now.

A shadow passed by the door at the opposite end. Too big to be Tori. She shuddered and felt for her phone. The one she'd left with Simon.

The shadow stopped at the door and tried to twist the knob.

Heart in her throat, Dani waited to see if it would open. It didn't. When he turned, she caught sight of the weapon in his left hand. No doubt that he had bad things on his mind.

An idea hit her. She went for the second set of stairs that would lead up to Tori's room and the upper deck. One by one, she climbed the stairs, listening for anything out of the ordinary that would come over the sound of the storm.

Where was Tori? Had the intruder caught her by surprise the way he had Janessa?

Fear for her new friend and for Simon nearly had her sobbing, but she had to keep going, had to help keep them safe.

At Tori's room, she went straight for the balcony that overlooked the larger deck below. She slipped out of the sliding glass door and immediately the rain lashed her, plastering her hair to her head and causing her to suck in a deep breath at the freezing cold. Teeth chattering, she walked to the edge and looked over.

She couldn't see him but thought that he was beneath the balcony. Frustration bit at her. Then she caught a glimpse of him. Pacing back and forth as though trying to decide what to do next.

She glanced at the heavy-duty glass end table next to the white Adirondack chair. Bolted to the floor. With locks she could easily open.

23

Adam stopped at the light and read the text from Tori.

Someone's on the boat. Send reinforcements. He caught me on shore. Knocked me out. Dizzy. I'm—

His stomach hit rock bottom. Someone? Someone who? How? And why did her text end abruptly?

It didn't matter. He pressed the gas and glanced at the clock. He would be at the marina in less than five minutes. His wipers sluiced the rain from the windshield.

He called her number and listened as it rang to voice mail. "Come on, Tori, answer the phone."

She didn't.

And now, neither did Dani.

A text message showed up across his screen.

HURRY ADAM. I'M SCARED. SIMON

Simon had Dani's phone? Why? "I'm coming, Simon, I'm coming." He texted the words and then pressed the gas pedal as hard as he dared. He wanted to go faster, but a wreck would further delay him. And neither he nor Dani could afford that.

The rain lessened abruptly. The sheets of water stopped and turned into a cold downpour, but the deafening roar of the storm had quieted.

The man who'd boarded the boat stayed out of sight just under the edge of the balcony. She didn't want to shoot him. She didn't want him dead, she wanted to talk to him, to question him. And if it wasn't Stuart, she wanted to know who sent him to the boat and how he'd found it. She set the gun aside and unlatched the locks that held the table in place. She picked it up and set it on the balcony railing, waiting for the right moment.

"Come on, come on," she whispered. Every once in a while she'd catch a glimpse of a shoulder or a foot. What was he waiting on?

With her right hand, Dani held the glass table on the rail. She shivered, wet and cold to the core, but she couldn't stop now. With her left, she tugged her heavy boot from her foot and tossed it over the side. It landed with a sound that was a cross between a thud and a splat.

Not a loud noise, but one not completely muffled by the roar of the lessening storm. The boot caught the intruder's attention.

And there he was just below her. Simon's big fish, dressed in a black suit, standing over the boot. Exactly where she needed him to be. With a whispered, "Oh please don't let this kill him," she released the table and sent it over the rail.

He looked up and gave a harsh cry but couldn't move fast enough. She dropped down and covered her eyes. Heard the sickening thud, then only the sound of the rain hitting the deck.

Shivering, shaking hard enough that she could barely control her muscles, she raised up and peered over the rail. Her intruder lay on his back, a ski mask on his head, rivulets of blood being washed away as the water drained toward the edge of the boat.

Adam heard the cry, then the crash, barely noting the rain had let up. Tori lay on her side, blood seeping from the gash in the back of her head. Sirens sounded in the distance and he knew help was on the way.

Didn't matter. He had to get Tori inside out of the cold. Her lips were already a pale blue color.

"Tori!" Kade reached for her.

"Bring her on the boat. Leaving her in the cold isn't an option."

Kade picked Tori up and cradled her in his arms. Her head lolled against his shoulder. Adam pulled his weapon and led the way.

"Dani?" He shoved through the door.

Kade followed, being careful not to bang Tori's head on the jamb. Adam let his eyes rove the area and found nothing amiss.

Kade laid Tori on the couch and hovered. "I know basic first aid, but she needs a doctor," he said, his voice low.

"I know, but we're going to have to deal with the danger first. Keep a close eye on her. Dani!"

"On the deck, Adam!"

"Stay here," he told Kade. He bolted to the door at the opposite end of the houseboat and looked through the window. About three feet in front of him lay a dark-clothed figure with blood coming through the mask and being washed away by the rain.

Adam stepped out and held his weapon on the still figure. Slowly, he made his way to the man and knelt beside him, feeling for a pulse.

"Is he dead?" Dani's whisper reached him.

He turned. "No. I've got a weak pulse. Cops should be here in just a few minutes."

"Who is he?"

Adam pulled the mask off. "I don't recognize him. Do you?"

When she didn't answer, he turned to find her backed against the wall, fingers pressed to her lips, shaking her head. "That's the guy who killed Trennan Eisenberg. He's an FBI agent. Ryan Blanchard."

Adam looked closer. Sure enough, it was the guy from the video. "Where's Simon?"

"Hiding." She whirled and raced back into the boat. Adam patted the man down, removed the weapon he'd dropped when the table hit him, and pulled a wicked knife from an ankle sheath.

Finding no more weapons, Adam stepped back and kept his Glock trained on him, but didn't think he'd be up and moving anytime soon. He had a nasty gash on his forehead.

EMTs made their way out onto the deck and Adam shifted to give them access to the injured man. He tucked his weapon into the shoulder holster. "Did you see the woman on the couch?" he asked the first one through the door.

She nodded. "We have two others behind us. They stopped to help her."

Relieved, Adam stayed with the EMTs to make sure Blanchard didn't wake up and decide to fight; however, he itched to check on Tori, Dani, and Simon. He pulled his phone from his pocket and tapped the fingerprint app. Pressing the man's thumb against the screen, Adam waited until he got the print approved, then sent it to his contact at the lab in South Carolina.

"You can do that?" The EMT stared, obviously impressed.

"I can."

"Are you a cop?"

"Yes." There was no way he was going into the long explanation of his organization and the powers he'd been granted by the government agencies. One of which was the ability to collect evidence and submit it. With a request for the lab to put a rush on it.

Even though he was quite sure who the man was, it wouldn't hurt to have it confirmed. Ryan Blanchard would be in the system.

Officers swarmed the boat. Adam flashed his badge and explained what had happened. As they took over, cuffing the man and patting him down once again, Adam moved back inside to find Tori sitting up, an ice pack on the back of her head, pain shining in her golden brown eyes.

He went to her. Shivers racked her even though she had a blanket wrapped around her shoulders. He gripped her upper arms. "You okay?"

"Yeah. I went hunting for him and he got the jump on me."

"Happens."

She grunted. "Not to me it doesn't. Simon even wondered if loosening the moorings was a trap." She sighed. "I took him seriously, wondering the same thing myself. The only problem was, our intruder was watching for me and saw me before I saw him." She glanced around. "Are they okay?"

"We're fine." Dani's soft voice filtered through the chaos and Adam turned to find her standing at the top of the steps. Simon stood next to her, a hard glint in his eyes, his lips pursed. The kid was mad, Adam thought. And he didn't blame him. Simon signed something, but Adam missed it. He looked at Dani. She interpreted. "He wants to know if it was Stuart?"

Adam signed, "No." He quit signing and said, "At least he didn't come here himself. I don't know if he hired the guy or not, but it wasn't Stuart."

Some of the tension seemed to seep from Simon's shoulders.

Simon moved to Tori. Kade shifted so he could sit next to her. "Are you okay?"

Tori gave the boy a hug and signed, "Just don't ask me to nod my head and I'll be fine." She glanced at the kitchen cabinet. "I could use a few ibuprofen pills, though."

188

"How many?"

She held up four fingers.

Simon went to get them.

Kade moved back close. Adam could tell the man was worried. And in love. He briefly wondered if Tori knew.

"So what do we do about him?" Dani asked Adam. "He's an FBI agent. He'll get off easy."

"No he won't. Not with this. There's no way to sweep this one under the rug, and I plan to make sure Ryan Blanchard goes away for a long time."

Just because he was no longer a US Marshal didn't mean he no longer had friends in convenient places. Jeb Owens with the South Carolina Law Enforcement Division—otherwise known as SLED—would run the print for him and confirm it belonged to Blanchard. The evidence would be admissible in a court of law and Adam would make sure he was there to testify.

"All right, ma'am, we're ready to transport you to the hospital."

Tori snorted. "Not me. I'll be all right."

Adam frowned. "You need to get checked out."

"I got hit on the head. I have a headache. If I start seeing double or throwing up, I'll go to the doctor." She downed the four orange tablets Simon handed her.

Adam grimaced. "How do you do that dry?" He'd never been able to understand how she did that without choking. He wanted to gag just thinking about it.

She smirked. "Some of us are just talented." She turned serious. "I'm not going anywhere, but you three are."

"Yeah. Which brings me to another question."

"How did they find us?" Simon asked.

"Exactly."

24

Dani also wanted to know how they'd been found and how they would avoid being found again. Simon sat in the backseat once again staring out the window, his jaw set, eyes narrowed. She wondered what he was thinking, but didn't have the energy to ask him.

The storm had moved on and the rain stopped. "Where are we going now?" Dani asked.

"Another safe house. We've got to figure out how Stuart—or whoever—keeps tracking us down. We're going to have more security too. Tabitha and Isaac are going to meet us there." He rubbed his face and shook his head. "I thought keeping it small and understated was the way to go. That the less people involved would make it harder to find you. Obviously, that didn't work." She thought he muttered, "Nothing's working." But wasn't sure she heard right.

"But how did they track us to the boat? How? You were so careful and even had us followed, backtracking, and making sure. I just don't understand."

"You're not asking any questions I haven't already been over in my mind a dozen times." He turned left, then right, glanced in the rearview mirror, and took the next right. "You see that helicopter up there?"

She glanced toward the clouds. It was dark outside now, but she saw the lights directly above them. Blades churned the air and she could hear it. "Yes."

"That's David and Kade. They're keeping watch from the air this time."

"But it's dark."

"They have the equipment they need. They can see." Adam pressed on the earpiece. He looked at her, then back at the road. "All clear."

"How can you guys afford all this? I mean, I'm not paying you anything and you have all this equipment and safe houses and—"

"We're a privately funded organization, but the governor is also involved. She's a friend of mine, and she believes in what we're doing. When David approached me about being a part of Operation Refuge, I asked the governor what she thought about it. She decided to get behind it as long as it could fund itself. She couldn't provide financial backing—and we didn't want it—but she could provide other things like law enforcement privileges and access to certain equipment."

"Like the helicopter. And Ron is your private funder?"

"Yes."

She nodded. "I got that impression. What's his story?"

"I don't really know. David is the one who would have to tell you that. All I know is Ron helped David out of a tight spot a couple of years ago. They've been tight ever since. And Ron has a soft spot for people in trouble. He goes out of his way to help others."

"Like the good Samaritan," she murmured.

He nodded.

"Did you talk to Ralph?"

"I did."

"What did he say about the key?"

"That it didn't go to any of the lockers they had on the premises and he wasn't sure what it went to."

She let out a sigh. "What did he say about Kurt?"

Adam talked and she listened, gaining insight into the man she'd married. "Did you know Gordon Faraday?" he asked.

"Yes, he was Ralph's partner. He died the same day that Kurt did." She twisted the Kleenex that had appeared in her hand. "I bought the snakes," she whispered.

"What?"

"The snakes that Kurt packed in that box. I bought them." Tears flowed freely now. "I didn't know." She gave a hiccuping sob and grabbed a breath. "I didn't know what he was up to or I would've warned Gordon." She gave a helpless shrug and mopped at the tears. "I'm so sorry."

"It's not your fault. It's Kurt's."

"A man died," she blurted. "How can someone be so evil?"

"It's a question people ask every day, unfortunately."

"Gordon has a daughter. Julie, I think her name is."

"Yes. I met her briefly when I went to talk to Ralph. She's still pretty torn up over her father's death."

"I'm sure." Dani gulped.

He squeezed her hand. "So apparently Kurt has a stellar reputation as an agent. But he's also known as a practical joker."

Dani shuddered. "Yes, but obviously, his practical jokes weren't harmless. They were mean and degrading. You didn't want to be the target."

"Sounds like you learned that the hard way."

"I did. I was on the receiving end of a couple." She drew in a deep breath. "I hate spiders and one time I opened my dresser drawer and he'd emptied a whole slew of them in there. I had to get rid of them. And I did, but I saw spiders everywhere for a month after that."

"He preyed on people's weaknesses. It made him feel superior. Powerful."

"Yes, I suppose it did." She sighed. "How's your mother?"

He shook his head and glanced at his phone. "I'm not sure. No one's bothered to text or call me." A muscle jumped in his jaw. He shot a glance at her. "You said you got married when you were nineteen."

"Yes." She could tell he was upset and didn't want to talk about it. She wouldn't push him to do so then.

"And you never went to college?" he asked.

"No. I wanted to, but Kurt wouldn't let me." She'd begged to take a few classes to work toward a degree in linguistics and he'd refused. "I have an affinity for languages and wanted to study them, but Kurt scoffed at the idea and told me my place was in the home."

She saw Adam's hands flex on the wheel and knew he was angry on her behalf. She appreciated it, but didn't need it. "You come across very educated."

Dani gave a watery laugh. "Well, thanks, I appreciate that."

He blew a raspberry. "I didn't mean it like that. I know people who don't go to college can still sound educated. I just meant—"

"I know what you meant. It's okay. I was very isolated in a lot of ways, but I read a lot. I mean, like all the time. There's a library across the street from our neighborhood. I spent a lot of time there. Especially when Simon was in school and Kurt was traveling. I would read for hours about different places, cultures, everything. And I found all kinds of ways to learn languages online." She shrugged. "Some of it rubbed off, I guess."

"I guess so." He shot her a smile.

She leaned her head against the window. "I want my life back."

"That's supposed to be how it works," he said. "We've done this dozens of times. We give you a new look, a new job, a new place to live—a new identity. You go about your business and only have to look over your shoulder every once in a while. No one we've ever relocated has ever been found."

"So I'm special, huh?"

He took her hand and squeezed her fingers. "Yeah. You're definitely special."

Dani felt the flush rise into her cheeks. "Thanks."

"Tell me about your life after Kurt."

She shifted to face him. "Life after Kurt, huh?"

"If you don't mind."

"I don't." She fell silent, thinking. "It was very strange at first as you can probably imagine. I had FBI wives and widows in and out of my house for nearly a month. They were so kind, so giving." She shook her head at the memories. "After being pretty much alone for so long, it was hard having them around—and wonderful too. Their kids would play with Simon and he finally started to smile easier. He lost his tension, his guard went down slightly. It was nice. I started jogging and getting to know some of the people in the neighborhood. Jenny and I became much closer."

"Jenny's house was where you were attacked?"

"Yes." She shuddered. "She's probably worried sick about me. I don't suppose I can call her."

"No. Sorry."

She sighed. "I understand, I just hate that I disappeared without even saying goodbye to her."

"That's the way it works, unfortunately."

"I know." Her throat tightened as tears threatened. "And I know Simon misses Mitchell something awful."

He grasped her hand again. "It's better to be safe and make

new friends than to contact old ones. If you contact them, you could put them in danger too."

"I know and I won't, I promise I'm smarter than that."

Adam decided the woman was absolutely brilliant. How she ended up with Kurt Harding was a question he didn't think he'd ever have an answer for. But Dani had been an impressionable teen and Kurt had been a charming older guy. He supposed he could see how it happened. What he didn't understand was how Dani had kept her softness, a quiet innocence, and her belief in God.

Having Simon probably kept that part of her from dying.

An hour later, after what should have been a five-minute drive, he pulled into the small airport Kade used and the three of them climbed from the vehicle. Simon looked interested in everything around him.

Kade met them at the door to the hangar. "You ready?"

"Ready."

"Anyone follow you?" Kade asked as he walked to the computer behind the desk.

"I want to say no, but at this point, I'm not making any promises. Let's just get out of here."

Kade held up a finger. "I've just got to log the flight." He looked up. "I assume you're all using aliases?"

"Of course."

Dani's quiet gasp caught Adam's attention. "What is it?"

She stared at the television above the desk. "The news clip. They're talking about a counterfeiting ring."

"Where?"

"At stores and restaurants I shopped at with the money I got from the safe. See? There." She pointed. "At the McDonald's and the Publix grocery store."

"What makes you think it's the money from the safe? It could be from anywhere."

"If it had been just those two stores, I wouldn't have given it another thought, but Simon's school reported a counterfeit twenty. I used one to pay for his lunches about three weeks ago," she whispered. She turned stunned eyes on Adam. "I'm telling you, the money from the safe is counterfeit."

Joe popped into Stuart's office. "How you feeling?"

Stuart grimaced and rubbed his side where the bullet had entered. "It's still painful, but I can cover it up. Guess the antibiotics are doing their job. So far no infection." He'd doubled up on the pills. "Thanks for your help."

Joe settled himself into the chair opposite Stuart. "You track down Dani yet?"

"No." He wiggled the mouse and brought up the program that would allow him to check on Dani's whereabouts. "Nothing yet."

Joe cocked his head. "Just out of curiosity, how are you tracking them?"

Stuart raised a brow and shot the man his most arrogant smile. "I have my ways."

"You keep showing up, they'll figure it out."

"Maybe, but not before it's too late to do anything about it."

Joe nodded. His intense stare made Stuart a bit uncomfortable. "What is it? Why are you looking at me like that?"

"I'm just thinking that you're really intent on getting Dani to fall in line with your plans. Are you obsessed or does she have something you want?"

Stuart blinked. Joe's directness sometimes took him aback. It annoyed him that he couldn't think as fast on his feet as he'd like when it came to the man. "Something I want? You mean as far as material things? No."

"So you just want her?"

"What's with the third degree?" Stuart leaned back and crossed his arms.

Joe shrugged. "Kurt said something to me one night when we were all out at Happy's."

Happy's. The local restaurant frequented by a large percentage of the Bureau. "What'd he say?"

"He said something about a letter in his safe."

Stuart sat up, his full attention on Joe. "He told you about a letter in his safe. Did he happen to mention what the letter said?"

"Yeah, but I'll warn you right now. You're not going to like it."

"Tell me," Stuart demanded.

Joe sighed. "You sure?"

"Joe—"

"Fine, fine. He said that he made sure Dani understood where her place was and that she was to stay away from you."

Stuart bolted to his feet, felt his face flush red. He narrowed his eyes, suspicion flowing through his veins. "Why would he tell you that? You just said you two weren't tight. Why would Kurt share something like that with someone he didn't even like?"

Joe's brow lifted in surprise. "What makes you think Kurt didn't like me?"

"Because you're my partner."

Joe grimaced. "Well, yeah, there is that, but Kurt and I got along okay." He paused. "Frankly, as long as you weren't the topic of conversation, we were fine. And besides, he'd had a little too much to drink that night. He said a few things he probably shouldn't have."

Stuart slumped back into his chair. "You got along okay? Just okay? I thought he saved your life."

Joe shrugged. "He did. But that's what we do when we're in the field. We look out for each other. We've got each other's backs no matter how we feel about each other outside of work. I didn't agree with the way he treated his wife, but that was his business. Kurt was a good agent."

Stuart studied the man. Was he lying? He couldn't tell. But he'd caught Joe in lies before, so Stuart was never sure what to believe when the man opened his mouth. Then again Stuart had lied to Joe on more than one occasion. "Kurt wrote a letter telling her to stay away from me." He couldn't wrap his mind around it. Had Kurt suspected Stuart's fascination with Dani? "Really?"

"Just telling you what he told me, man."

Kurt must have figured it out. Stuart was usually pretty good about hiding his emotions, but when he got around Kurt . . . Stuart blew out a breath. If Joe had noticed Stuart's fascination with Dani, then it went to reason that Kurt might have too. Maybe he and Joe even discussed it. Even laughed about it.

The thought sickened him.

Stuart wiggled the mouse to life. "We'll see about that."

25

At the safe house off the coast of North Myrtle Beach, Adam examined the contents from the safe once more. His main focus was on the stack of twenties. One by one, he went over them, examining each and marking them with his pen. He looked up to the faces surrounding him. "They're excellent forgeries."

A collection of sighs filtered from the group. Dani picked up one of the bills. "How can you tell?"

Adam rubbed the bill. "The paper feels the same as the real thing. And see the colored fibers?" He used a magnifying glass to point them out. "You can't re-create that."

"Then why would you call them counterfeit?" Simon asked, his attention glued to what was unfolding in front of him.

"See this edge?" Adam pointed. "It's got some broken spots going around the bill. They're very faint and you wouldn't notice unless you were looking for them. That's the only thing that's tipping me off. The ink is slightly raised, the paper is authentic, but in a genuine bill, you wouldn't have the break in the ink around the border."

"How did they get the paper?" Dani asked. "I mean you can't just walk into the nearest Office Depot and buy currency paper."

"True." Adam leaned back and looked at Blake, Tabitha, and

199

Isaac. "I'm guessing they bleached lower denominations and then printed the twenties. You've even got a few fifties in here."

Dani shook her head and paced to the nearest window. "Unbelievable." She spun back to those gathered around the table. "So this is why someone broke into my house? They wanted the counterfeit money?"

"Probably."

Isaac blew out a breath. "We need to let the Secret Service in on this. They're the ones who investigate these reports."

Adam nodded. "We'll contact them eventually." He glanced at the twenty-four-hour news station playing on the television. The finding of the counterfeit money was the top story of the day. "Right now, I don't want to do anything to draw attention to Dani and Simon." He looked at Dani. "Could this be why Stuart's been so determined to get to you?"

"What do you mean?"

"I mean, he came to the house the day Kurt died to get something from the safe, right?"

"Yes."

"What if he was after the counterfeit money?"

Dani nodded. "Maybe. Stuart never said what Kurt told him to get. It's very possible he was coming after the money."

Adam glanced at Isaac then back to her. "What about this black box with the key?"

Dani cocked her head. "That keeps nagging at me. I just don't remember that being in the safe."

"It was in the bag."

"Then it must have been in the safe." She rubbed her eyes. "Maybe Stuart knows what the key is for."

Adam shook his head. "Maybe, but I'm willing to bet he wouldn't tell us even if he did know. I'm not exactly his favorite person right now."

"He'd probably lie," Dani agreed.

"I get the feeling that Stuart would lie about anything as long as it suited his purpose. He was going to get something out of that safe, just a small box. But we know he agreed to get it, as it gave him a reason to see Dani."

Isaac cleared his throat. "So either Stuart is really obsessed with Dani and agreed to get whatever it was Kurt wanted as an excuse to see her, or there's something in the safe he actually wanted and is trying to get it."

"But he's had six months to get it. Why start now?" Tabitha asked.

"That's the big question," Adam said. "What's triggered the action six months after the fact?"

"Was he at your house a lot after Kurt died?" Tabitha asked.

Dani rubbed her forehead and closed her eyes. "Yes, he was, but he never said anything about the safe or anything in it."

"Because he didn't want you to know he was interested?" Blake asked.

"Or because he didn't care," she said.

Adam pulled his phone from his pocket. "Dani, I've got to share something with you and I'm hesitant because it's going to be another shock."

Dani pulled in a deep breath and braced herself. "What is it? Just tell me."

"Someone has cameras set up in your house."

"What do you mean . . . cameras?"

"Surveillance cameras. The crime scene cleanup crew found one in the guest room and in the hall. They were pretty well hidden, but these guys clean every nook and cranny, so I'm not surprised they found them. The camera in the hall was in the fire alarm. The one in the guest bedroom was attached to the lamp."

Dani stared at him. She knew her jaw practically rested on her chest, but she couldn't find any words to respond.

Isaac took pity on her. "Would Kurt have done that?"

"No," she gasped. "No. I mean I don't think so."

"Then who?"

"Stuart. He's the only one."

Adam and Isaac exchanged a look. Isaac rubbed a hand over his chin. "I think we need to pay Stuart another little visit. I'm not sure I buy into the fact that he wasn't interested in what was in the safe."

Isaac shifted and pulled the box with the key toward him. "You said there were security cameras. Whoever was watching wouldn't have any trouble figuring out the combination."

"Stuart didn't need the cameras to find out the combination," Dani said. "He already knew it. Kurt would send him over to get things out of the safe." Her head was on the verge of exploding. Cameras in her house? She shuddered. "Who was watching? Where are the monitors or whatever you use to watch the cameras?"

"They didn't find any. That means whoever put them in is watching from a remote area."

"Probably via his computer," Isaac said.

Dani felt sick. Violated yet again. "I want them gone and I want that house put on the market. I never want to go back there again."

Adam nodded. "I can have someone arrange that. I can also call in a professional moving company to pack everything up and move it to storage."

"Yes, please do."

"Consider it done." Adam stood. "Where's Simon?"

"In his room, on his Nintendo."

Isaac looked up. "Nintendo. He's not on the internet, is he?"

Adam blinked. "Internet? No. It's a video game with cartridges."

"Yeah. A video game that can connect to the internet. Kids play each other all the time on those things. My niece and nephew each have one. JJ plays someone in China."

Dani gasped. "He plays his friend Mitchell Lee, but where would he get the code for the wireless here?"

"Off the modem," Adam said on his way to the back of the house.

Dani followed behind him. Adam rapped on the door. Dani would have laughed if she hadn't been so stressed. "He can't hear the knock."

Adam flushed. "Right."

She opened the door and stuck a hand inside to flip the light switch off and on.

Within seconds Simon stood at the door. Dani's hands flew as she asked him, "Are you on the internet?"

Simon frowned. "Yes, I'm playing Mitchell. Why?"

Before Dani could explain, Adam took over. "Interpret for me, will you?"

"Sure."

"Simon, have you gotten on the internet at all of the safe houses?"

Her son shrugged. "Yes. I got the password off the modem."

Dani closed her eyes, praying for strength. "Okay. Thanks for letting us know, but from now on, you can't play Mitchell, okay?"

Simon's mouth flattened and his nostrils flared. "Why not?"

"Because anyone after us can trace us through your game. They probably know you're friends with Mitchell and are connecting his game to yours. That's how they're finding us."

His anger faded and his eyes widened. "Really?"

"Yes," Adam said. "We wouldn't just tell you that you couldn't play the game. I know this whole thing is crazy and totally boring at times and I'm sorry, but it's the only way to keep you and your mom alive. Understand?"

Simon shut off the game. His face had paled about three shades and Dani wanted to pull him to her and protect him, tell him everything was going to be all right.

But she couldn't.

His hand shook as he held the game out to her. "I'm sorry, Mom, I didn't know. I mean I knew I couldn't get on a computer and use the internet, but I didn't think about the game. I'd never put you in danger, I wouldn't, I promise." His voice shook.

Tears clogged her throat. Dani nodded and took the game. "I know you wouldn't, hon, I know."

Dani looked at Adam. "We're going to have to move again, aren't we?"

———

Stuart almost had the next location, but just before he nailed the exact address, the tracker went blank. The kid had shut off the game. He swore. Then sat back in his chair. He'd come back online again sometime soon and Stuart would have him.

Joe stepped into his office and Stuart wanted to growl.

"Glad you're here late," Joe said. "Saves me a phone call."

Stuart shrugged. "What's up?"

"We've got a case."

Stuart stood and grabbed his wallet and cell phone. "What is it?"

"Disappearance of a kid."

"Abduction or runaway?"

"Not sure yet, but we've been called in on it because it looks like it's gang related. They left some symbols."

"Great." Together they headed for the parking garage. Stuart pulled the keys from his pocket. "Where to?"

"That ritzy neighborhood on the west side of town. Stone-bridge?"

"I know where it is."

He clicked open the locks and within minutes they were on the way.

Joe looked at him. "I had an idea about how you could get Dani to come around to your way of thinking."

"Really." Stuart didn't bother to hide his cynicism. "Because your last idea worked so well, right?"

"Hey, I didn't say it would work, I just said you should try it."

"And I did." He paused. "So what's your next brilliant idea?"

"You've got to get the kid in your corner."

"And how am I supposed to do that when she won't even talk to me? When she's running from me and has people helping her run?" He made the next left onto 29. The subdivision was a straight shot about four miles ahead.

His partner remained silent and Stuart figured it was because the man couldn't come up with a good answer.

They parked at the curb and Joe said, "You'll think of something."

"Why do you care?"

A smirk crossed his partner's face before he turned serious. "Because that woman is distracting you and I don't need a distracted partner. So let me know what I can do to help you out."

Made sense.

Stuart took a deep breath and focused on the frantic parents waiting on the front porch.

Adam stood in the doorway watching for Isaac, who would be arriving any moment with another car. Blake and Tabitha scouted the area around them and Simon looked dejected. Adam shifted, praying for the right words. When Simon looked up, Adam caught his eye. "Don't feel bad," he signed slowly. "We all make mistakes."

Simon's brows rose and Adam thought the boy almost smiled.

Almost. Simon signed, "Thanks." He paused and chewed on his lower lip.

"What is it?"

"You've made mistakes?"

Adam curled his lips into a rueful smile. "I've made so many mistakes, you'd be an old man before I finished telling you about them."

Simon didn't look like he was sure he could believe Adam, but the tension in his shoulders relaxed a fraction.

Adam's phone rang. He snatched it and recognized Ralph Thorn's number. It hadn't been twenty-four hours yet. That surprised him. "Hello."

"I checked you out."

"Figured you would. Is this a secure line?"

"Yeah."

"Good. Do you have anyone in mind I can turn this video over to?"

"I want to say it's all good to give it to the Special Agent in Charge."

"But?"

A heavy sigh came through the line. "I'm just not sure. When I wasn't clearing you, I was tracking the movements of the guys in the video. Ryan Blanchard is in the hospital."

"Yeah. He showed up at our safe house ready to do harm. Fortunately Dani outsmarted him."

"*She* put him in the hospital?"

"She did."

"Impressive."

"I thought so." Enough chit-chat. "So do I hold on to the video?"

"For now. I want to figure out who the other person is in that room before I start throwing that evidence around. I don't want to give it to the wrong person and have it disappear. And I don't want to end up dead either."

"I understand." Adam hesitated, then decided to go for it. "I need you to do me a favor if you don't mind."

"What kind of favor?"

"I need you to gain access into someone's house."

A snort. "I won't do anything illegal."

"Then do it legally. I don't want you to take anything except maybe some pictures. I need to know if this guy has been playing Peeping Tom with my client."

"Why me?"

"Because you know him. Stuart Harding had cameras set up all over my client's house. At least we suspect it's him and I need confirmation. There would be monitors that would allow him to keep track of the cameras."

"Stuart Harding."

"Yes."

"Special Agent Stuart Harding?"

"That's the one."

Ralph grunted. "Always thought he was a bit odd. Any ideas on how I'm supposed to accomplish this?"

Adam laughed. "You're FBI, I'm sure you can come up with something."

"Right."

"So you'll do it?"

"I don't know why, but yeah, I'll see what I can find out. And hang on to that video, I'm still checking on a few people."

"What about OPR? The Department of Justice? Or at the very least, the local US Attorney's Office?"

"I'm going to send it to OPR. Just double-checking to make sure the person who gets it isn't Stuart's golfing buddy or something."

"Right. Let me know."

"I will."

"Thanks."

26

Simon had had enough. With the danger, the moving, the boredom. But mostly with his mother's sadness about their inability to live life the way it was meant to be lived. How many nights had she sat on his bed and talked to him, weaving story after story about people who didn't live like them and that one day he would be able to escape and be happy?

Too many to count.

It was time to go after that life.

Christmas was coming and it was going to be another fiasco if things kept on this way. The adults were trying, but what they were doing just wasn't working, in his opinion. Stuart needed to be stopped and Simon decided he would have to be the one to do it. And he'd figured out exactly how he was going to get to Stuart.

He glanced at the clock. Three in the morning. Everyone except whoever was on night duty should be asleep. He hoped it was Adam who was awake and not Isaac.

Simon slid from the bed, careful not to wake his mother who slept in the other full bed against the wall. A sharp pain in his stomach made him gasp. He pressed a hand against his belly button and waited for the moment to pass. It finally eased enough that he was able to move.

Even though he couldn't hear himself or any noise he might make, he'd learned over the years how to be quiet. Thanks to his dad. It didn't pay to make any sound that might attract his father's attention, therefore, he simply learned how to avoid it. He removed the batteries from his hearing aids and pushed them deep into the pocket of his sweatpants. No sense in having the dumb things start to whistle and announce his departure.

Simon reached for the end table and, with his eyes on his mother, eased the drawer open. She stirred and sighed, but didn't wake. Simon reached in and wrapped his fingers around the butt of his father's Glock, then shoved it into his pocket. It weighted down his sweats and he quickly tightened the waistband's drawstring. The gun was a little different than Adam's but similar enough that he didn't think he'd have any trouble figuring out how to work it. He knew it didn't have a safety so he'd have to be extra careful.

He snagged his shoes and his hoodie, leaving his heavy coat behind. He hated the thing. In socked feet, he climbed the stairs and paused at the top to shove his feet into his shoes and pull on the hoodie over his sweatshirt. He'd gone to bed in his sweatpants, planning the move on the way to the new safe house. A split-level that smelled like mold. It made his nose itch just thinking about it and he stifled the sneeze he felt building.

Simon peered around the edge of the wall into the living area. Seeing no one, he walked up the next set of stairs to the bedroom he knew Isaac was using.

The bathroom door to the right was cracked. Light filtered through, allowing Simon to see the sleeping man. Isaac dwarfed the double bed, and while Simon couldn't tell if he was snoring or not, the even rise and fall of his back said he was asleep. Moving carefully, cautiously, using the light from the bathroom, Simon made his way to the end table.

Just what he wanted. Isaac's iPhone.

He knew that he would only be able to use it on a limited basis, but that was fine. Once he had the information he needed, he'd turn it off. When he found Stuart, he'd turn it back on. He definitely wanted them to trace his movements, just not too fast. Guilt over using the Wi-Fi and leading Stuart to his mother hit him hard. He hadn't even thought about it, hadn't known they could trace them through the game. His jaw tightened. Stuart had probably planned it that way.

He was still confused how they did it, but vowed not to get on the internet again with the game.

He knew Adam and Isaac would figure out he took Isaac's phone, but there was no way Stuart would know, so there was no way the man could track him. Confident in his ability to talk Stuart into leaving his mother alone, Simon slipped the phone into his pocket and headed for the walk-in kitchen pantry. When Adam went outside the front door to check the perimeter, he would turn off the alarm for a brief moment.

Simon had watched and learned. With Isaac's phone, Simon punched in a text to his buddy, Mitchell Lee. He waited for the confirmation vibration and gave a silent nod of satisfaction.

From the cracked door of the walk-in pantry Simon stayed still, barely breathing while keeping his eyes on the alarm panel, waiting for it to indicate it was off. He just hoped Isaac didn't wake up and discover his phone missing before Simon had the chance to slip out the back door. He grabbed several bags of chips and stuffed them into his backpack. He'd need some fuel before he got to his destination.

Dani rolled over to see Simon's lump under the covers. She gave a brief smile. He'd flourished under the attention of Adam in the last couple of weeks.

She swung her legs over the side of the bed and froze. The end table drawer was open and her Glock was gone. The dread that she'd become so familiar with was back and had settled firmly in her gut.

"Oh Simon, what have you done?" she whispered to the empty drawer. She sank onto the bed next to Simon and reached for his shoulder.

And grasped a pillow. Dani yanked the covers off and gasped. "Simon?"

She threw on her clothes and raced for the kitchen. "Adam?"

Isaac stumbled down the stairs. "Anyone seen my phone?"

Adam opened the kitchen door and stepped inside to rearm the alarm.

Dani absently noted he looked tired. "Have you seen Simon this morning?"

"No, I just got back from checking the perimeter. When I glanced in earlier, he was sleeping."

"No, his pillows were sleeping." She ground her molars and forced herself to calm down. "He's not in his room."

Adam frowned. "He didn't come outside, I would have seen him."

"Did you take the gun from my end table?" she asked Adam.

Adam's eyes sharpened. "No. What gun?"

Impatience bit at her, but succumbing to it would do nothing for Simon. "The Glock I had. It was Kurt's and it was in the safe. I took it from the bag and carried it in my purse. When we got here last night, I put it in the drawer of the nightstand." It was heavy and unwieldy, but she'd felt safer for it.

"Do you know how to use it?"

She looked him in the eye. "Yes. I don't know what compelled me to do it, but shortly after Kurt's death, I started going to a firing range three times a week. I know how to shoot and I know how to hit what I aim at."

"But you had me teach Simon."

A hint of a smile wanted to break loose. She held it back. "Yes."

A glimmer of an answering smile graced his lips. "Ah."

She shrugged. "I'm sorry. And I'm not. Simon needed—needs—a positive male influence in his life even if it is for a short time." Her frown returned along with her panic. "And now I don't have the gun in my drawer or Simon in his bed. I need to know where my son is."

"Is anything else missing?"

"You mean besides my phone?" Isaac asked.

"Yes."

Barely controlling her panic, Dani hurried back to the bedroom and went through Simon's stuff. "His dirty clothes are here. His backpack, Nintendo DS system, clean clothes, shoes, and hoodie are gone." She clutched the heavy coat to her. "Of course he didn't take this."

Adam blew out a sigh. "How did he get out of an alarmed house and past *me*? Because he had to be the one to leave. No one came in here and took him."

Dani shook her head. "It never occurred to me he'd do something like this. Not that he couldn't, you understand, I don't underestimate his intelligence. He's borderline genius. But I didn't think he *would*." She was rambling, her words tumbling over one another as her fear attacked her. Where had he gone? What was he *doing*? And how long had he been gone? And had he had help? If so, who? *Why?* The questions ran circles in her brain.

Adam got on his phone.

Adam tried to figure out how Simon could have gotten past him and decided the kid had waited until the alarm was turned off and then slipped out the door before it was turned back on.

He led Dani to the couch and she dropped onto it. He sank down beside her. "Where would he go?" Dani stared at him, the terrified, lost expression nearly his undoing. "Come on, Dani, think. Where would he go?"

She spread her hands. "I don't know. The only friend he has is Mitchell."

"You have his mother's number?"

"Of course." She gave it to him and Adam passed it on to Isaac.

Who held his hand out. Adam lifted a brow and then remembered. He handed Isaac his phone. "Get someone over to his house, make sure he's safe and watch for Simon."

The man stepped aside and dialed the number.

Tears slipped down her cheeks and she shivered, clasping her arms across her stomach. "He's got to be okay, Adam. He just has to."

"He will be."

She bolted to her feet. "You can't promise that!"

He stood too. "No, I can't, but I can promise that we'll do everything possible to get him back."

"Just like you've been doing everything possible to keep us safe?" she lashed back. She slapped a hand to her mouth and stared at him, eyes wide.

Inside, he flinched. He knew Kurt would have backhanded her. And while her words wounded, he simply held out his arms. Shock seemed to hold her still for a second, then she moved toward him to bury her face against his chest. For the next few minutes Adam let her cry, feeling the wetness of her tears through his heavy sweater.

"Come here," he whispered. He led her back to the couch. She settled down beside him and pulled away at the same time. His arms ached with the emptiness. Unfortunately, he didn't have time to analyze his growing feelings for Dani.

She stood and scrubbed her eyes with her palms and drew in a ragged breath. Then firmed her chin and stared at him. "I'm scared to death, Adam. No. I'm terrified, but I won't give up. I won't let them win." Her fingers curled into fists held tight at her hips. "And I won't let them have my son." Adam watched her eyes harden to a coldness that almost scared him. "Are you driving me or am I going alone?"

Dani sat next to Adam in the front seat while he drove with determined purpose. His phone rang and he snagged it. "Yes?" While he listened, Dani watched his face for any clue as to what the call might be about. He glanced at her and nodded. "Great."

"What?" She pounced as soon as he hung up.

"Our buddy Ralph got a hit off the Lee phone line."

"What did he find out?"

"Someone—probably Mitchell—sent a fax to the bus depot, supposedly with your signature on it, authorizing Simon's bus ride."

She gaped. "What? How—never mind. So we just go to the stop and get him?"

"No, the bus left at 6:00 this morning and it's only a three, three-and-a-half-hour ride, depending on traffic."

She glanced at the dash clock. "It's 9:30 now. Has the bus gotten there yet?"

"A few minutes ago."

"Too late to send someone to meet him." She gasped as a thought hit her. "And if we can find out that easily, so can someone else, right?" He didn't say anything and her heart thudded against her chest. "Stuart won't hurt him," she said. "He'll just use him to bring me to him. Probably."

"If it's Stuart that's after you."

"Why do you say that?"

"I can't help but think there's something else going on. I know Stuart works for the FBI and he's not exactly a standup guy, but Blanchard killed a man in your house. Then he shows up on the boat. Something is off."

"But what about Stuart showing up at the first safe house? We know now he tracked us through the game. Not once, but twice." She thought about that. "And if he could do it, so could someone else, right?"

Adam shrugged. "Of course."

"But who?"

"Whoever knows you saw the murder."

She closed her eyes. "Kurt is dead, Ryan is in the hospital, Trennan is dead." She opened her eyes and looked at him. "Those are the only three I could see from my vantage point by the door."

"So the only other two who were there are the person taking the video and the shadow by the door."

"Yes."

His phone rang again. "Hello." A pause. "See if you can track him down. They're probably together." He hung up. "Mitchell left right before Isaac got ahold of his mother. Any idea where they'd meet up?"

Dani groaned. "No, not really. Since Kurt's death, they've gotten together almost every day. We've met at different places or they've gone to each other's house. We live about two miles apart."

"All right, see if you can find a piece of paper and a pen in here and list all of the places you think they might go."

Dani searched the glove compartment and came up with a gas receipt and a pencil stub. It would do.

27

Simon avoided the woman who seemed to be looking for him. He'd told her his mother was in the bathroom and that he was waiting on her. The three-hour ride had seemed to go on forever. He couldn't relax for thinking someone was going to stop the vehicle and drag him off of it.

But nothing had happened and he now found himself back in Greenville trying to gather his courage to face down his uncle. Simon took a deep breath and headed for the door.

He glanced over his shoulder to see the woman bearing down on him. He burst through the glass door and raced down the sidewalk toward the school where he'd told Mitchell to meet him. Thankfully, the bus station was only about a mile from his school. Getting from the school to Stuart's house would take a little more thought. He'd worry about that later.

He looked back to see that he'd lost the woman, but was willing to bet that she'd called someone to report him. Whatever.

It took him about fifteen minutes to make his way to the school. By the time he arrived, he felt nearly frozen and wished he'd brought his heavier coat.

He rounded the building, staying out of sight of the road or the main office. Simon slipped up next to the building and shivered.

The low roar of a motor caught his attention and he peeked around the corner.

Mitchell. But what was he driving?

Simon walked out to meet his friend. "What's that?" he signed.

"Our ride, my man," Mitchell signed back and grinned. "Hop on."

"No way." Relieved, Simon climbed on behind Mitchell and held on tight. The motorized bike was small, but when Mitchell gave it gas, Simon realized it was also quite powerful. He held on to Mitchell with his left hand and moved his right hand in front so Mitchell could see him sign. "Turn left."

Mitchell did. Simon looked back and noticed the black car. "Turn right," he signed.

For the next five minutes, he took them on a meandering route. The black car followed, staying back, but keeping pace.

Dread centered itself in his gut. With his right hand, he signed, "Someone's following us."

Mitchell gunned the bike and it shot forward.

Simon tightened his grip on Mitchell. "Where are we going?"

"Going to lose them."

The black car moved closer. Mitchell made a sudden right turn into a neighborhood. His friends were still there. Then Mitchell turned off the street and onto a walking trail.

Where no car could follow. He looked back to see the car stopped and no one behind them.

Simon breathed a sigh of relief.

That was very short-lived. He motioned for Mitchell to stop. He needed more than one hand to get his point across.

Mitchell braked and turned so he could see Simon. Simon looked around. Could see the roofs of houses through the thick trees. "You think you could get this thing into that other neighborhood?"

"Through the trees?"

"Yeah."

Mitchell shrugged. "We can try and walk it and see what happens."

"Good, because those guys following are going to be waiting where this walking trail ends."

"Who are they? Why are they following you?"

"I think they're people my uncle Stuart hired to find my mom. Only I'm going to make him stop them before that happens." He saw Mitchell swallow hard and felt a twinge of guilt for getting his friend involved in something that might be dangerous. He hadn't stopped to think about that when he'd hatched this plan. Nothing he could do now. He thought about turning Isaac's phone on, but wasn't quite ready for that yet. "Come on, let's go."

Mitchell didn't ask any more questions. Together, they pushed the bike, forging their own path through the dense trees. By the time they reached the edge, they were both sweating.

At least there wasn't a fence. They pushed the bike through the backyard, around the side of the house, and into the street. Mitchell climbed on and cranked it. Simon resumed his position in the back and held on as Mitchell led them out of the neighborhood and back onto the main road.

Simon kept watch over his shoulder, but didn't see anyone. He gave the directions to Mitchell who followed them without question.

Within fifteen minutes, they pulled up in front of Stuart's house.

Dani stared at the blank paper in front of her, depressed to realize she had no idea what her son was thinking or where he would go. She had one name written down. Mitchell.

With doubt in her heart, she wrote, *Home.*

"Anyone and everyone, Dani," Adam said. "Even the most unlikely ones."

218

"Well, I know he wouldn't go to Stuart. Maybe Jenny? He likes her."

"Put her down. We'll get in touch with her and have her on the lookout."

His phone rang while she wrote.

"That's what I figured," he said. "Thanks."

She looked up. "What?"

"That was Ralph. He said they found a whole setup in Stuart's home office. He's been watching you probably since Kurt died."

Nausea welled. "That's so sick."

"He's a sick person."

She shook her head. "What did I do wrong?"

Adam shot her a quick frown, then looked back at the road. "What do you mean?"

Dani sighed and looked in the mirrors. She could see Isaac behind. Tabitha was in front. "I don't really know what I mean or if I could even explain it."

"Try me."

"My life has been one struggle after another. I look around and see others who have it so easy, are so privileged. And then I look at my life and I just wonder what I did that was so awful to deserve such pain." She flicked her gaze out the window, wondering why she was baring her soul to a man she'd only known such a short time. But she needed someone to talk to and he seemed willing to listen. Why not see if he had some answers? "My childhood wasn't horrible, but my father was killed in a car accident when I was little. I have almost no memories of him. My mother worked three jobs to support us. I was the nerdy one in high school, the one that got bullied and picked on."

"But you stuck with it and graduated."

"I knew if I dropped out, I would never be anything." She lifted her chin. "That was so important to me. I wanted to be something. Someone."

"And then you met Kurt."

"Yes. Then I met Kurt."

"He swept you off your feet?"

"Oh boy, did he."

"Tell me."

She pushed out her lip. "It's a rather sad story. Sad in the sense that I was so vulnerable and stupid. And starstruck."

"Starstruck?"

"He was a big bad FBI agent." She gave him a self-deprecating smile. A smile she felt slip into a frown. "I was looking for a hero, someone to rescue me from my sad little life. I thought I'd found that in Kurt."

"What about your mother?"

Pain lanced her. "She lives in California. I haven't seen her since I graduated from high school."

He shot her a startled look. "Why not?"

"Kurt wouldn't let me. And she didn't have the money to fly out here anyway. After Kurt died, I tried to get her to come visit, but she wouldn't." She shrugged and tried not to let the pain of her mother's refusal drag her any lower. "And then Stuart started all of his weirdness and I let the subject drop. I still want her to come. Or to go visit her. I want her to meet Simon."

He reached over and took her hand and squeezed. She felt the warmth from his touch race up her arm. "We'll see if we can't make that happen after we get this little mess cleared up."

"Little mess?" She gave a low laugh even as worry for Simon nearly consumed her. "You have the gift for understatement, don't you?"

"Maybe, but one way or another, we're going to make sure we find Simon and get you two safe."

"Safe. I've forgotten what that feels like," she murmured and closed her eyes. *Please, Lord, let Simon and I know what that feels like. Please. Soon.*

"You didn't do anything to deserve it."

She blinked. "What?"

"You didn't do anything wrong. You didn't bring on the rotten deal you've gotten in your life. God didn't decide to just zap you for some perceived wrong. He doesn't work that way."

"I know he doesn't. In my mind, I know that. My heart wants to argue sometimes. Especially when I was the one who made the choice to marry the man. It's like I made that bad choice so I deserve to be punished for it. One bad decision that has led to one bad consequence after another."

Adam sighed. "Yeah. I know what you mean."

"Are you referring to your uncle?"

He shot her a sidelong glance. "Tori told you?"

"Yes. I hope you don't mind."

He shrugged. "No, it's a story that was in all the papers. It's not a secret by any means. I wasn't keeping the details from you, I just haven't had the time to explain."

"I know."

"My uncle was a very high-ranking judge. He had his hand in a lot of pies. He found out that David and Summer had been compromised in the WITSEC program. But they were still under marshal protection. He convinced me that I would be helping him by getting on the protection detail."

"Help him how?"

"He needed a crucial piece of information from a laptop. He said he had a key witness who wouldn't turn over the evidence, but he was worried about how admissible it would be anyway. He asked me to get the information. David had the laptop with the information and David wasn't talking. I planned to see what information he needed and find a way to get it to him without any kind of ethics breach." He drew in a deep breath. "But I saw pictures on the laptop that proved my uncle was being paid off by Alessandro Raimondi, an organized crime boss."

"Oh. Wow. That's . . . crazy."

"Yeah. When I realized what I was looking at, everything became crystal clear. I knew what I had to do. But—I hesitated. For just a brief few hours, I kept my mouth shut. When we were on the way to nab Raimondi, I called my uncle and told him I'd discovered what was going on and the deal was off. He put a hit out on me and—" He shrugged, but she could see the pain on his face. He tossed her a twisted smile. "Thankfully, it failed."

"I'm so sorry, Adam. You've had a rough time yourself, haven't you?"

"Yes. Betrayal leaves a bitter taste in your mouth no matter what form it takes." He flexed his fingers on the wheel.

"Betrayal is betrayal," she muttered. "And you quit the marshals."

"I didn't feel like I was worthy to work for them anymore."

"But you didn't do anything wrong."

"I didn't immediately act on information I had. I did something wrong."

"Would they have fired you?"

He pursed his lips. "No. I had a moment of poor judgment. I would have probably received a reprimand, if that." The conflict raging inside him was evident as he raked a hand through his hair. "I didn't purposely set out to do anything wrong. I thought I was doing a favor for a man who held justice to the highest degree. I thought I was helping put away a bad guy. My actions weren't listed in the rule book, but my intentions were pure. It just didn't work out that way and so I quit. I needed time to recover. To forgive myself and work through the angst and consequences of my uncle's actions."

"And have you?"

He shot her another glance. "Worked through the angst?" He shrugged. "Most of it."

"Do you want to go back to the marshals?"

He shook his head. "I've found my calling. I'm doing what I'm meant to do."

"When did you come to that conclusion?"

He reached over and took her hand again. Squeezed her fingers and let his gaze linger a bit before turning back to the road. "When you walked into my office."

Her breath caught and she gazed at him. A ligth blush crept into his face, matching the warmth she felt rising within her. He cleared his throat and put his hand back on the wheel as he pulled into the hospital parking lot. Tabitha parked to their left, Isaac to the right.

Adam looked at his phone. "Nothing on Isaac's phone. Simon still has it off. Mitchell hasn't shown up yet. And your friend Jenny texted to say she hasn't heard anything from Simon." He slid the device into his pocket. "Let's go see if Mr. Blanchard is awake yet." He studied her. "I don't suppose you would allow Tabitha to take you somewhere safe? I'm not sure going into the hospital is the wisest move."

She opened her car door and stepped into the cold. Snowflakes greeted her and she raised a hand to swipe them away from her cheeks.

A light dusting of white appeared and disappeared as soon as it hit the ground. She jutted her jaw at him. "Probably not, but that's my son who's in danger, and if this man knows anything about who might hurt him, I'm going to get it out of him."

28

Simon walked up the front porch steps to his uncle's front door, took a deep breath, and rapped his knuckles against the wood. His heart thundered in his chest and he thought even he could hear it. His hands shook and he hoped Mitchell thought it was because he was cold.

In actuality, he was sweating bullets beneath the hoodie and sweatshirt. And the pain in his gut was still there. He pressed his hand against his belly and fought off a wave of nausea. He briefly wondered if food would help, but was shocked to realize he wasn't hungry. Weird.

Snowflakes drifted down, and for the first time in his life, he prayed they didn't stick.

He felt the weight of the backpack pulling on his shoulders. He'd had to ditch the gun when he got on the bus. How could he have forgotten about security? He'd put it in a safe spot, so hopefully they could get it later. When all of this was over.

He rubbed his palms down his sweatpants and looked at Mitchell. "What if he's not home?" he signed. "What's today anyway?"

Mitchell looked at his phone. "It's Friday morning. You think he's at work?"

"Of course he is. I should have thought of that first," he signed and grumbled at the same time.

"So call him and get him here."

"I would think he would know I was here with the way he's been following us all around the United States." Simon sat on the porch step and stared at Mitchell and his phone. He jumped to his feet, then doubled over, grasping his belly. He sank back onto the step.

A hand landed on his shoulder and he looked up to find Mitchell staring at him with concern. "You okay?"

"Yeah, yeah." He bit his lip and sucked in a deep breath. "Forget that. I just realized that they're not tracking me, they're tracking you."

"What?"

"Just like the game. They're probably tracking your phone. Turn it off."

Mitchell did and Simon ran his hands through his short hair that still felt weird to him. "Okay, so he's not here. Can you take me to his office?"

Mitchell's brows rose. "His office? Where is it?"

"Downtown."

"That's a pretty long way. Dude, are you sure?"

"I'm sure. How much gas you got?"

Mitchell shrugged. "Enough to get us downtown and back." He reached into his pocket and pulled out a twenty-dollar bill. "Plus money if I need more. Hop on."

"We lost him, but the phone says they went to Stuart's house," his source said.

"Stuart's? I didn't think Simon even knew where he lived," Joe said.

225

"Guess he knows how to work a GPS."

"Guess so."

"So what now?"

"Head over to Stuart's and see what's going on. Stuart's here at the office, not at home."

"Maybe we should watch the office and see if he shows up."

"I can take care of that part. You head over to Stuart's."

"On the way."

Joe hung up the phone and glanced at his watch. After he'd read Kurt's letter, he'd made contact with a buyer for the counterfeit plates Kurt had stolen from one of the Bloods' gang members. Only the Bloods weren't aware of who stole them, so they wouldn't be in on the action. Only Joe knew who had them—or at least had access to them. Access to the plates and everything else Kurt had left behind. A new will that had been notarized and signed by three different lawyers. Bank account numbers in the Cayman Islands, a Swiss account. More money than Joe had ever seen in his life.

All he had to do to get it was to kill Dani Harding.

Adam kept an arm around Dani's shoulders and decided he liked the way she felt snuggled up against him. He looked over to catch Tabitha's eye. And raised brows. Adam refused to acknowledge the flush he felt climbing up his neck.

He cleared his throat and led the way to the room. Ralph had sent him the room number about thirty minutes ago. In front of the door, they found Ralph standing guard. "You?"

Ralph shrugged. "I volunteered."

"Is he awake?"

"Yes. But he's on some serious pain meds." He looked at Dani. "Hello again."

Dani stepped forward and gave the man a hug. "Hi."

Ralph looked surprised. Then pleased. "I'm glad you're okay."

"Me too. But Simon's not and I really need to talk to Ryan and find out if he knows anything."

Ralph nodded and shared a glance with Adam. "Help yourself."

Adam pressed the door open and stepped inside to find the man with his eyes closed and his head bandaged. An IV trailed from the inside of his arm to a bag hanging on the pole next to him.

"Mr. Blanchard?"

Nothing.

Dani moved past him to the bed. "Look at his face."

Bright pink patches, blistered and peeling skin. "Looks like he's been burned by something."

"Like boiling water?" She placed a hand on his shoulder and shook him. Hard.

Special Agent Ryan Blanchard blinked, then his eyes fluttered closed again.

"Wake up," Dani demanded. She gave him another rough shake.

"Wha—?" He sniffed and drew in a breath. Adam watched the man work hard to force his eyes open. "What?"

"Who hired you? Stuart Harding?"

"I want a lawyer." His eyelids fluttered shut.

Dani gave his shoulder a viciously hard shove and Blanchard gasped. But he looked at her, eyes narrowed in pain and anger. His gaze shuttled to Adam. "Get her away from me."

Adam shrugged. "Sorry. I don't tell her what to do, trust me on that one. You might as well tell us where Simon is."

"Simon," he mumbled. "Kurt's kid."

"And mine," Dani said, leaning in. "Where is he?"

"I don't have a clue."

"You tried to kill me at Jenny's house. I threw hot water on you. That's why your face is burned."

"Don't know what you're talking about."

"Did Stuart hire you to kill us?" Dani demanded.

The man gave a low, pained laugh. "Wasn't going to kill you. Stuart talked about all you were going through. I was just there to make sure you were okay."

Dani snorted. "Right. Dressed in a black drysuit, a mask, and carrying a gun with a suppressor."

"It's cold outside. The ski mask and drysuit kept me warm. Found the gun on the deck. Wondered who it belonged to."

Adam sighed. "Come on, Dani, you're not getting anything from him."

She pursed her lips and he could see the desperation in her. He knew she was wildly worried about Simon. He was too, but Blanchard wasn't going to talk. Adam grabbed her hand. "Come on."

She whirled away from him and charged at the man in the bed. "Where's my son? Where's Simon?" When Blanchard simply closed his eyes, Dani grabbed him by the collar of his hospital gown and shook him. "Where is he? Tell me!"

Blanchard howled with pain, his eyes rolling back in his head as his hands lifted to press his palms against his bandaged head.

Adam grabbed her arm and pulled her. "Dani, stop."

"I can't until he tells me," she sobbed.

She jerked from his grasp and made another lunge for the writhing man. Adam finally snagged her around the waist and hauled her away and out the door.

"Dani, you've got to stop."

She leaned against him and he held her while she took deep breaths and stopped fighting him.

"I'm sorry," she whispered.

"It's okay."

"No, it's not. I'm just so scared, Adam. So scared . . ."

"I know."

"I've got to trust that God is taking care of him, but it's so hard."

"I know," he said again.

Ralph caught his attention. "Nurses are coming. Better get going."

Adam pulled her down the hallway in the opposite direction of the approaching medical staff. In the stairwell, he led her down and stopped on the first landing. She leaned against the wall and stared at the ceiling.

"How can they do this?" she whispered. "How can they hurt a little boy?"

He couldn't help it. He pulled her against him once again and stroked her short-cropped hair. "He's going to be okay. We're going to find him."

"You can't promise me that!"

Adam sighed. "No. I can't. I'm sorry."

"No. I'm sorry." She sniffed and palmed her eyes. A thought seemed to hit her. "Is your mother in this hospital?"

Pain shot through him. "Yes."

"Then you need to go see her."

"Not right now. I will later. Once you and Simon are safe."

Dani bit her lip. "Adam, you need to go to her."

"I can't. If someone sees me going in her room and connects us, they might hurt her to get me to give you up."

She gasped. "Oh. I didn't even think about that."

"I know. I'll make it up to her. She'll understand, I promise."

"What about your sister?"

He sighed, but his heart twisted at the concern on her face. Concern for him and his family. "I appreciate that you want to help me, but let's worry about you and Simon for now, okay?"

She nodded. "Okay, so where are we going? What do we do next?"

"Call your friend Jenny, and see if Simon's shown up at her house." He handed her his phone.

Isaac stepped into the stairwell. "There you are."

"What's going on?" Adam asked.

"Tabitha just radioed me. Two guys just walked into the hospital and are on their way up."

"What makes them stand out?"

"They're in a government-issued vehicle."

"FBI?"

"Looks like. Tabitha spotted weapons in shoulder holsters. And one of them is Stuart."

Adam took Dani by the elbow. "Find out who the other one is. Time to go."

She hung up the phone and handed it to him. "Jenny hasn't seen him."

"He and Mitchell are together," Isaac said. "We've got someone tracking Mitchell's phone."

Adam started to lead them down the stairs, then paused.

Isaac stopped. "What?"

"Go up."

"Why?" Dani asked.

"They'll expect us to go down. Let's go up. We can take the crosswalk over and then down to the parking garage. Tell Tabitha to meet us there." He pulled his weapon from his holster. "Stay close."

"How did they find us now?" Dani asked.

"I don't know. We're not exactly laying low and hiding out at this point. It could be that they had someone watching Blanchard's room and called when we showed up. Who knows?"

"You don't sound too concerned."

"Oh, I'm concerned. I'm concerned we're going to be dodging bullets. I'm concerned Simon hasn't shown up and I'm concerned no one has contacted us about him." He pulled her up the stairs. She kept up.

"If someone has Simon and wants to contact us, how will they know how?"

He paused and opened the door to the floor that would lead them to the crosswalk. He looked at her. "Simon knows my number. And he has Isaac's phone. If someone wants to talk, he'll be able to find us."

She nodded. Then looked around. "Now what?"

"That way."

He kept a good grip on her hand. Isaac brought up the rear. "Tabitha's waiting with the car."

"Good. Let's try to get there without anything newsworthy happening."

The three of them dodged hospital workers and patients as they raced across the plastic-covered walkway. At the end, they stepped into the next building and Adam led them to the next set of stairs.

Joe Duncan flashed his badge to the hospital security officer. "I need to look at your monitors if you don't mind."

"FBI? Is that thing real?"

Joe sighed. "Yeah. Now you mind?"

He was running out of time. He'd managed to send Stuart on a wild-goose chase to check on Ryan. He wanted to get to Dani before his partner and he didn't need the man in the way. But he had to hurry before Stuart called him to tell him he hadn't found out anything.

The officer hesitated, then moved out of the way. "Help yourself."

Joe did. He settled down in the vacated chair and started clicking on the different views of the hospital. He saw Ralph outside of Ryan's room. More clicks, more views. And then he spotted them. On the crosswalk. He spoke into his phone. "Fifth floor, the crosswalk." He looked back at the security guard who was watching. "Which way would you go if you wanted to get out of the hospital?"

"Down to the first floor and through the lobby. Or through the side door and out into the parking garage."

Joe spoke into his phone. "Cover the lobby door and the side door." Then he walked to the door. "It's all yours now."

"Glad to help." The officer settled himself into the chair and turned back to the monitors.

Joe pulled his weapon—the one he'd already prepared with the suppressor—walked up behind the man, placed the barrel near his head, and pulled the trigger. All in less than a second. The guy never knew what hit him.

He shoved the weapon into his waistband, walked over to the monitors, and erased the path he'd taken from the point of entering the hospital to walking into the security office. Then he shrugged off his sports coat and shoved it in the backpack. Pulled out a hoodie and slipped it on. He yanked the hood up over his head and opened the door.

29

Simon looked up at the FBI office and almost changed his mind. Then he remembered his mother's fear and squared his shoulders. He could do this. He pressed a hand against his belly and took a deep breath. The pain had gotten worse since he'd left the boat this morning. A wave of nausea washed over him and he swallowed hard, ordering his nerves under control. Shivers racked him and he felt hot and cold all at the same time. Vaguely he wondered if he had a fever.

He swung off Mitchell's bike. "Don't turn your phone on, okay? They'll be tracking it," he signed.

"I won't. Hurry up. I'm freezing."

"You can come in with me."

"No way. I'm going to get out of sight. If someone decides they need to call parents, I don't even want to be in the area."

"Where will you hide? You won't leave me, will you?"

"Of course not." Mitchell shot him a frown, then looked around. "See that bush?"

"Yeah."

"I'm going to hide behind it and watch the door. I'll pull up when you come out."

Simon took a deep breath. "All right. Wish me luck."

Mitchell shook his head. "I think this one calls for prayer."

"Yeah. Me too." He started up the steps, trying to figure out exactly what he was going to say to Stuart and praying he didn't throw up thanks to the growing pain centering itself in his lower right side.

Dani paused on the third floor when Adam tugged on her hand. "That way."

"I thought we were going all the way down."

"We were. I'm changing directions."

"Okay." She stepped from the stairwell onto the patient floor. Nurses and doctors brushed past her without a second look. "Where to?"

"The service elevator."

"Where is it?"

Adam glanced at Isaac, who nodded. He stopped a woman with a cleaning cart. "Where's the service elevator?"

"Around the desk and on to the back wall." She grabbed her mop and headed for the newly vacated room. "But that's just for hospital personnel who have keys. You'll have to use the elevator through that door there."

"Right. Thanks."

Adam cupped her elbow and guided her toward the service elevator.

"What are we going to do?" Dani asked. "We don't have a key."

"Actually, we do." Isaac held it up with a triumphant smile. "Sometimes my shady past comes in handy."

Within seconds Dani found herself staring at a pair of stainless steel doors. Adam swiped the key and the doors opened. They stepped inside and began the descent to the bottom floor.

Adam called Tabitha. "Where are you?" He listened, then nodded and hung up. "When we get out of the elevator, hang a left.

Walk down the hallway to the end and out the door. Summer is waiting with a vehicle."

"What happened to Tabitha?"

"She's still waiting."

"A decoy?" Dani murmured.

"Yep."

The elevator gave a slight bounce and the doors parted. Isaac and Adam had their weapons drawn and held slightly behind them.

The hallway loomed empty and Adam motioned for Isaac to lead the way. Dani followed and Adam brought up the rear.

Dani could see the car through the glass doors at the end of the hallway. Within seconds, they were settled in the vehicle.

Summer glanced in the rearview mirror. "Glad you could make it." She pulled away from the curb.

Dani turned to look over her shoulder out the back window.

So far so good. She let out a relieved breath, closed her eyes, and sent up a prayer. When she finished, she asked, "Has anyone found my son yet?"

"Not yet," Summer said. "We're still watching Isaac's phone and his friend's phone. If they turn them on, we'll have them."

"And if they don't?"

Adam reached over and took her hand in his. "Then we'll have to figure out another way to find him."

"How?" She couldn't keep her frustration from spewing forth. "This is what I was afraid of. This is why I wanted to run. My nightmare is unfolding before my very eyes and you and your company seem to be powerless to stop it from happening. I trusted you and I—" Dani couldn't believe the words she let spill from her lips, but she was afraid, so very afraid. She snagged the ragged fragments of what remained of her self-control and closed her eyes. She leaned forward to rest her head against the seat in front of her and let the sobs explode.

Adam drew in a shaky breath, unsure of how he should respond. Unfortunately, he had a feeling anything he said or did wouldn't be the right thing. He shot Summer a frantic look in the rearview mirror. She raised a brow and tilted her head toward Dani. Adam ground his teeth with indecision. So what did *that* mean?

Dani's thin frame shook, her racking sobs easing to hiccuping gasps. With one last look at an exasperated Summer, Adam finally moved. Summer nodded her approval.

Adam placed his hands on Dani's shoulders and turned her to him. She took one look at him and resisted. He tugged. She gave in and allowed him to pull her against his chest.

"I've got to stop doing this," she mumbled. "It's not solving a blessed thing."

"You're letting off steam." He stroked her short hair and rubbed the nape of her neck.

"I'm being a crybaby."

"I'd say that was allowed in this situation."

She sat up and sniffed. He handed her a tissue Summer had slipped to him. She used it, then clutched it like a lifeline. "I can't think of where he'd go. Jenny said she hadn't seen him. He wouldn't go to Stuart. He'd only go to Mitchell."

"What about a church?"

"We don't have one. Kurt wouldn't let us go. At least not very often."

"A teacher? An administrator at his school?"

She shook her head. "No. No one."

She knew it was pitiful. She and Simon had been so isolated when Kurt was alive. And now that he was dead, Dani realized how alone she still was. The thought saddened her.

Adam's tug on her fingers brought her eyes up to his. "You're not alone," he said. She gulped. Was she really that easy to read? He simply smiled and turned to Summer. "Where are we?"

"Almost to Dani's subdivision."

Dani leaned forward. "You think he would have come home?"

"Won't hurt to check."

He spoke into his phone. "Isaac, you close by?" He listened. "Right." He looked at Summer. "Drive on past the subdivision. I want Isaac and Tabitha to do a sweep before we go in."

Summer did as he asked. Dani saw Tabitha and Isaac turn into the subdivision. Summer made a U-turn and parked on the side of the road.

"Where's Blake?" Dani asked.

"His mother had a heart attack," Adam said. "He had to fly home about an hour ago."

"Oh." No one had said anything.

Adam held up his phone. "He texted me and said to offer his apologies."

"No, it's no problem. Of course he'd go be with his mother." Unlike Adam who'd chosen to stay with her. A gratitude like nothing she'd ever felt before rose up within her. God had his hand on this situation. She knew he did, she just needed to keep giving it up to him every time the terror threatened to overtake her.

For the next ten minutes, Dani waited with barely concealed impatience. She could imagine that Simon had gone home and was holed up in the bonus room playing his video games. *Oh please, God. Please let me hold him again.* She would hug him to pieces.

Before she grounded him for life.

While the scenario played out in her head and she hoped with all her heart it was true, deep down she knew Simon wouldn't do that to her.

Although he *had* left. Who knew what he was thinking?

"How mad would Simon have to make you in order for you to give up on him?" Adam murmured.

"What?" Had she heard him right?

He flushed. "Nothing."

Dani gripped his forearm and felt his muscle contract beneath the long-sleeved shirt. Almost like an afterthought, she realized she wasn't afraid of Adam and probably never would be. He'd never use his strength against her. He was nothing like Kurt.

"Adam, Simon could never do anything to make me so mad I'd ever give up on him."

"Nothing?"

"I really can't think of anything. I might be really mad, but I'd never stop loving him, praying for him."

He nodded.

"You think your mother's given up on you?" she asked.

He flinched. "It occurred to me that she might."

"Because you haven't been there for her through the surgery?"

"That and the thing with my uncle."

Guilt pierced Dani to the core. "I'm sorry."

Adam gripped her hand. "I am too, but this isn't your fault. None of it is, so don't you dare try to shoulder the blame, okay?"

She nodded. "I'll try." A pause. "I don't know your mom," she said. "But if she loves you with even a drop of the love I feel for Simon, then she won't give up on you. Ever."

He stared a moment longer, then leaned over to kiss her forehead. "Thanks."

She gave him a shaky smile and turned her gaze back toward her house. A house she never wanted to set foot in again.

His phone rang. He listened and nodded. "Okay. Thanks."

She looked at him and didn't even have to ask. "He's not there."

"No. And he's not at Jenny's either. She's not home. If Simon's hiding out somewhere in her house, he's not answering the door. Isaac didn't want to break in. But your movers are cleaning the

238

place out and putting everything in storage. The realtor is putting the house on the market tomorrow."

She blinked at the news. "Oh. Wow! That was fast."

"Do you regret it? You can always stop it. Just don't sign the papers."

She lifted her chin. "No way."

Adam smiled. "I didn't think you would."

"So now what?"

He thought. "I think we need to go by Mitchell's house."

"Why?"

"Because we know for sure he and Simon were in contact. Simon probably arranged for Mitchell to meet him somewhere. Mitchell has to come home sometime, right?"

Simon signed and spoke to the man at the desk. "I want to see my uncle. Will you tell him I'm here?"

"Who's your uncle?"

"Stuart Harding."

The man's brows rose a little higher on his wide forehead. "Stuart Harding, huh? What's your name?"

"Simon Harding."

"Kurt's kid?"

"Yes sir." He kept a hand pressed against the pain in his stomach.

"All right. Have a seat over there. We'll see what Stuart says. He just walked in not two minutes ago."

Simon settled himself on the hard plastic chair and watched the man's lips as he spoke into the phone.

"Thank you." He looked at Simon. "He'll be right here."

"Thanks."

"Sure." The man looked down. Then back up. He said something, but Simon missed it.

He frowned. "What?"

"I said, how are you doing since your dad's death?"

"We'd be doing just fine if Uncle Stuart would leave us alone."

The man blinked. Stared. Then blinked again. "Oh. Huh?"

"Never mind." He winced and leaned forward to press his face into his hands. He'd never felt this kind of pain before.

The touch on his shoulder brought his head up. He looked into the concerned eyes of the man from the desk. "Hey, I'm Buddy Faust. Are you okay, kid?"

"Yeah. Yeah, I'm fine."

Mr. Faust's hand moved to his forehead. "You've got a bit of a fever."

"It'll go away."

The elevator door opened and Stuart stepped into the lobby.

Simon went rigid. His stomach hurt so bad, he wanted to vomit. His uncle looked so much like his dad he couldn't help the small gasp that slipped from his lips.

Stuart walked over to him and hunkered down in front of him. Mr. Faust returned to his position behind the desk. "Simon, glad to see you. What are you doing here?" His eyes slipped to the door and the man behind the desk taking everything in, then back to Simon. "Where's your mom?"

Simon stood. "That's why I'm here," he said, doing his best to keep his words clear and firm. "I want to talk to you about my mom."

Stuart raised a brow. "Why don't you come on up to my office and we'll talk?"

"No. Here's fine." No way was he going up to Stuart's office. And besides, he was beginning to think he might need to find a doctor.

Stuart reached out and gripped his upper arm. Simon winced and tried to pull away. His uncle waited until Simon turned to look at him. "Then we'll step outside. No sense in having an audience."

240

An audience? As his uncle dragged him to the door, he realized Stuart didn't want Mr. Faust to hear the conversation. That was fine with Simon, but he didn't like being manhandled by Stuart. He'd had enough of that from his father.

Outside the building, Stuart jerked him around to face him. "Where's your mother, Simon?"

"Hiding from you." Simon yanked on his arm. His uncle's grip never budged. Simon's fear escalated, but he refused to give in to it or the pain raging through his abdomen. "I wanted to come ask you to leave us alone. Leave her alone. She doesn't want to date you or marry you or even be with you. Now stop following us." He pulled again and Stuart's hand dropped.

Simon turned to leave, but Stuart grabbed him again and spun him back to face him. The dark look on his uncle's face scared him. Slowly the look faded and Stuart dropped his head and released Simon's arm.

Simon watched, his insides screaming at him to run. A sudden sharp pain wrenched at him and he grabbed his belly with a cry. He dropped to the ground, gasping. He pressed and the pain eased to an intense ache.

He looked up to see Stuart standing over him, the frown on his face one of confusion, not anger. Stuart asked, "Are you all right?"

Simon shook his head and felt the sweat pop out on his forehead. Then he jumped to his feet and raced to the nearest bush to lose what little he'd had to eat today. He looked up to see Mitchell staring through the bushes with wide eyes. Dizziness hit him. Simon signed, "Get your phone. Turn it on."

Before he could sink to the ground, he found himself swept off his feet and being carried in Stuart's arms. Mitchell's scared face disappeared. Simon put up a token struggle, then gave up, resting his hot head against Stuart's shoulder.

"I want my mom," he whispered.

30

Stuart paced his living room. Simon lay on the couch curled into a ball, sleeping now after downing two ibuprofen Stuart had insisted he take. He wasn't sure what was wrong with the kid, probably a stomach virus.

He swigged back a beer and thought about what he should do. He had Simon. Now he just had to figure out the best way to use the boy to get to Dani. So, what now? A phone call?

Simon stirred and blinked. His gaze focused in on Stuart and fear flashed across his face. Good, fear would make him more agreeable to deal with. He still didn't look good though. "Use the trash can if you need to puke again." Stuart pointed just in case Simon didn't understand his words.

Simon dropped his eyes to the bucket next to the couch. "It doesn't hurt as much."

"Good."

Simon looked at him. "Will you call my mom, please?"

"You have the number?"

"Yeah." Simon rattled it off.

It probably belonged to one of the goons she'd found protection with. Stuart entered it into his phone. "Lie back down."

"You calling my mom?"

"Yes, yes. In a minute."

Simon pressed a hand to his stomach and groaned. "I really feel sick."

Stuart sighed. "You'll live." He paused, then snorted. "For now."

"I've gotta go to the bathroom. Where is it?"

Stuart pointed. "Down the hall to the left."

Simon made his way in that direction. Stuart pulled his attention from the kid and decided he'd better call in with an excuse for disappearing. He punched in Joe's number and paced while he waited for Joe to pick up.

"Are you working today or not?" Stuart winced at the ire in Joe's voice.

"No, ah, something's come up."

"What kind of something?"

"I've got Simon with me. He's sick and I need to take care of him."

Silence. Then Joe's low voice came through. "How did you get your hands on him? I didn't see you leave."

"You were in the meeting with the SAC when Faust called me down to the lobby." Stuart laughed, but there wasn't any humor in it. "And he came to me. Found me at the office. I don't know where Dani is. I'm getting ready to call her now."

"The one day you're actually in the office and Simon finds you?"

"I know. It must mean Dani and I are meant to be."

Joe blew out a sigh. "I'm not sure how you get that as a sign you're meant to be with Dani, but whatever. I don't really care. Look, just . . . take care of the kid. I'll cover for you with the SAC."

"Thanks."

Stuart hung up and began his pacing again.

Dani thought she might come out of her skin. The not knowing was killing her. She prayed until she felt prayed out. Mitchell's phone had come on and they'd been able to track it. Straight to Stuart's office building. Summer tapped her fingers against the wheel, humming a song Dani thought she'd heard before but didn't have the mental energy to come up with the title.

Adam returned moments later and climbed back in the car.

"Go to Stuart's house."

"What?" Dani gaped. "Why?"

"The guy at the desk inside said Simon came here asking for Stuart. Stuart came down and moved Simon outside to talk. He said it looked like the two of them were arguing though. And he said Simon didn't look like he felt very good."

"He's sick?"

"I don't know. Why don't we get to Stuart's house and find out?"

Summer was already pulling out of the parking lot. Dani's heart felt ready to beat right out of her chest. "What's wrong with him?" She pulled her cell phone from her pocket, the one she'd been given with strict instructions to only use in an emergency. She figured this qualified.

"What are you doing?"

"Calling Stuart." She dialed his number and waited. Voice mail. "Stuart. This is Dani. I know Simon's with you. I'm on the way to your house. He better be all right. Call me back." She hung up and clutched the phone. "How far away are we?"

"Fifteen minutes, maybe. It's five o'clock traffic, so it may take a bit longer than that."

Fifteen minutes. She could hang on for fifteen more minutes. Her arms ached to hug her son. She desperately needed to know if he was sick, to touch his forehead to feel for a fever.

Oh please, God, take care of him. I can't. He's in your hands. But let him be in mine soon.

244

Adam barked into his phone and Dani did her best to pay attention, but praying for Simon won out. When he hung up, he looked at her. "I called the authorities in on this."

"Why?"

"Because I'm not sure about Stuart's mental well-being. I don't know what he's thinking or how he's feeling right now and that makes him dangerous."

Dani gulped. "You're thinking he might use Simon as some sort of hostage, aren't you?"

He reached over and grasped her hand. "I don't want to go there yet, but I want to be prepared if it happens."

Dani fell back into prayer.

She prayed until Summer pulled to the curb of Stuart's house. A house Dani had never seen before. It sat on a gently curving hill, a nice brick two-story with black shutters and a matching front door. The well-manicured front yard invited one to approach.

She wanted to shrink into her seat. And if Simon hadn't been inside, she might have done just that. Instead, she reached for the car door.

Adam grabbed her arm. "Wait."

"What?"

"Backup will be here soon. I want to make sure it's not a trap."

"A trap?"

"Sorry, I'm a little paranoid these days."

She could understand that.

Within minutes, three squad cars pulled around them.

Dani swiveled her neck, hand on the door handle. "I just want to get to Simon," she whispered.

"I know, Dani, I do too. But I want to make sure he stays safe in the chaos, okay?"

She met his gaze, and nodded. Adam climbed from the car and flashed a badge. She looked at Summer. "Is that real?"

"Real enough. The governor issued all of Operation Refuge law enforcement badges. We only use them in extreme cases."

"So Adam considers this an extreme case."

Summer nodded. "Yes."

"Okay then."

She couldn't pull her eyes away from the house. Simon was behind that front door and she wanted to kick it in and grab her baby.

Instead, she watched the officers swarm the house. Three in one direction, three in another. Two walked with Adam to the front door. Adam lifted his knuckles and rapped.

Silence.

"Stuart, answer the door, I know you're in there."

"We got cause to believe a kid is in danger?" the officer to his left asked.

"Yeah."

"Then let's go in."

The knock on Stuart's door took him by surprise. He wasn't expecting anyone. He'd made no calls other than the one to Joe and then turned his phone off.

He glanced out his window.

Butterfly. He opened the door. "How'd you know to come here?"

"Because you weren't at work and you weren't at home."

He sighed and let her in. "This place has become more home than anywhere else."

Butterfly wound her way into the den. "What made you come here?"

He shrugged. "I felt like being on the water."

The den windows opened to the lake. The house wasn't large,

but it was definitely peaceful. Isolated. Calm. All the things Stuart wasn't. He'd bought it for Dani, but so far she hadn't seen it. But she would. Soon. "I'm kind of in the middle of something right now."

"So I'll help you." She hefted her purse on her shoulder.

"Look, my nephew's here. He's sick. You need to leave."

"Why don't I just check on him?" She headed down the hall.

"Fine. Check on him."

While she was gone, Stuart paced, wondering how to get rid of her. He glanced at his weapon on the counter. He could take care of her very easily if it wouldn't leave him a mess to clean up.

He walked to the couch and picked up a pillow. He could suffocate her.

While he was pondering his options, she returned to the den, her purse clutched in front of her. "He's sleeping on your bed. I think he has a fever."

"I told you he was sick. Now leave and I'll call you when things are settled down."

"No you won't."

"What?"

"You won't call. You don't want to be with me, do you?"

"Butterfly—"

"Don't bother."

She paused in front of the windows and didn't speak for a moment. Stuart sighed, then ground his teeth. He didn't have time for this. When she turned, Stuart found himself staring down the dark barrel of a gun.

He froze. "What are you doing?"

"You're never going to give up on her, are you?"

His mind clicked. Her steady hand and unwavering gaze chilled him to the bone. "Butterfly. Put the gun down."

"Answer the question, Stuart. You're so obsessed with Dani you can't see what you have staring you in the face."

His jaw tightened as he tried to think through how to handle her. "I don't know what you mean."

She barked a harsh laugh. "You know I've been in love with you since you pulled me from the gang."

Going deep undercover could mess with your mind sometimes. He'd come across Butterfly and she'd been different than the others. Hard, but not hardened. Willing to kill, but innocent of doing it. But she had information. Lots and lots of inside information that helped him look good. Allowed him to one-up Kurt a little more often.

She sighed and shook her head. "You killed for me."

"And I'd do it again. No one messes with my property."

"Your property?" Another laugh, this one disbelieving. "But you don't love me."

"I don't know. I'm not sure I know what love is."

"But you love Dani."

"No. I don't think I do."

That took her by surprise. She blinked and Stuart moved closer.

"Then why are you so determined to have her?"

He shrugged. "Because she was Kurt's. Once I have Dani, I will have taken everything from Kurt."

"Kurt's dead, Stuart. What does it matter now?"

"Oh, it matters. And yes, he's dead. We all die. But once Dani belongs to me, Kurt will have died with nothing."

"That doesn't even make sense. She doesn't want you."

A smile tugged at his lips. "She will now."

Confusion pulled her brows together. "What do you mean?"

"I mean I have Simon. When she comes to get him, she won't be leaving."

Butterfly studied him, the gun still steady. Stuart waited, biding his time. He was fully confident in his ability to take the weapon from her.

"You know, it's funny, this rivalry between you and Kurt. Apparently he felt the same way you do."

Now it was Stuart's turn to be confused. "How would you know that? You didn't even know Kurt."

"Of course I knew Kurt."

"How?" Uncertainty hit him. He hated the feeling and his anger surged. "You're lying."

"Why would I lie about knowing your brother?"

"When did you meet Kurt?"

"I introduced myself to him at your office."

Stuart felt the vein in his forehead begin to swell and throb. In a deadly quiet voice, he said, "You went to my office? I told you, never go to my office." He took another step forward. The gun lifted to center itself on his forehead so he stopped.

"And, of course, I'm supposed to do everything you say, right?" she sneered.

"Tell me."

She gave a delicate shrug. "I wanted to see where you worked. I dressed up in this killer business suit and went. When you weren't there to see how I could dress when the occasion called for it, I was crushed. But then the elevator opened and out walked a man who could have been your twin. And I realized it was Kurt, the brother you hated so much."

Stuart forced himself to unclench his teeth. "And what did Kurt have to say?"

"Once he found out I was your girlfriend, he had a lot to say."

"You were never my girlfriend."

"Whatever. All that mattered was that Kurt thought I was. He took me out for coffee and we became very good friends."

Stuart felt the rage build. This was not what he'd had planned. "No. You wouldn't do that."

"Why wouldn't I? Oh, at first, I didn't believe him when he

249

told me of your obsession with his wife. I defended you, I really did. But he just laughed and told me to watch and learn. So that's what I've done this past year, Stuart, I've watched and I've learned. Oh boy, have I learned."

Stuart wanted to howl his fury. Instead he narrowed his eyes. "So why have you continued to lead me on? Let me believe you loved me?"

Some emotion he couldn't identify flickered in her eyes, then they hardened. "I suppose because part of me hoped you would get over this thing with Dani. And part of it was that you were the only one who could *lead* us to Dani."

"Lead you to her? And who's us?"

"Kurt wrote me a note to be delivered in case he died. Do you want to hear it? I have it memorized."

"Sure." Somehow he got the word out through clenched teeth.

"'Dear Butterfly—I have to say the nickname fits—I guess I'm dead, but I have something I want to make sure I leave you with. You see, my brother Stuart is obsessed with my wife and that's just not going to happen. As soon as he hears I'm dead, he'll move in on her and knowing Dani, weak woman that she is, she'll fall right into step with whatever plan he has. I repeat: That. Can. Not. Happen.'"

Stuart felt the heat start at his feet and work its way up. He opened his mouth to speak, but she wasn't finished.

"'The plan is for Dani to join me in the hereafter. Wherever I am. So here's the deal. Send Dani to me. If you want your reward, you will have to get Dani to help you. She holds the key to your wealth.'"

Stuart frowned. "Key to your wealth?"

"I know. As soon as Dani tells me what I need to know, she's dead and I get everything."

"He sent you a letter? He left instructions for you to kill Dani?"

"Yes. And it gets even better. I quote, 'The only way to make sure you stay out of prison is to make sure Dani dies. Get rid of her and claim the prize.'"

"What prize?"

"Kurt really didn't tell you anything, did he?"

He balled his fists at his side and turned his back on the woman with the gun. He glanced down the hall, wondering where Simon was. If only the kid would show up and distract her. He could get the jump on her and—

"Turn around, Stuart." Her low silky voice made him wonder if she'd come to her senses.

He turned.

She smiled. "Time for you to join Kurt so you two can battle it out for all eternity."

His anger fizzled like cold water on a flame. Fear blossomed.

He lunged toward her. The gun cracked.

Pain exploded through his head, then nothingness covered him.

31

Dani wanted to scream, to wail her despair. Stuart's house was empty with no sign that he or Simon had been there recently. She sat in the car and chewed on her thumbnail while her mind spun. He wasn't here. But Stuart had him. Where would he take him?

Adam returned to the car, his face grim, jaw tight. "Nothing."

"Did David get ahold of Mitchell yet?" Summer asked.

"Yeah. David texted me while I was inside and said to call him as soon as I could talk."

"So call."

Adam dialed the number and pressed the speakerphone button.

David got right to the point. "Mitchell Lee came home. I've been talking to him for the last two hours. Simon stole Isaac's phone and texted Mitchell to set up how Simon would get back to Greenville. Mitchell stole his mother's credit card and reserved the bus ticket, faxed the information needed for a minor to travel alone to the bus depot, and arranged to meet Simon at the school."

"How old are these kids again?"

"I know, right?"

"What else?"

"Mitchell said they met and went to Stuart's house. Stuart wasn't home so they headed over to the Bureau office."

"And the rest is history."

"Pretty much. Mitchell said he saw Stuart pick up Simon and rush him to his car. Simon managed to sign to him to turn the phone on, so he did, knowing we'd trace it."

"But he didn't call 911."

"No. He said Simon made him promise not to call anyone, just to turn the phone on."

"And of course he had to be loyal to his buddy and do what he asked."

"Of course."

Adam sighed. "All right, thanks."

Simon rolled over and threw up over the side of the bed. He couldn't remember when he'd felt this bad. Maybe when he'd had the flu last year. Maybe. The dull ache in his belly had moved back into the arena of severe pain. He pressed a hand to his side and let the tears flow. He wanted his mom. She would know what to do.

When he finished retching, he wiped his mouth on the comforter, not caring if Stuart got mad. At this point, he would welcome a fist to the face. At least it would be a pain he could deal with. This hurt in his stomach—

He looked around. Where was he? He didn't recognize the room. It was different than when he'd fallen asleep. Where had Stuart brought him now?

A shadow moved across the bed and he looked to the door. The man seemed vaguely familiar.

Simon blinked. "Where's my mom?"

"Call her." The phone landed on the bed beside him.

Simon grabbed the phone and looked at it. If he called her,

would he be putting her in danger? He lobbed it back. "I'm deaf, moron."

The man moved fast and was beside the bed before Simon could take another breath. Hard fingers twisted themselves into the collar of his shirt, knuckles pressing against his throat, cutting off his air. Fear, fast and furious, flowed through him. "Dial the number, kid, if you want to see tomorrow." The man shoved him away to stand over him and stare down at him.

Simon hauled in a deep breath and felt another wave of nausea ratchet through him. He gagged and the man nearly tripped in his haste to avoid getting spewed upon. Simon looked at him. "Who are you?"

"You mean you don't recognize your own uncle's partner?"

Recognition swept through him. "Joe."

"Yeah. Now that the introductions are over, I need your help."

Simon squinted. Without his hearing aids, he was having to rely solely on speech reading. His head pounded with the effort to concentrate. "What?"

Joe turned to the door.

Simon sighed. "If you're saying something you have to look at me, I'm deaf."

Joe turned, his irritation apparent. "I said, your mother has something I want. She and I are going to make a trade and we'll all live happily ever after, got it?"

Looking into the cold brown eyes, Simon felt sure the man didn't have a happily ever after in mind for him and his mother.

"Got it." He shot a glance toward the door. "Where's my uncle Stuart?"

"He's tied up with something right now. Quit yakking and start dialing."

Simon stared at the phone. He looked up. "I don't know her number." Again the man started for him and Simon held up his hands as though in surrender. "I really don't know. They . . . they gave her a new phone and I don't know what the number is. I don't, I swear." His words tumbled fast from his lips. He wished he could hear how he sounded because he wasn't sure he was making any sense to the man standing over him.

Without another word, Joe turned on his heel and left the room. Simon lay back against the pillow and groaned. No way was he calling his mom and leading her into danger. He knew the number. Had memorized it the moment she'd gotten it. But he wouldn't dial it.

He gathered his strength and rolled off the bed, walked down the hall, and saw a woman's back. She faced Joe. Joe faced Simon. Joe yelled something and the woman looked like she yelled back, her hand movements choppy and agitated. Joe grabbed the woman by the back of the hair and pulled her closer, talking the whole time. Simon wished he could see more of his lips. Then Joe let her go and this time Simon managed to see the words. "I have a plan and I need your help to make it work."

Simon sank to the floor and leaned his head back against the wall. He felt so weak, so tired, so sick. He closed his eyes and kept them closed. Even when someone shook his shoulder he didn't open his eyes to acknowledge he was awake. He felt a cool hand on his forehead. A smaller hand that probably belonged to the woman. He pretended it was his mom. Then rough hands grabbed him and carried him back to the bed.

They sat in front of Stuart's house, not moving, just thinking, planning. Adam knew the minutes counted and he had to make the right decisions. He prayed for divine guidance. "Does Stuart own any other property other than the house that we just left?" Adam asked.

Dani leaned her head back against the headrest. "No. Not that I know of. Stuart never talked to me about that kind of thing."

Adam called David. "Are you back at the office yet?"

"I am. Sitting here in front of the computer. What can I do for you?"

"Can you look into Stuart's real estate holdings? He's not at home, but I'm wondering if he's got another house somewhere."

"A lake house," Dani whispered.

"What?" Adam shot her a questioning look.

"The night Janessa was killed, Stuart came to the door and said he wanted to take me away, let me use his lake house to relax and get away from it all. I just remembered. What's the nearest lake?"

"Lake Bowen? Lake Greenwood? Lake Hartwell?" Summer suggested.

"Keowee?" Adam said.

"Hold on. I'm checking," David said. He would access a secure database used only by law enforcement personnel. Thanks to the governor, Operation Refuge also had permission to use it.

"Come on, David."

"Hey, I'm only as fast as this computer."

A few seconds later, David came back on the line. "He has a lake house at Lake Keowee."

"About an hour from here. What's the address?"

David gave it to him and Adam repeated it so Summer could put it in her GPS. Adam made a decision. He dialed another number.

"Ralph Thorn."

"This is Adam Buchanan. I need your help again."

"How?"

Adam filled him in. "I trust you, Ralph. Dani trusts you. We don't have anywhere else to turn for this one."

A slight pause that was only a brief two or three seconds, but felt like minutes. Finally Ralph agreed. "I'll call the Seneca police and have them head out to that address. I also have a friend, an agent, who's there for the weekend. I'll call him and have him scope out the house."

"Let us know as soon as you hear something."

"Will do."

"Wait a minute," Dani said. "Aren't we going out there?"

"No."

"Why not?"

"Because if he's there, the FBI will let us know and we can set up a plan of action to get Simon away from Stuart."

"Stuart is the FBI. He knows all of the plans of action. I need to talk to him. I need to be there. He'll listen to me. I'll beg, I'll lie. I'll do whatever it takes to get my son away from him."

Adam gripped her fingers. "I know you would, Dani. But trust me. This is the best way to handle this."

Tears swam in her eyes and he expected her to flat-out refuse. If she did, he had no idea how he was going to convince her to sit tight.

Her phone rang. She glanced at the screen, then up to him. "It's Stuart."

Dani answered the call and put it on speaker. "Stuart. Where are you? Where's Simon? How could you do this to your own nephew?"

"Dani, so good to hear your voice."

Dani froze. "You're not Stuart."

Adam's eyes slammed to hers. He lifted a brow. She shrugged.

"No. I'm afraid Stuart wasn't invited to this party."

"What party?"

"I have your son, Danielle Harding, and if you want him back, I'm going to have to insist you give me my plates."

"Your . . . what?"

"Plates. I'm sure you've seen the news and figured out the money you've been passing around is counterfeit. Very good counterfeit. Almost exactly like the real thing. I'm actually surprised someone caught it. But that's beside the point. Those plates were very expensive and I want them back."

Dani shot a look at Adam. He waved a hand encouraging her to keep talking. "Stuart had Simon. How do I know you have him now?"

"Hold on for a minute."

Heart in her throat, desperate to find her son, Dani held. Within seconds her phone beeped. The man came back on the line. "Check your messages. I'll call you back soon."

He hung up and she clicked over to the messages. And gasped. "No. Oh no. My baby. He really has him and he looks so sick."

Adam took the phone from her hand and looked at it. "We've got to find him fast."

"How many hours is it that hostages have before they're living on borrowed time?"

"Don't go there."

"I don't know where else to go, what to do, or how to do it. I'm completely dependent on you and your agency to get my son back." A slight pause. "And I don't like it."

Adam rubbed his chin. "We could not wait on Ralph. I could call in the FBI."

"They're probably the ones who have him," she snapped. She rubbed her eyes. "Sorry. No, I don't want to call in the FBI or any other law enforcement. I want to give them what they want, get my son, and move to an island in the Caribbean."

"Then we need to know where the counterfeit plates are."

"I have no idea."

Adam thought for a moment. "I'm willing to bet if we find out what that key from the safe goes to, we'll find the plates."

Her phone rang and she didn't bother waiting for it to finish the first ring. "I'm here. What's wrong with my son?"

"Nothing he won't recover from, I'm sure. Assuming you will cooperate."

"Of course." Somehow she found the strength to keep her voice steady. Somehow she found a way to press down the terror raging inside her. Simon needed her calm. He needed her to think. "Where are the plates?"

A moment of silence stretched her nerves to the breaking point.

"You have them," he said.

"No, I don't."

"They were in the safe."

"Trust me. We've gone through every item in that safe and there were no counterfeit plates in there."

"Then I suppose you'd better find them. Kurt would have left some kind of clue so they would be found. He left me a letter, you probably have one too. You have twelve hours and then I start sending your son to you piece by bloody piece."

The phone clicked off and she simply stared out the window barely controlling her need to scream.

Adam took the phone from her. She thought she heard him ask for David, then she shut her mind off to everything around her except for her prayers for her son.

32

"Let's go to the office," Adam told Summer. "We have the items from the bag. The key. Everything. The guy's right. If Kurt wanted those plates hidden, yet found when necessary, he would have left some kind of clue. Instructions. Something." He rubbed his eyes. "We need to go over that letter again."

She shivered and he knew she wasn't interested in seeing it again. Unfortunately she didn't have a choice.

"You said the letter didn't sound like Kurt."

"No, not really. Other than the fact that he would arrange to have me killed so we could be 'together forever.' Unfortunately, I can see him saying that. Followed by his stupid 'Gotcha.'" She shuddered. "It's gotten so I absolutely hate that word."

Summer drove with skill and speed and soon Adam found himself helping Dani out of the vehicle and into the office building.

Within minutes, they had the safe contents once again spread out on the conference room desk.

"I feel like we're spinning our wheels," Dani said.

"Give me the letter," Adam said.

David passed it to him. Adam looked at Dani. "Okay. Come look over my shoulder and tell me what jumps out at you as being out of character for Kurt."

Dani stepped behind him and again he was struck by his acute awareness of her as a woman. A very attractive woman. And a very scared mom.

She cleared her throat. "'You know my job is dangerous, it's never safe. I take risks everyday. Risks that ensure I'm making huge deposits in the bank for our future.' Okay, that right there."

"What?"

"That sentence about making huge deposits in the bank for our future. If he knew I'd be reading the letter, why talk about our future. He's talking in the present tense. Should he say, 'I was taking risks'? Or something? And the whole 'making huge deposits in the bank' thing. It just doesn't sound like him."

Adam nodded slowly. "Okay, that makes sense. What else?"

She swallowed. "'They're risks you'll never know about. One day those risks might get me killed. I'm not planning on it, of course, but you never know. One other thing. You may think I'm not aware of Stuart's obsession with you, but I am. Let me make myself clear, Dani. Only you hold the key to my heart.' Everything else up to this point sounds normal." She snorted. "Or abnormal, depending on how you look at it."

"Definitely abnormal," he agreed.

She took a deep breath and continued. "'There's no one else for me and there's no one else for you. He will never have you. Once Stuart finally realizes that, he will understand that I will always win and he will always lose. I'll see you soon, my darling. Kurt.' The rest of it sounds exactly like him."

"So let's isolate those two sentences. What do we have?"

"'I'm making huge deposits in the bank for our future,'" she said.

"And 'Only you hold the key to my heart.'"

"Why would he put those sentences in there? He'd never say that."

"And he knew that you would know that."

"He expected me to find this letter long before I did, didn't he?"

"Yes, I would think so."

She tightened her lips. "I'm glad I didn't."

Adam looked back at the two sentences. "So what words stand out to you?"

"Huge, deposits, bank, future, key, heart." She muttered each word. Then drew in a deep breath.

"What is it?"

"The bank that Kurt used. I think it was called Future America?"

Adam circled the word future. "So, we're dealing with a bank?"

"Not just any bank. The bank of Future America."

"Okay, I'm going to take a wild guess here and say that this key," he picked it up and held it out to her, "is a key to a safe-deposit box at the bank of Future America."

"But which one?"

"Whichever one is closest to your house."

"No." She shook her head slowly. "The one closest to his office."

Adam nodded. "All right, let's check that one out."

"But it's in Kurt's name. They won't let me in."

David cleared his throat. "You're assuming it's in Kurt's name. What if he put it in your name?"

"But wouldn't I have to sign some papers? I think I'd remember."

Adam nodded again. "Let's just see what happens when we request to get into the box." He looked at Dani. "I have all of your old identification that you would need."

His phone rang and he answered it on the first ring. "Hi, Ralph."

"We found your man."

"Stuart?"

"Yes."

"And?"

"He's dead. Bullet got him right between the eyes."

Hearing that Stuart was dead registered, but emotionally she felt numb. All she could think about was her son. Her heart ached with a fear she'd never felt before, but right now she had it under control. Being proactive, doing something to help get him back, helped tremendously. Earlier, waiting for the team to come up with a plan had nearly had her climbing the walls.

Adam retrieved her old identification documents and she dyed her hair back to her original color so it just looked like she'd gotten an extreme haircut. She ditched the glasses and dressed in khakis and a baby blue sweater Summer had unearthed from somewhere in her office.

When she walked into the conference room to announce she was ready, she found the team around the table, heads bent, hands clasped. Adam glanced up and motioned for her to join them. She walked over and took his hand and joined her heart to his as he prayed aloud. "Lord, we ask you to protect Simon. He appears to be a sick kid, God, and needs your healing hand. Let us get him back safe." Dani felt tears slip down her cheeks as she listened and prayed right along with him.

After each person petitioned God for safety, protection, wisdom, and supernatural protection for Simon, they ended the prayer with a unanimous "Amen."

Dani wouldn't say she felt peace when they were done, but she felt stronger, ready to face whatever was coming and deal with it head-on. She was ready to get her son back and didn't care what she had to do to accomplish that. Having God in her corner brought comfort.

"Ready to go?"

"Yes, please."

"I'm going to be right with you every step of the way."

"Do you think they'll be watching?"

"I have no way of knowing. Probably. We've left your cell phone on. Whoever it was that called has your number, and if he's FBI, he'll be tracking it."

She pulled in a deep breath. "Good."

Adam narrowed his eyes at her. "Good? Why? You're not thinking of doing anything stupid, are you?"

"Of course not. I just want my son."

"We tried to trace the number that called you, but it was encrypted, no way to track it."

She nodded. "I'm not surprised."

"Your phone, however, is traceable."

"You did that on purpose, didn't you?"

He gave her a slight smile. "Yes."

"With the intention of being able to track me if you needed to or were you planning on setting some kind of trap?"

"No trap. I just wanted to be able to keep up with you should the need arise."

They climbed into the SUV and Adam took the wheel. Isaac and David followed behind. Adam drove to the bank and pulled into the parking lot.

Dani shoved open the passenger door and waited for Adam to come around. He looked her in the eye. "Are you sure you can do this?"

"I can do anything if it means getting Simon back."

"He could have been bluffing. He might be waiting for you in the bank. Keep your eyes open."

"I will."

"All right then." He took her hand and helped her from the vehicle. She made a beeline for the glass doors. Adam kept pace with her, covering her from behind. "I think you're safe for the moment."

"Why do you say that?"

"Because whoever wants those plates doesn't want you dead."

"But as soon as I give them what they want, they'll no longer have a use for me, will they?"

"True."

"And Simon? Would they kill a child?" She coughed on the knot that formed in her throat.

"I don't know, Dani."

"They would, wouldn't they?"

"Right now, Simon's still alive. Let's figure out how to keep him that way."

"Yes. Let's do that."

She took a deep breath and stepped inside the warmth of the bank, praying the cold pit of terror wouldn't take over and render her incapable of saving her son.

Joe lowered the binoculars. "They're in the bank. Text Dani the message."

Butterfly sat beside him. Simon lay on the backseat. The kid was so weak with whatever virus he had, Joe hadn't bothered to tie him up. And gagging him would only cause him to asphyxiate on his own vomit. He just hoped the kid didn't puke in the car. That would really put him in a bad mood.

Butterfly took his phone and texted Dani.

We're watching u. We have Simon. Get out of the bank alone. Any dumb moves and your kid dies.

Joe held the gun against Simon's temple and Butterfly snapped the picture while the kid trembled, eyes wide, face pale.

Once Butterfly had hit Send, Joe lowered the gun.

Butterfly opened the door. "I've got something to do. I'll meet you at the warehouse."

"Where are you going? I might need help with the kid."

Butterfly glanced in the backseat. "I think you can handle it." She slammed the door and walked across the street to the Sassafrass Boutique. A known place to acquire high-quality drugs. Joe gritted his teeth. He'd thought she'd kicked that habit.

He sighed and settled in for the wait.

Dani glanced at her phone when it vibrated. The text message notification zipped across her screen. She'd look at it in a minute. Right now, Adam was leading her to an official-looking bank representative.

The woman looked up and smiled. "How may I help you?"

Adam took the lead and she checked her phone. She held back her cry with effort. Adam was saying, "We're here to retrieve the contents of a safe-deposit box."

"Certainly. I'm Heather Gillespie and I'm happy to help you. May I have your ID and key?"

With a shaky hand, Dani handed over the items. Mrs. Gillespie scanned the picture and looked Dani over twice. "That's a pretty drastic change."

Dani gave a self-conscious laugh. "I know. It was a spur-of-the moment thing. I'm letting it grow back out."

Mrs. Gillespie clicked a few strokes on the computer keyboard. "Glad to have you back in, Mrs. Harding." She stood. "Follow me."

Dani gaped at Adam. "I've never been here," she whispered.

"Kurt was FBI, Dani, he could do a lot of things. Getting a safe-deposit box in your name probably wasn't real hard." He glanced at the woman walking at a jaunty pace just ahead of them.

"Getting a fake ID and someone to impersonate you wouldn't be any big deal."

"I can't believe Kurt. This is just insane."

"Sounds like Kurt might have just had a little insane in him."

Her mind on the message, Dani gave an absent nod and stopped when Mrs. Gillespie pulled open a large steel door. She stared at the screen of her phone, the text message sending her heart into overdrive.

"You all right?" Adam asked.

"Yes, just hoping they'll call." It wasn't a lie. She desperately wanted to see her son safe.

"Right this way." Mrs. Gillespie led them to box number 421 and inserted her key. She motioned to Dani. "Mrs. Harding?"

Dani placed the key into the hole and twisted. Mrs. Gillespie removed the box and carried it to the room at the far end where they would be able to have privacy in case anyone else came in. "Take as much time as you need, Mrs. Harding." She turned and left them.

"Do you want me to open it?" Adam asked.

"No." She tried to steady her trembling fingers and couldn't quite get them to cooperate. The text message played over and over in her mind. She felt Adam's hands on her shoulders and turned to look him in the eye.

"You can do this," he said. "You're a strong woman, Dani. You've come a long way. You're a great mom and your son needs you."

She nodded. "You're right. You're very right about the fact that he needs me." She lifted the lid and blinked. "It's another box."

Adam pulled it out and set it on the table. While his attention was on the box, she texted,

?

A simple question mark, but whoever was on the other side of the conversation would understand.

The immediate reply told Dani it had been ready to send before she even asked the question.

Bring everything. Pull the fire alarm in the hall and go out the door on ur left. A taxi will be waiting. Get in. He knows the address.

Adam looked up. "It's got a lock that can only be opened with the right sequence of numbers."

"Then how do I know I've got the plates?"

"We'll take it back to the office and I'll bust it open."

"Right. Okay. Here, will you put it in the bag?"

"Sure."

As he did, she checked her phone again. "I just want this to be over. I want to hold my baby in my arms again."

"You will. Let's go." He took the bag and she placed a hand over his.

"I want it."

"It's kind of heavy."

"Not as heavy as my heart. Let me have it please."

He passed it to her with a quizzical look. "All right."

She pressed the bag with the box to her chest and wrapped both arms around it. Should she tell him about the message? "Adam—"

"Yes?"

A picture of the gun against Simon's temple flashed across her mind. "Nothing. Let's go."

He led the way.

Dani followed behind, looking for the fire alarm. As she walked beside him, she glanced side to side, searching, her brain spinning. Tell him, her fear whispered. Agony scorched her. She couldn't.

The red-and-white box on the wall was just ahead. She moved closer to the wall until her shoulder almost brushed it.

Almost there.

Three more steps.

And pull.

33

The alarm startled the woman in front of him so much, she stumbled. Adam grabbed her, steadied her. "Are you all right?"

"Yes, I am. Thank you." She patted her hair back into place. Adam turned to check on Dani.

Only she wasn't there. "Dani!" He spun in a one-eighty. Two doors. One to the left, one to the right. "Which way out of the building?" he yelled over the screech of the alarm.

"There." She pointed. "Where did she go? Why did she run out that door?"

"I don't know." He bolted through the door and stopped, looked one way, then the next. He got on his phone.

David answered.

"I lost Dani."

"You what?"

Adam winced. "The fire alarm went off and she disappeared in the chaos."

"Does she have the contents of the safe-deposit box?"

"Yes."

David sighed. "They got to her."

Adam wanted to pound his head against a wall. "It was too

easy. I should have suspected something when she wanted to hold the box."

"She decided to go out on her own."

"The only reason she would do that is if they threatened Simon."

"How would they get ahold of her?"

"The phone I gave her. The guy has that number." He sighed. "I let her keep the phone and answer it to give her a sense of control. She needed it."

"And now he's contacted her without you knowing it."

"It looks like it." Adam ran toward the end of the street, looked one way, then the next. No sign of Dani. He never would have thought she had it in her to go off on her own.

"Do we have that number?"

"Yes. I've got it."

"I'll get a trace on it. The first thing he'll do is take her phone, though."

"I know. Do it anyway." He blew out a breath. "Where would he take them?"

"I don't know. We don't even know who has her."

Adam's heart constricted. "I know." His phone beeped with an incoming call. "I've got to take this. I'll get back to you. Let me know if you get anything on the phones."

"Will do."

Adam switched lines and headed for the front of the bank where Isaac would be waiting on him. "Hello?"

"Ralph Thorn here."

"Hi, Ralph, I'm kind of busy at the moment."

"You're not too busy for this."

"What do you have?" He climbed into the passenger seat and switched his phone to speaker so Isaac could hear.

"I hand delivered that video to one of our lab technicians. I trust him implicitly. He's my son-in-law."

"And?"

"He managed to ID the man next to the door on the left."

"Who is it?"

"Special Agent Joseph Duncan."

Shocked, Adam looked at Isaac. "Go toward East Main," he said. "See if you can spot her." To Ralph, he said, "Stuart Harding's partner?"

"Yeah. I decided to chance it and took the video to the Special Agent in Charge. He was . . . well, let's just say outraged is putting it mildly. I've never seen him so furious. And embarrassed that these guys are a part of his team. He vouched for Kurt's promotion. Word is filtering down that he didn't follow up on some previous complaints about Kurt and now his own job is on the line."

"Is it really going to matter?"

"In the long run? Probably not. He'll clean house, but he'll still be a part of OPR's investigation. Too many people know what's happened now. The only thing he can do now is be aggressive and work hard to arrest everyone involved and hope that'll count in the long run."

"That's good to hear, but this thing may go higher than those in that video."

"I know that. I've still got a copy."

"And I sent a copy to the governor early this morning," Adam said. "I don't know if she's seen it yet."

Silence. "That was probably a wise thing to do."

"I guess we'll see. Right now, Dani is missing."

"Missing?" Ralph's voice sharpened. "You've lost her as well as Simon?"

"Unfortunately, Dani decided to take matters into her own hands. She pulled the fire alarm at the bank and bolted out of a side door. They must have had a car waiting for her. I need access to the security video footage. And if I give you a number, can you get me the content of the text messages?"

A sigh. "I need both phone numbers. I'll have to get a subpoena."

"Dani and Simon don't have much time. At the very least, Simon's a missing child. I would think this would qualify as exigent circumstances. We should be able to get the information we need from the wireless carrier immediately. They'll accept the subpoena later, so put a rush on it, will you?"

"I'll do my best."

Adam gave him the numbers even while his eyes roamed the streets for Dani's familiar face and form. He probed each car they passed.

"I'll need some time," Ralph said. "I'll call you if and when I have something."

"Any idea where we can find Joe Duncan?"

"We're looking for him now. If you find him first, let me know, will you?"

"Right."

Adam let out a breath. "Okay. We're running out of time, Ralph."

"Yes. You are."

Adam looked at Isaac. "Go back to the bank. I want a look at the surveillance video." His next call was to the governor to request her cooperation and ability to expedite everything.

———

Dani sat in the back of the car and held Simon's head on her lap, stroking his flushed cheek. His eyes had flown wide when he'd seen her and he'd started crying. She'd grabbed him and held him close even while her heart stuttered in fear, not only with the danger they were in from Joe, but from the fact that he looked really ill. "He's sick, Joe. He needs a doctor."

Joe snorted. "Nobody needs a doctor. I've given him some medicine."

"What did you give him?" she cried.

"Calm down. It was just some ibuprofen. He said his stomach hurt."

Miraculously, Simon was now asleep, leaning against her. At least she hoped it was sleep and not that he'd passed out. "Why are you doing this?"

"Money."

Dani tried to settle on what to say. There was no way she was going to give him some speech about the sanctity of human life. She knew her words would fall on deaf ears. More deaf than Simon would ever be.

So now it was up to her to get them out of this. "So what are you going to do with us now?"

"We're going back to my office—er, my other office—and I will decide what to do with you then."

"You're going to kill us, aren't you?" she whispered.

He glanced in the rearview mirror at her and she read the truth in his eyes.

Dani cleared her throat. "Okay, so then you won't mind telling me what this is all about."

"Like I said, money."

"Whose money?"

"Kurt's. He wrote a new will and left everything to me. The will is in the safe-deposit box. The plates should be there too. I've already got a buyer for them."

"So this isn't about the murder of Trennan Eisenberg?"

"Yes. Actually it is. Trennan was the one who acquired the plates. He'd been paid well. Then he decided to extort more money in order to hand them over. I didn't like the idea too much and neither did my partners."

274

"So you killed him?"

"Only after he told us where the plates were. He knew he was going to die anyway. He gave up the plates so we'd leave his wife and kids alone."

"And you really left them alone?"

"Yeah. She was clueless."

Dani barked a laugh. "So was I."

"No, you were spending the counterfeit money, you saw the murder. You were far from clueless."

He had a point. "So why did Kurt have the plates?"

"He got them from Trennan. When he got back, he put them in his safe and ordered the man's execution."

"Which Ryan Blanchard carried out."

"Yes."

Dani trembled hard at the complete lack of emotion in Joe's voice. "Kurt moved them, though. The plates weren't in the safe."

"So I found out when I broke into your house and opened the safe. Stuart said you'd cleaned it out the day you decided to run." A muscle jumped in his jaw. "Guess you didn't put the stuff back."

"I didn't." They rode in silence a few more miles.

Adam watched the security video. "Rewind it." Mrs. Gillespie complied. "Zoom in on Dani's phone, will you?"

"Of course." She did.

Adam glanced at Isaac. "See how she's holding the phone? It's aimed toward the camera. She left the phone face up on purpose."

"So we could see the messages."

"She got in a taxi. Let's see the outside footage."

Mrs. Gillespie clicked a few more keys and maneuvered to the camera that would show the door Dani exited.

"Back it up to the time she ran out the door."

She did.

"There," Adam pointed. "She's going out the door and getting in the cab. She's gone within seconds."

Isaac let out a sigh. "She may not even be alive at this point."

Adam couldn't speak for a few seconds. He finally found his voice. "We're going to go on the assumption that they're alive and waiting for us to come rescue them."

"I know," Isaac agreed, his voice soft.

Adam was on the phone to the taxi company before Isaac even finished the two words. "I need to know who's driving the taxi with the license plate number GSO049."

"Why do you need to know?"

Instead of getting angry, Adam explained the situation, adding, "If you could just get me that information, you might help save a woman's life."

A pause. "Seriously?"

"Never more serious in my life."

"Give me one second to pull up the screen on my computer." Adam heard the clicks in the background. He wanted to be standing over the guy's shoulder so he could see what he was looking at. "His name is Henry Reston. If you'll hold, I'll try to raise him on the radio."

"I'll hold."

Again, time seemed to crawl, but in reality took only about sixty seconds. The man came back on the line. "He said he dropped your woman at six-oh-four Persian Avenue."

"That's only about five blocks from here."

"Said she got in another car."

"Another car. Can you ask him what it looked like?"

"I asked him that, seeing as how this woman is in trouble. He said it was a white Beemer. Four door."

"He didn't happen to get the license plate, did he?"

"Nope, but he said the woman acted scared and jumpy, then saw a kid in the backseat and grabbed him in a big hug."

Adam sent up a prayer of thanksgiving. Simon was alive. The man spoke again. "He actually followed them to a building downtown."

"You're kidding. Where?"

The man gave Adam the address.

"Could he identify the driver?"

"I don't know, I'll ask him."

"Thanks for your help. You and Henry may have just saved this woman's life."

"No problem." A pause. "Hey, will you call me if she's all right? My name's Scooter."

"Of course, Scooter."

"If she ain't, don't call."

"Yeah. I'll be calling you real soon."

"Praying it's so."

Adam hung up and called Ralph. Thankfully the man seemed to keep his phone nearby. "Ralph, I've got a witness who says he saw them take Dani to this address." He rattled it off. "Can you get a team out there?"

"On the way."

Isaac looked at Adam. "You should be a detective."

Adam shrugged. "You know I was a cop before I was with the marshals. I learned how to run down a lead." He grabbed his coat and shook Mrs. Gillespie's hand. "Thank you so much."

"Of course. I do hope everything turns out all right."

"It's going to take more than hope to make this turn out all right."

34

Joe had parked the car and led them up the steps of a large farmhouse. Several acres of land surrounded the house out back with trees bordering the land. Inside, the place had been gutted and gave new meaning to the term "open floor plan." Dani looked around and realized the main area had been made into some kind of office. The kitchen opened into the den area. Supporting beams held up the ceiling. Two rooms had been left at the end of the hallway. Stairs at the end of the den disappeared into a second floor. She guessed the entire area to be somewhere around five or six thousand square feet. It looked more like a warehouse with a kitchen than a house.

Joe pointed to a small table and chairs in the kitchen breakfast nook. "Sit over there and keep quiet." Without another look in her direction, he carried the locked black case she'd pulled from the safe-deposit box to a larger conference-sized table that sat in the middle of the room.

She finally noticed the smells. Ink. Smoke. Alcohol and ammonia? Dani gripped Simon's hand. His flushed cheeks and glassy eyes worried her. Somehow, she had to find a way out.

Simon let go of her hand, bypassed the table and chairs, and slid down the wall, holding his stomach. He leaned his head against his knees.

"Oh God, help me, please," she whispered. "Help me help my son." Joe still turned his weapon in her direction every few seconds, but he knew as well as she did she wasn't going to do anything that put Simon at risk. Any more than he already was.

Dani ignored the chairs and went to sit beside Simon. He resisted her efforts to pull him into her arms and she let him be. He was miserable and in pain. He gave her a small shove. "Sit in the chair, you'll be more comfortable." Dani eyed him. "Please. Go. Just do it, will you?"

Dani moved to sit in the chair. If it would bring him some kind of peace of mind, she'd do it.

A door opened and she looked up as the woman entered the room. Dani gaped. "Jenny?"

Joe smirked. "Dani, meet Butterfly."

Jenny gave her that sweet smile that had often brought Dani comfort in the past year. Now it made her skin crawl as though she had a million tiny ants just beneath the surface of her skin. "Hello, Dani." She glared at Joe. "You left me."

"You didn't give me a choice."

Dani's gaze jumped between Joe and the woman she'd called a friend. "I don't understand."

Jenny shrugged and moved closer, fingering her necklace. Five black beads, one white and five red. "I tried to get you to leave Kurt, but you just wouldn't do it."

Dani was having trouble processing, so she simply stared. This time the woman she thought was her friend, her best friend, sighed. "The women's shelter pamphlet?"

"Oh." She frowned. "Why did you want me to leave Kurt?"

"Because we were much better suited for one another than you and him."

While her fear wanted to swallow her, anger also started to rear its head. "I won't argue with that. And for the record, you know I tried to leave him. I told you what happened."

"Yes, Kurt and I had quite the laugh over it. Who do you think warned him you were planning to run?"

Dani couldn't breathe. The betrayal was just too much. "Then why give me the pamphlet? Why help me set all that up if you were going to just tell him? He almost killed me and Simon!"

Jenny frowned back. "Exactly."

Dani flinched. "But . . . why?" She just wanted answers. Her life had taken such a twisted turn, she wasn't sure she could think straight.

"Because Kurt had what I wanted. Money, position, power, respect, everything. If you were gone, I would move in to comfort the grieving man. I'm very good at comforting men and convincing them that they're not bad people, just misunderstood. And they're very good at being grateful and taking care of me." Her expression darkened. "Except Stuart. Stuart just wouldn't let go of his fascination with you. It was maddening." She turned her sultry smile on Joe. "But Joe knows my true worth, don't you?"

He winked at her and turned back to the box.

Dani was stunned. All fear had left her. Numbness had set in. How had she surrounded herself with such deviant people? She hadn't. She'd married one, and while he'd isolated her on the one hand, his actions had brought these people into her life.

She couldn't help compare her past life—life with Kurt—with her present. Adam, Summer, Isaac, Tori, David—

If she and Simon somehow got out of this, she would make sure they surrounded themselves with people who loved others rather than people who loved self and used others. She looked into Jenny's eyes and wondered why she'd never noticed the emptiness before.

LYNETTE EASON

Because she hadn't been looking. Because she'd been so grateful to have someone who seemed to care, someone she could call friend. So desperate she hadn't looked beneath the surface. Her stomach twisted. And part of her just wanted to give up. To throw her hands up and declare herself done. She wanted to stop fighting and let them win because she was almost too exhausted to care anymore.

"Who used whom?" she asked.

Jenny lifted a brow. "What do you mean?"

"Stuart, Kurt, and now Joe. Who's using whom?" Jenny frowned as though the question was beyond her. Dani sighed. "You moved into my neighborhood. Was that just a fluke?"

"Of course not. After Stuart got me out of the Bloods, he set me up in that house." She closed her eyes as the mere memory brought her joy. "I'd never seen anything so fancy. At least, not that wasn't on television. But to live there? Oh my, what a dream. Fancy house, perfect man? I was set." Her jaw tightened and she opened her eyes. "That is until I found out why he wanted me there."

"To spy on me."

"Yes," she hissed. "I was in love with him, I would have done *anything* for him, and all he wanted from me was to spy on you." She sighed. "So, I figured it was some kind of phase he was going through. You were married to his brother. He'd get over it, right? I'd give him time and he'd realize he was wasting his time." She shook her head. "Nope. Then I met Kurt and figured out who the alpha male was in *that* relationship."

"So you moved in on Kurt."

"He didn't mind." She gave Dani a wicked smile. A smile so evil it made Dani sick.

"And now Joe?"

"Yeah. Once he told me about the money and how I could

help him keep up with you through Stuart, I couldn't turn him down." She glanced over her shoulder. "What's taking so long? Open it up already, would you?"

Joe shot her an irritated glance. "I'm kind of in the middle of making sure the buyers are on the way."

Jenny sauntered away as though Dani had just bored her completely.

Simon shifted beside her. She pressed a hand to his head to get his attention, but realized he was already looking up. "Can you hang on just a little longer? We're going to get out of this. Adam will find us," she signed.

He nodded and did the same. "It just hurts. Bad."

Dani tried to slow her racing thoughts. She needed to get to a phone. "We may be on our own, Simon. We may have to rescue ourselves."

He studied her for a long time, then gave a slow nod.

"Hey," Joe said. "Butterfly, the buyers will be here any minute. Let's get this done."

"How can you do this?" Dani bit her lip, then blurted, "Did you arrange to have Kurt killed so you could keep all the money?"

Joe snorted and moved to stand in front of her. "No, I didn't even know about his money until I got his letter."

Dani frowned. "What letter?"

Joe reached into his pocket and pulled out a piece of paper. He held it up and began to read.

"'Hey Joe, guess this is it, man. I guess I've gone and done something stupid or someone has betrayed me and killed me. Either way, that leaves me in quite a quandary. You see, I may be dead, but my wife is still alive. She and Simon. And that just can't be. So, I've got a plan, but I'm going to need you to implement it. You've bugged me for three years about how you could pay me back for saving your hide, not once, but twice. Well, here's how you can make things even. I want Dani and Simon to join me in the hereafter. Wherever that may be. My idiot brother has been lusting after my wife since the day he met her. There's no way that's going to happen. So, yeah. I'm asking you to kill her. Sorry to be so blunt, but I've never been one to mince words.'"

Dani began to shake, the shivers racking her.

Joe frowned. "What's wrong with you?"

"I'm terrified and cold and worried sick about my son. And now you're reading a letter from my husband asking you to kill me and Simon. It's . . . just . . . a . . . reaction. Keep going." She clasped her hands together and prayed Simon wasn't paying attention.

Joe kept reading. "'You may be asking what's in it for you. Here it is. I know you need money. Well, I've got lots of it. Plus a house. In a safe-deposit box is a new will, notarized, signed and witnessed by my lawyer. Dani doesn't know about this one. But in the will, I leave you everything to the tune of two million dollars. This will is dated after the will that gives Dani everything, so the old will is null and void. It's all legal. No court of law will be able to find anything wrong with it. You ought to be able to get out of that trailer and take care of your sister just fine. Or gamble it away. I don't really care just as long as Dani's dead. And you can kill Simon too, if he's in the way.'"

Dani thought she was going to be sick. So this was how the man who'd promised to love, honor, and cherish her had arranged to have her killed even after his death.

Joe didn't look up as he finished the letter.

"'The combination for the box with the will and some other things you can have—yeah, the plates are in there—is my birthday, October 3rd. 1-0-3. Got it? Don't let me down, Joe. I'm counting on you.'"

Joe folded the letter and looked at Dani and Simon. Dani was stunned. Her heart beat in her chest like a trapped bird. Her breath felt short and she wondered if she'd pass out. No, she couldn't. She had to get Simon away from these people. "What are you going to do?"

"First, I'm going to open the box." He placed it on the table and spun the numbers. She heard the soft click. Joe gave a triumphant smile and opened the lid. With a reverence that made her nauseous, he lifted three wrapped rectangular shapes from their resting place, one by one and set them on the table. Then he pulled a manila envelope out. When he had the flap open, he removed the papers from the envelope. "The new will. Shall I read it?"

"Please don't do this," Dani whispered.

"Too late, Dani. I owe Kurt to fulfill his last wish."

"Not to mention collecting a lot of money," she spat.

He shrugged. "Yes, that too. I'm looking forward to spending the rest of my days on a small private beach." He looked down at the paper, tossed aside a blank top sheet, and gaped.

"What is it?" Butterfly moved in close and looked over his shoulder to read. "What is this?" she cried and snatched the paper from his hand.

Dani stood, her trembling finally under control. "What is it?"

"This! This is what it is!" She shoved the paper at Dani who read it.

"Gotcha!"

35

"As soon as we know where they are, will you be ready to roll?" Adam asked.

"We'll be ready." Ralph Thorn barked orders on the other end of the phone, then came back on line to Adam. "The address the taxi driver gave us checked out, but they weren't there. We've got video footage from traffic cams showing us the vehicle, but Joe's no dummy. He'd know we'd track him with the cameras."

"Then what is he doing? Is it a trap?" Adam's belly clenched as his mind scrambled to figure out what Joe was doing. "He's luring us with the cameras while going behind the scenes somewhere? Dani and Simon don't have time for us to be following a wild-goose chase."

"I'm open to suggestions," Ralph said.

"You know Joe. Where would he go?" Adam asked.

Ralph sighed. "I *thought* I knew Joe. Obviously not." He paused. "Wait a minute."

"You thought of something."

"Yeah."

"What?"

"I'm checking something."

Adam waited, impatient, breath whooshing through his lungs, desperate to find Dani and Simon. "Well?"

"The white Beemer was stolen and has been abandoned. But Joe's car is on the move."

Adam felt a surge of excitement. "He's in his car and you can track it."

"As long as he doesn't disable the GPS in it."

"He doesn't know we're on to him, though, so he'd have no reason to disable it."

"Unless he's just being extra cautious, and let's hope that's not the case."

"Hey!" Jenny's yell brought Dani's head up. "Where's Simon?"

"What?" Dani blinked. She swiveled to look where she'd last seen Simon.

His empty spot mocked her. Her heart lifted. He'd taken advantage of the adults' distraction and slipped off. "Oh Simon," she whispered. *Oh please God, get him to safety.*

She stood and Joe shoved her back into her chair. "That's what I get for being nice." He shot a dark look at Jenny. "Find that kid. He can ID us."

Dani ran to the nearest window. "Go, Simon, go."

A hard hand jerked her away. "Get outside and find that kid," Joe yelled at Jenny.

With a murderous glare toward Dani, Jenny bolted through the door. Joe threw Dani back into the chair, grabbed the paper he'd thought was going to be Kurt's will, and shoved it at her. "What's this? Gotcha? Gotcha? Where's the will?"

Dani pushed the paper away. "How am I supposed to know? I didn't have anything to do with this. I just wanted to live my life with my son and forget the last twelve years ever happened. You and Kurt dragged me into this!"

Joe grabbed his head and pressed. "I can't believe this. Kurt wouldn't do this to me," he roared. "He wouldn't!"

"Why not?" Dani said quietly. She stared at him. "Why not you?"

Joe froze and stared at her. "What do you mean?"

"Kurt picked on anyone he considered weaker than himself. If you let him know about a weakness, he would exploit that."

"Just like he did with Faraday," Joe whispered.

Dani knew he was talking to himself, but she answered him anyway. "What?"

"Nothing. Nothing." Then he pulled his gun and started shooting.

Adam heard the gunshots as he pulled to a stop at the base of the drive. A rambling house loomed before him. Ralph pulled in behind him, along with other law enforcement officers who'd been ready to move when called. Adam shoved open his door and pulled his weapon, prayers on his lips. *God, please don't let them be dead. Please.*

He moved toward the house, hunched over and running. David moved beside him. Isaac branched out around to the side of the house. FBI agents followed, weapons ready, fanning around the house.

Adam knew the SWAT team was setting up, a hostage negotiator was on the way, and pretty soon Adam knew he would be relegated to the backseat when the ASAC, possibly even the SAC, arrived and took over.

He had to get Dani and Simon out of there before that happened. Letting this turn into a hostage situation and dragging it out with negotiations that would go nowhere wasn't going to work. Not in this case, not with Joseph Duncan.

Joe had inside information. He knew the game plan and playing by the rules wouldn't work with him. Joe would expect them to do so and would figure he could outsmart them in some way. He wasn't aware of Adam's feelings for Dani and Simon. He didn't know about the desperation racing through his veins.

And Adam planned to use that to his advantage.

Dani stayed in her chair as Joe paced and muttered in front of her. His uncontrolled anger had resulted in a wild spray of bullets that littered the far wall, but thankfully he hadn't turned the weapon in her direction. Her gaze flitted from one corner of the house to the other, probing the shadows, wondering where her son had gone and how he was managing to be so quiet.

Simon hadn't been outside. At least she hadn't seen him from the window. When she'd encouraged him to "go," she'd been praying out loud. Joe had misunderstood and thought she'd actually seen Simon. But her whispered prayer had sent Jenny outside. Now she just had one of them to deal with. The kitchen was bare. Nothing stood out to her that could be used as a weapon.

A shadowy figure slipped past the window and Dani blinked. Stared. The blinds were open just enough to let a bit of light in. With one eye on Joe, who now spoke into his cell phone and had his back to her, she reached for the rod and gave it a twist. The kitchen brightened, but Joe didn't appear to notice.

She looked out and saw nothing.

No more shadows, no Simon. Just a vast expanse of rolling brown land.

Joe grew even more agitated, spitting and cursing. He'd unwrapped the plates. Or what were supposed to be the plates. Instead, he'd found bricks engraved with the words "Gotcha." Just like the paper.

She thought he might just have a stroke. Dani stood, the door across the room her goal.

He whirled and caught her in the face with a backhanded punch. She went down, ears ringing, head throbbing.

"Stay there!"

Pain spiked through her head and she lifted a hand to wipe a trickle of blood from her lip. Anger and fear boiled within her.

"Find the kid and find him now!" He slapped the phone onto the counter and glowered at her. "I need to know where those plates are."

"I have no idea."

He swung his weapon around and aimed it at her head. "Then I have no more need of you."

Adam's face appeared in the window behind Joe. For a moment, she thought she might be hallucinating.

Adam had his weapon raised, looking like he desperately wanted to pull the trigger. But she saw his problem immediately. She was in the direct line of fire. If Joe moved unexpectedly at the wrong moment, Dani would take the bullet.

Then a high-pitched squeal reached her ears the same time it reached Joe's. He spun. Adam disappeared.

Dani bolted to her feet. "Fine! Then just shoot me! Just do it! I don't even care anymore."

Joe spun back. "What is that?"

The squeal continued and Dani felt her heart stop. Simon. And he wouldn't realize his hearing aid was whistling. "How would I know?" Joe started toward the sound and Dani followed. "What if I know where the plates are?"

He spun back. A cruel grin crossed his lips. "Do you?"

"Maybe." The whistling continued. Dani nodded. "But you have to let me get Simon some help first."

"Not a chance. I'm going to kill that kid when I see him. I don't need him, just you."

"Then you might as well kill me too. I'll never tell you where they are." She spoke the words with deadly intent. Her eyes never left Joe's and he blinked. Then swore. "Where is he?" he shouted.

"Where's Jenny?" Dani countered.

"Good question." He got on his phone and Dani waited, tensed and ready to move as soon as she got the opportunity.

Jenny didn't answer and Joe let out another string of curses that blistered her ears.

She moved toward the door. "I'll take you to the plates, let's go."

"This isn't the way this was supposed to go down," he muttered.

The whistling never stopped.

Joe growled and moved toward the sound, his determined footsteps slamming terror for Simon into her very soul.

She started to follow and stopped when Simon stepped from a room around the corner, finger to his lips. Simon grabbed her hand and they raced for the door.

Dani threw it open and came face-to-face with Jenny.

And the gun now jabbed into her midsection.

Adam froze. He'd seen Dani, but not Simon. Had wanted to take the shot, but had hesitated. If he missed, if Joe moved, the bullet would have gone straight into Dani. He couldn't take the chance.

And then Joe had whirled and Adam had to duck to avoid being seen. The shots fired spurred him on. He was out of time. He raced up the front porch steps and kicked the door in. It slammed back against the wall. He went in low, gun held ready. He heard Isaac behind him. "Clear." The SWAT team flowed through the house, clearing it. The door to his right slowly opened toward him. He moved to the side and waited. No one on the other side. Someone had pulled the door shut and it hadn't latched. Now, unbalanced, it swung back open.

He nodded to Isaac, who moved opposite him. Adam reached for the knob and pulled it. MP5s pointed toward the now fully open door.

Adam motioned for the other cops to go around him. The gunshots had come from the back. The large open area stood empty. Three officers moved to the back. Adam went for the stairs.

At the top, he rounded the corner and came face-to-face with Joseph Duncan. The man stood, weapon in hand, eyes flitting wildly from one window to the next.

Adam kept his weapon trained on Joe. "It's over, man. Don't make me pull this trigger."

"It's not over."

"Of course it's over. Cops are all over this place. You of all people know how this is going to play out." He held his gun steady on Joe's chest. "Now put the weapon down."

"I can't go to prison. I'll rot there."

"And I can't let you go."

Joe moved the barrel of his weapon to his chin in one smooth move. "I'd rather be dead."

"No! Don't do it, Joe. That's not the answer."

Joe met his gaze. Adam lunged.

Joe pulled the trigger.

Adam hit his knees and rolled. His heart heavy, he had to push Joe aside and focus on Dani. He whirled back through the house and bolted back to Isaac's side. "What do you have?"

Isaac held up a mirror. "From what we can see, there's a woman with a gun on Dani and Simon."

Dani felt hopelessness sweep over her. So close. They'd been so close. The back door had been almost within reach. She'd cried out for Adam, and instead, Jenny had shoved the barrel of the gun into her stomach. "Back, get back. Move."

Dani had done as ordered, keeping Simon behind her. Her son who trembled and shook. Jenny shoved them through another door, down the stairs, and into the basement. Where was Joe? What had he been shooting at?

In the basement, Simon slumped to the floor and placed his head against his knees. Dani went to him and placed her hands on his shoulders. He looked up. "I'm sorry," he signed.

She stroked his cheek and watched Jenny from the corner of her eye. The woman paced.

"What are you doing?" Dani asked. "The cops are here. It's over."

Jenny shook the gun in her direction. "It's not over until I say it's over."

Would this never end?

Dani heard running footsteps above. "Adam!"

"Shut up!" Jenny screamed. "Shut up!"

The basement was one big concrete room that ran the length of the house. A storm shelter of sorts with an outside entrance.

Dani hovered next to Simon, praying Adam had heard her cry. The door flew open and light spilled down the steps. Dani sucked in a deep breath as her eyes fell on a two-by-four inches from her fingers.

Before she had time to think about it, she grabbed the board and swung it around in one smooth move. The side of it caught Jenny on the forearm. The woman cried out and the gun dropped to the floor.

She scrambled for it as footfalls landed heavy on the steps. "Freeze! Police!" It wasn't Adam's voice, but it was a sweet sound to Dani's ears. She dove for the weapon even as Simon moved faster than both of them. His small hands wrapped around the butt of the gun and he brought the weapon up to center it on Jenny's chest.

Fear latched itself around her throat. "No, Simon," Dani signed. "Put the gun down."

"Not yet," he said. He panted, the fever flushing his cheeks. His glassy eyes darted from Jenny's stunned face to the bottom of the stairs where Adam held his hand up to the others on the way down. "Stay there," he ordered.

He looked at Simon, gesturing as he said, "Simon, I need you to put the gun on the floor."

"No." His jaw jutted. Jenny moved slowly, scuttling sideways toward the door centered on the opposite wall. Simon followed her with the gun held exactly how Adam had taught him to hold it.

"I'm going out the door," Jenny said. "I'm going to disappear. You'll never see me again." Her hand fumbled for the doorknob behind her.

Simon didn't speak, he simply tracked her with the weapon.

Jenny found the knob, turned it.

And stepped outside into the waiting arms of the SWAT team.

Simon's eyes rolled back in his head and he dropped to the floor, the gun skittering across the concrete.

Dani ran to his side and grabbed him up in her arms.

Adam waited for one of the SWAT members to cover the gun, then slid to his knees beside Dani and Simon. He felt Simon's pulse and placed a hand on his forehead. "We've got an ambulance upstairs. Let me carry him."

Dani didn't even realize she was crying until she nodded and felt the tears drip from her chin. "What about Joe?"

"He's not a threat anymore. He's dead."

Adam gathered her son in his arms and carried him up the stairs.

36

Three hours later, Adam found Dani dozing in the chair next to Simon's hospital bed. Even the creaking of the door didn't rouse her. She looked innocent. Vulnerable.

Kissable.

He didn't want to wake her. She needed to sleep. He took a step back and his rubber sole squeaked on the tile floor. She jerked. Blinked. And immediately her gaze went to Simon. He watched her relax at the sight of her son sleeping peacefully. She finally turned her attention on him. "He's going to be all right."

"Yes."

"The doctor said his appendix was ruptured, but that the antibiotics should take care of the infection." She swallowed. "Thank you for coming after us."

He moved closer and touched Simon's hand. "I was scared for him," he whispered. "And you."

Dani went still, her gaze searching, curious . . . disbelieving. Then tears filled her eyes. "You really were, weren't you?"

He nodded. "I really was. He's a great kid."

294

She looked back at Simon. "Yeah. He is." She took a deep breath and thanked God once again for sparing her son. And herself. "Have you seen your mother?"

Pain darkened his eyes. "I tried. My father told me she didn't want to see me."

Dani gasped. "Adam, I'm so sorry."

He shrugged. "I guess she just needs more time."

Dani stood and gripped his hands, then she leaned in to kiss him. A deep heartfelt kiss through which she did her best to convey her compassion, her need to comfort him. And he let her. He wrapped his arms around her and held her close. When he lifted his head, she offered him a smile.

"I want to be there for you, Adam."

She saw his eyes darken. And a measure of peace fill them. "I want that too, Dani."

Simon stirred and Dani turned her attention to him. She lifted her hands to sign. "Hey, darling, how are you feeling?"

Simon lifted a weak hand and drew a finger down his throat. Adam handed Dani the cup with the straw. She blinked and smiled. "You're getting good."

Adam shrugged and held up his iPhone. "I've been watching sign language videos when I can."

Dani helped Simon take a sip of the ice water. When he lay back against the pillow, he let out a breath. "Thanks."

"Go back to sleep, hon."

He closed his eyes and Dani rubbed hers. Adam placed a hand on her shoulder and she realized the relief she felt in just his presence. It felt so good not to be alone, to share the burden of her sick child with someone else.

"You need to get some rest yourself," Adam said.

"I know. I slept a few minutes, but feel thickheaded and groggy."

"You *look* great."

She felt the heat climb up her neck and into her cheeks. "Ah . . . well. Thanks."

He stuck his hands in his pockets. "Sorry. I didn't mean to make you uncomfortable."

Dani let her gaze meet his. "I just laid a kiss on you, Adam. You didn't make me feel uncomfortable."

"Did too."

"Did not."

They fell silent, then burst into laughter. Adam kissed her, then Dani looked over at Simon and caught him watching them. His eyes bounced between them, then he smiled and let his lids flutter shut.

37

Dani pushed the door open and stepped inside. An older man who looked a lot like Adam glanced up. Confusion creased his brow. "Hello."

"Hi." Dani cleared her throat and ran her damp palms down her jean-clad thighs. "Hi."

"Can I help you?"

"Are you Adam's father?"

"I am." Confusion turned to curiosity. "Who are you?"

"I'm Danielle Harding. Adam's latest client."

The man's jaw tightened. "What are you doing here?"

Dani glanced at the woman in the bed. She slept, her deep, even breaths barely raised the sheet. "I wanted to talk to you. To both of you if you would be so kind as to hear me out."

A brow raised. "Adelle's sleeping right now."

"I see that. So maybe I can just talk to you and see what you think?"

He waved a hand toward the window seat. A bench that was also used for family members staying overnight. Dani sank onto it, wishing she had her purse so she would have something to do with her hands. But she'd left it in Simon's room. She cleared her throat and clasped her fingers together in front of her. "I wanted to meet you because Adam and I have grown close over the last week."

"Close?"

"Yes. He kept a killer from succeeding in his quest to kill me and my son."

That got his attention. "You don't say."

"I do say. We spent a lot of time together when we weren't running for our lives or fighting off attacks from people who were supposed to uphold the law instead of take advantage of the fact that they could circumvent it and get away with their illegal activities."

He blinked and Dani hauled in another fortifying breath. "Adam was coming to be with his mother when he got a call from Tori that someone had found us. It's my fault he wasn't here when Mrs. Buchanan had her surgery. But he wanted to be here, he really did."

"But he put you first."

Dani nodded. "He said she would understand. That she wouldn't want me or my son to die because he chose to be with her." Mr. Buchanan seemed to be at a loss for words, so Dani pressed on. "He misses you. You're keeping him at arm's length and it's killing him slowly. Please forgive him for whatever it is that's keeping you apart. He needs you."

"And we need him." The soft voice behind her had Dani swiveling to find Mrs. Buchanan awake with tears streaming down her cheeks. "Of course I understand. He has a dangerous job, one of those jobs that demand much of him." She lifted her wet eyes to her husband. "Much like a politician who has to miss certain events in his child's life, Adam's had to choose what he can and can't do according to the demands of his job. He's had to make some very difficult decisions over the past year and I'm going to have to stop wallowing in my self-pity if I want to have a relationship with him again." She sniffed and Dani handed her a tissue. She took it, but kept her eyes on her husband. "I want to see my son."

"He's a wonderful man, your son."

Adam's mother's eyes narrowed and then her lips rose in a small smile. "Well, well," she whispered.

"What?" Dani asked.

"Nothing." She lifted a brow at Mr. Buchanan. "Well?"

Dani caught her breath as hope rose. She looked at Mr. Buchanan, almost daring him to refuse.

Instead, she watched his eyes fill as he nodded. "It's time."

"Well, thank goodness you guys have finally come to your senses." Dani turned to find a woman in the doorway holding two bags from a local fast-food chain. Sarah, Adam's sister. She had to be. The resemblance was uncanny. She looked back at Dani and simply said, "Thank you."

38

Dani still couldn't shake the feeling that she was missing something. She frowned as she loaded the dishwasher and put the soap in. Simon was still in the hospital, but she'd left him in good hands. Her mother had flown in from California and the two of them were getting to know one another. Simon was thrilled to have his grandmother at his side.

Her mother had encouraged her to take a break, so Dani had decided to go home. She'd been sleeping at the hospital with Simon, rarely leaving his side.

Yesterday, Adam had presented her with the keys to her new home. She'd found it online and said she thought it would be a great fit for her and Simon. Ron had insisted on helping with the rental expenses and Dani promised him when her house sold she'd pay him back. She really wasn't comfortable with the arrangement, but it was what it was and Ron had insisted.

Dani decided to be grateful.

Adam's attention meant a lot to her and she appreciated his help. She refused to allow herself to be suspicious of his motives. She'd seen him angry, she'd seen him tenderly care for Simon, and she'd seen him come after her with a desperation in his eyes

300

that had stunned her. A desperation to make sure she and Simon were safe.

She turned on the machine and listened to it start up with a quiet hum. She liked her new house. A small rental in a nice neighborhood. Adam was right. It fit her and Simon. No bad memories came with it. Only the promise of the future. A good future.

Outside the sun shone bright, deceiving one into thinking it was a warm day while the temperatures hovered just above thirty.

All should be right with her world now that she didn't have to worry about Stuart or Kurt or Joe or Jenny or anyone trying to kill her.

And yet it wasn't. All wasn't right.

Because something was still very, very wrong.

But what?

She realized it was the letter. The one that Kurt wrote and left in the bag with the other items. Her subconscious had been working on it, and the more she thought about it, the more she didn't believe Kurt wrote it.

But he had to be the one who wrote it. Who else could have? And for what reason? Dani sighed. She was just going to have to accept that her husband had pulled the ultimate practical joke from the grave.

It was over.

The hairs on the back of her neck spiked and she froze.

And slowly turned to come face-to-face with a woman who looked familiar, but one she couldn't place. Dani lifted a hand to her chest as though that would calm her racing pulse. "Who are you? Why are you in my kitchen?"

"I was looking for you."

"Most people knock when they want to enter someone else's home." She could feel her pulse beating at the base of her throat. She reached for the cell phone she'd left on the counter.

"I'm not most people." The woman moved closer.

Dani's fingers closed over the phone. "Wait a minute, I recognize you. You came to see me after Kurt died."

"I did."

"Why?"

"To put the plan in motion."

Dani blinked. "What plan?"

"Do you know who my father was?"

Dani pressed one button and hit Send. The woman still stood on the other side of the counter, the raised bar hiding Dani's actions. She looked for a weapon, but the woman's hands were by her side so she couldn't see one. But that didn't mean she didn't have one.

Confused, Dani frowned. "No. I don't even know who *you* are."

"I'm Julie Faraday. Gordon Faraday was my father."

Dani gasped with shock. "I'm so sorry! I heard about his death. It was terrible."

"Is that all you can say?"

"What else can I say that would help?" Dani tried to soothe. The longer they stood there, the more agitated the woman became. "What can I do? What do you want from me?"

"I want you to know."

"Know what?"

"Know that your husband and his stupid practical joke killed my father. Your husband *murdered* my dad and all he could say was 'Gotcha.'"

Dani held out a beseeching hand. "Please . . . I don't understand."

"Then let me explain it." She lifted her right hand and pointed a gun at Dani's face.

Adam heard Dani's voice and another woman talking. She'd called but hadn't answered his hellos. Adam frowned, wondering

302

if she'd dialed the number accidentally. With his feet propped up on the desk, he'd been contemplating calling her to ask her if she and Simon would want to have dinner with him.

Just as he was about to hang up, he heard her say, "Why don't you put the gun down?"

His feet hit the floor with a thud and he stood to bolt over into Blake's office. With a jerk of his hand, he motioned for Blake to follow.

Blake lifted a brow, but must have sensed his urgency as he stood and grabbed his coat from the back of his chair. "You drive," Adam mouthed and punched the mute button.

"Where?" Blake asked.

"Dani's new place."

Blake nodded and together they hurried out to Blake's red truck. Adam put the phone on speaker.

Dani was talking, her voice a little shaky, but firm. "I can't change whatever it was that Kurt did."

"My father was deathly afraid of snakes after being bitten last year. Almost seven months ago, several of his friends at the FBI threw him a birthday party. Your husband put snakes into a box—" Her voice cracked.

Adam looked at Blake. "Faster."

* * *

"—and when my father opened that box, all those snakes popped out all over him and he had a heart attack and died." Tears dripped down Julie's cheeks and Dani's heart went out to the woman even as she prayed Adam was on the way.

"But I didn't have anything to do with that," she whispered. "My husband was an evil, evil man. If he found a weakness in someone, he preyed on it. He did the same thing to me and our son."

Doubt flickered in Julie's eyes. Then hardened. "For six months

I've planned my father's revenge. Do you know, I went up to that office and pumped those agents for information?" She gave a hiccuping laugh. "Ralph was more than willing to let me ask questions and talk about my father. He thought I needed to, that it was therapeutic. So I made it a point to go to his office a couple of times a week. Other agents felt sorry for me and told me stories about my father. Like his suspicions about Kurt Harding and how he'd gone to his superior and said he shouldn't get that promotion."

"I'm so sorry," Dani whispered.

"I planned it all, you know. I planted the letters. I set up the safe-deposit box, everything. A couple of weeks before my father died, I was at the office waiting to go to lunch with him and overheard a conversation between Peter Hastings and another agent about some plates they needed but couldn't get their hands on. And Peter said that whoever had those plates was dead. At the time, it didn't mean much, but later, as Ralph filled me in on more details, I realized how to set everything up. I wanted Joseph Duncan dead. He was as bad as your husband. All he cared about was money. He stood there and watched my father die. He didn't even care! Ralph said he even laughed. *Laughed!*"

Dani prayed Adam was listening. "But your father died the same day as Kurt. How did you put it all together so fast?"

"It wasn't hard. Ralph was at the hospital with my dad when I got there. We were both grief-stricken. He talked and I listened. And the more I listened, the angrier I got. It didn't take long to plan everything. I had time because I couldn't sleep, couldn't eat, could hardly do anything except plan. Within a few days, I had it all laid out."

Dani's mind spun, reeling with the information. "Did you plant the letter in my end table?"

"Yes, and the safe-deposit key, and I sent letters to Joe and that witch down the street, Jenny. And Stuart—" She gave a derisive laugh. "Stuart was so blind with his infatuation for you, I didn't know if he'd even care about the letter, but he did."

"And you impersonated me at the bank."

"You wrote checks for bills and put them in your mailbox. All I had to do was steal one and practice your signature, get a fake ID with all of your information on it, and I was in."

She made it sound so easy. Dani blinked and forced her mind to work.

"But why hurt me? I didn't have anything to do with your father's death. I was scared of Kurt and only stayed with him because I was afraid he'd kill me if I left him."

"Why hurt you? Because you bought the snakes."

Dani blinked. "How did you know that?" She could almost hear the woman's teeth grinding.

"Because the receipt was mixed in with the disgusting creatures. Your name was on it."

"Kurt sent me into the store. I have a debit card that he allowed me to have and use occasionally. But I only bought them on his order."

"Then I guess that was one order you should have disobeyed." She lifted the gun higher and raised her other hand to steady the weapon. "Now you can join him."

The gun cracked. Dani dove for the floor, expecting to feel the bite of a bullet. She waited for the pain. Instead she heard a thud and, pulse racing, looked up to see Julie Faraday on the floor, a black hole between her eyes.

Adam's tense face appeared in the window that had been shattered by the bullet.

Dani placed her hands over her face and cried.

Adam watched Dani pour herself a cup of coffee. "You want to sit outside on the balcony?"

"Sure." She offered him an easy smile and followed him to settle into the three-seater swing.

"It's Christmas Eve."

"Yes, it is. And it's a lovely sixty-five degrees."

"Unbelievable." He let out a contented sigh, sank down beside her, and took a sip of his tea. "We're going to my parents' for lunch tomorrow, right?"

"Wouldn't miss it."

"And your mom's coming?"

"Yes." Dani's mother had moved one neighborhood over from Dani, and Adam knew she was loving the proximity. She and her mother were closer than ever. Her happiness reflected on her face.

"Where's Simon?" Adam asked.

"Playing that game with Mitchell. I would fuss about him spending too much time on it, but he's doing *math*, for goodness' sakes."

"You do realize he's probably got a genius IQ, don't you?"

"I do."

"It's going to take a lot of energy to keep up with him."

She gave a low laugh. "Yes, I'm aware of that too."

Adam cleared his throat and looked down. She must have sensed his nervousness. Or something. "Adam?"

"Yes?"

"Are you all right?"

"Why do you ask?"

She frowned. "Because you're acting a little weird."

He stood and walked to the rail of the balcony. "That's because I've been doing a lot of thinking."

"About?"

He turned to face her. "Us."

"Us. Okay."

He couldn't read her. That fact scared him to death. He was going to have to jump off the cliff without a safety net. "Dani, we met in a crazy way."

"Yes."

He found the seat beside her again. It was easier than standing on shaky legs. "But I'm glad you found us. Found Operation Refuge, and I'm glad God brought you into my life."

Dani leaned forward to kiss him. A long, sweet, lingering kiss that he wanted to deepen and definitely prolong. Instead he pulled away and cleared his throat. "Okay, as much as I enjoy it, stop distracting me. I've got stuff to say."

She blinked and tilted her head. "All right. Sorry."

Adam groaned and leaned over to plant another kiss on her lips. "No, no. Don't be sorry. Just . . . listen."

"Sure." She smiled up at him, curiosity burning in her gaze.

He took a deep breath. "Dani, I love you."

She smiled.

He stopped. "What's that smile mean?"

"It means, I know you love me. You've loved me for a long time."

Adam gaped. Dani laughed and tapped his chin. He shut his mouth, then opened it. "Well, yeah. Practically from the moment you walked into my office."

A cloud settled over her face. "I was another woman that day. Broken. Scared—"

"Strong, a fighter."

"I didn't feel strong," she whispered.

Adam wrapped an arm around her shoulders. "You were. Still are."

"Thank you for giving me time. Time to figure out my life and

307

get it back on track. Time to spend with Simon and just—be. Thank you for not pushing. We both needed the space and the time to heal and figure out what it means to live and not be afraid every moment."

"And if you need more time, I'll wait."

———

Dani shook her head. "I don't need any more time. I know my heart." She placed her hand against his chest. "And I know yours."

"I love you, Dani," he said again. This time with more confidence.

Tears flooded her eyes and she blinked to hold them in. "I love you too, Adam."

"And I love Simon like he's my own."

"I know, I've seen it."

"And so," Adam signed, "why don't you come on over and join us, Simon?"

Simon stepped out onto the balcony, the sheepish expression on his face betraying his eavesdropping. Dani shot him a frown and her son shrugged.

Adam pulled Simon down next to him and grabbed him in a loose headlock. When he let go, Simon grinned and gave Adam a light punch on the arm.

Men. Dani sighed. But then smiled. How she loved these two.

Adam signed, "Ready?"

Simon nodded.

Dani lifted a brow. "What are you two up to?"

Adam shoved his hand in his front pocket and pulled out a small box. Dani gasped. Then noted the fine tremor in his fingers as he popped it open to reveal a gorgeous square-cut diamond. She gulped and looked into his eyes, absently noting Simon's gleeful expression.

"Dani, I know I'm nothing fancy and I've made a lot of mistakes in my past, but this last year has been one of the best in my life because you and Simon were a part of it. I was ready to marry you eleven months ago, but knew you needed time. So, if you're ready, I'm ready."

Dani couldn't speak through the lump in her throat. Could barely see through the tears in her eyes, but she managed a nod. Adam slipped to the floor in front of her and removed the ring from the box. He took her left hand. "Will you marry me?"

Dani blinked. Felt a tear slip down her cheek. Looked at the ring and the man behind it. Thought of all the reasons she should say yes. Then tried to think of why she should say no.

Adam's hand tightened on hers. "You're scaring me, Dani."

She took a deep breath. "I'm trying to think of a reason to say no."

His face fell and he lost all color. He started to pull away from her and she clasped his hand tighter. "But I can't think of a single one," she whispered. "Yes, I'll marry you."

He slid the ring on her finger, then grabbed her to place a firm, hard kiss on her lips. He gave a low, shaky laugh. "Don't torture me like that ever again."

"Sorry, I didn't mean to."

"So, when are you getting married?" Simon asked.

Dani shuddered from all the emotion rolling inside her, but turned to Simon. "You knew about this?"

"Of course."

"Of course," she murmured.

Adam shrugged. "I couldn't ask you without getting permission from the person you love most."

She leaned over and kissed him again, then smiled. "*One* of the people I love most."

He lifted her hand to his lips and kissed the finger that now held his ring. "To forever?"

"Forever."

"Thank goodness," Simon declared. "Now, I'm starving, where are we going to eat?"

PROLOGUE

FRIDAY, NOVEMBER 20TH
ATLANTA, GA—CENTER FOR DISEASE CONTROL

"It's time," the voice said. "Remember what we told you."

CDC employee Anwar Goff wanted to rip the small piece from his ear and stomp it into oblivion. But his tormentors had been very clear about what would happen if he did so. "If at any time we can't hear you, they will die. Ask for help, they will die. Write a message, they will die. Use your phone, they will die. Am I clear?" So Anwar left the earpiece alone and slipped from the bathroom. His footsteps echoed on the tile flooring as he walked down the empty hall.

CDC Building 18 had shut down about an hour ago. Anwar moved with slow, hesitant strides that all too quickly ate up the distance between the bathroom and the Biosafety Level 4 lab. Sweat threatened to drip into his eyes and he drew his left arm across his forehead.

With shaking fingers, he swiped the key card, and the first set of doors opened, then closed behind him. For a moment, he just stood there, trembling. "God, help me," he whispered, then moved once again.

"God can't help you. Only I can," the voice whispered, then gave a small laugh. Evil clung to the words and Anwar clamped his lips shut.

Once inside the changing area, he set his briefcase on the bench next to the lockers and drew in a deep breath. He couldn't help the stifled sob that slipped from him as he opened the third locker from the left.

Don't think, just do it. Within seconds he was in protective clothing, complete with mask, gloves, and gown.

Next, he rolled the combination on the briefcase to unlock it. With short, sluggish steps, Anwar left the changing room and approached the next set of doors. He swiped his card again. The doors opened with a soft whoosh and he stepped into the BSL-4 lab.

His target lay in the locked freezer just ahead. Muttering another prayer, he crossed the room, opened the freezer door, and found what he'd come for. He paused and swallowed hard as he simply stared, feeling paralyzed. Helpless. For the past seven years, he'd worked his way up the ranks of the CDC, gaining the confidence of his superiors. And now all of his hard work had brought him to this.

"We're waiting. Your family is waiting."

He thought of his wife and two teenage children. With another deep breath, he reached into the freezer. Carefully, he transferred the tray that held the one-inch-long plastic vials topped with the plastic screw caps. The vials sat in seven little white cardboard boxes. One by one, he removed the boxes and placed them in the black case. There they would be kept frozen by the dry ice during transport.

Anwar snapped the briefcase closed and rolled the combination to lock it.

He'd done it. He'd really done it. Tremors raced through him as he glanced at the clock on the wall. He had very few minutes to spare, but he wasn't quite sure his legs would be able to carry him back through the two sets of doors. He didn't move. Couldn't. He simply couldn't do this. "I can't do this," he whispered.

"But you will."

Yes. He would.

So this is how he would go down, how he would be remembered. *Don't do it!* But the faces of his children, his wife, rose up before him. He squared his shoulders and tightened his grip on the bag.

He left the lab, not looking back, not thinking about all of the people who would soon die. He was only thinking of the three people he was trying to save. With hurried, erratic movements, he entered the lobby and waved to the security guard who barely looked up from the computer.

"Night, Anwar. See you next week."

Anwar didn't answer, just strode through the glass doors and out into the night. He shivered as the wind cut through his heavy coat. Even Atlanta had its fair share of cold weather.

For a moment Anwar hesitated. If he went left—

"Why aren't you moving, Mr. Goff?"

Anwar jerked. They were watching him. He moved to his car and climbed in. He placed the briefcase on the seat beside him. Just earlier that day, his wife had sat in that spot and they'd talked about their plans for Thanksgiving. His parents were coming, but hers couldn't make it. With a tight throat and tears in his eyes, he cranked the car and pulled from the curb.

ACKNOWLEDGMENTS

Thanks to Dru Wells for your invaluable input in the world of the FBI.

As always, thanks to my awesome family who let me spend hours on end at the keyboard to produce books. My agent, my editors, and I appreciate you!

Lynette Eason is the award-winning, bestselling author of several romantic suspense series, including Women of Justice and Deadly Reunions. She is a member of American Christian Fiction Writers and Romance Writers of America. Lynette graduated from the University of South Carolina and went on to earn her master's degree in education from Converse College. She lives in South Carolina with her husband and two children.

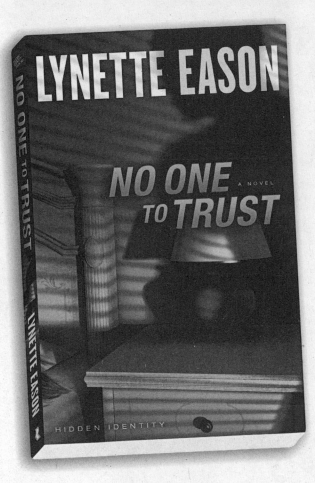

Also from Lynette Eason:
The **WOMEN OF JUSTICE** series